MADEMOISELLE PERLE
AND OTHER STORIES

T0349949

MADEMOISELLE PERLE AND OTHER STORIES

Guy de Maupassant

Translated from the French by
Ada Galsworthy and Elsie Martindale

Selected, with a preface by
Robert Hampson and Helen Chambers

riverrun

This collection is drawn from *Yvette and Other Stories*, by Duckworth, 1904; reprinted n.d. [c. 1914] and *Stories from De Maupassant*, 1935, by Jonathan Cape, London

This edition published in Great Britain in 2020 by

riverrun

An imprint of

Quercus Editions Ltd
Carmelite House
50 Victoria Embankment
London EC4Y 0DZ

An Hachette UK company

This selection and preface © 2020 by Robert Hampson and Helen Chambers
Robert Hampson and Helen Chambers assert their moral right in the copyright of the preface.

A CIP catalogue record for this book is available
from the British Library

PB ISBN 978 1 78747 928 9
EBOOK ISBN 978 1 78747 927 2

10 9 8 7 6 5 4 3 2 1

Typeset by CC Book Production

Printed and bound in Great Britain by Clays Ltd, Elcograf S.p.A.

Papers used by Quercus are from well-managed forests and other responsible sources.

Contents

Preface

GUY DE MAUPASSANT is probably one of the world's greatest story-tellers. He was certainly one of the finest short-story writers of his generation in a period recognized as the golden age of short fiction in France. He was an immensely productive writer, and, during his relatively short lifetime, he was the most popular author in France after his friend, Émile Zola.

Maupassant was born in Normandy on 5 August 1850. His father was a worldly, lazy man-about-town with a private income; his mother, a cultured, well-read woman, was the daughter of a wealthy Rouen businessman. The marriage did not take, and the couple had effectively separated by 1860. Guy and his brother were brought up by their mother in the fashionable Normandy resort of Étretat. After a short, unhappy period at the seminary of Yvetot, which ended with his expulsion, he became a boarder at the Lycée Corneille in Rouen. During this period, he came under the mentorship of a family friend, the novelist Gustave

Flaubert. Flaubert trained him in the art of writing, impressing on him the importance of precision and of learning to see with his own eyes.

In July 1870, France declared war on Prussia, and Maupassant joined the army. The Franco-Prussian War (1870–71) was short-lived but had a lasting effect on Maupassant, as evidenced in the many stories he wrote dealing with the war and its aftermath. The war also ruined the family business, and Maupassant moved to Paris and became a civil servant – first in an unsalaried position, then in paid posts in the Admiralty and later the Ministry of Education. He also turned to writing and became part of the 'Naturalist' group led by Zola. In 1880, his novella 'Boule de Suif' was included in Zola's collection of Naturalist stories about the Franco-Prussian War, *Les Soirées de Médan*.

'Boule de Suif' established Maupassant's reputation as a writer. It was followed by an immensely productive decade, in which Maupassant published seven novels and more than three hundred stories. However, as the decade advanced, Maupassant also increasingly suffered physical and mental problems caused by the syphilis that eventually killed him. He attempted suicide in January 1892 and died in a mental hospital in July 1893.

Reception

French Naturalism had a troubled reception in Britain. Zola's novels *Pot-Bouille* and *La Curée* were published in translation by Henry Vizetelly in 1885 with a Preface by the Irish novelist George Moore. Moore's own best-selling naturalist novel, *A Mummer's Wife*, was published in the same year. However, Zola's work was controversial: its open-eyed observation of the social world challenged Victorian publishing conventions. Moore's novel, with its focus on female sexuality and adultery, was banned by libraries, and W.H. Smith's refused to sell it. Undaunted, Vizetelly went on to publish Eleanor Marx Aveling's translation of *Madame Bovary*, Flaubert's great novel of adultery, the following year. Another social reformer, Beatrice Webb, recorded her embarrassment at having a copy of a Zola novel in her pocket when she shared a compartment with a Liberal MP on a train journey in 1887. The MP then produced his copy of Henry James's attempt at naturalism, *The Princess Casamassima* (1886). In 1888, Vizetelly, as the publisher of Zola's works in Britain, was tried and convicted for publishing 'immoral literature'.

In that same year, Henry James entertained Maupassant in London. He then published an essay on Maupassant in the *Fortnightly Review*, and another in the following year in *Harper's Weekly*. The latter was used as the introduction to *The Odd*

Number, a selection of thirteen of Maupassant's stories, translated by Jonathan Sturges, published by Harper's in New York in 1889. In his Introduction, James praises Maupassant for his 'first-rate style', but also warns his American readers of things they might find difficult: above all the fact that Maupassant's 'vision' was 'altogether of this life'. James then teases out what this implies: Maupassant 'takes his stand on everything that solicits the sentient creature who lives in his senses'; his fiction assumes 'the immitigability of our mortal predicament'; and then, in the clearest warning to the readers, the stories are characterized by a 'strong, hard, cynical, slightly cruel humor'. In his piece for the English *Fortnightly Review*, after noting Maupassant's 'essential hardness — hardness of form, hardness of nature', James welcomes Maupassant's insistence on the artist's primary duty as faithfulness to his own perceptions, expressing himself in the form that best suits his temperament 'with all the contrivances of art that he has learned', whereas by contrast (he continues) the British and American novelist is 'misled by some convention or other' and surrenders to self-censorship. He praises the acuteness of Maupassant's senses, and the 'economy of means' by which he renders the particular instance, but this emphasis on the senses also makes him an embarrassing case — 'and mystifying for the moralist'. At the same time, for James, Maupassant's pessimism, cruelty, and cynical view of mankind stands in contrast to the compulsory optimism of the English novel, whose 'optimism of ignorance as well as of delicacy' he explicitly associates with women readers. Of course, the issue which James has difficulty discussing in a Victorian periodical is Maupassant's direct treatment of sex and sexuality: as he says, 'we have reserves about our shames and sorrows'. He nevertheless uses Maupassant's example to plead the case for the freedom of the artist to choose their own subject. And he has no trouble praising Maupassant's style, where 'every phrase is a close sequence, every epithet a paying piece, and the ground is completely cleared of the vague, the ready-made and the second best'.

Maupassant was particularly popular in the Francophile literary circles around Henry James and Joseph Conrad, which included Ford Madox Ford and John Galsworthy. In his 1924 'personal remembrance' of Conrad, for example, Ford noted how, when they first met, what brought them together was 'a devotion to Flaubert and Maupassant', going on to record that they knew 'immense passages' of both writers by heart. Both were attracted by these authors' aesthetic concern for form and the art of writing. Indeed, in his 1930 book *The English Novel*, Ford claims Maupassant as the major influence 'on the Anglo-Saxon writer of today', before proceeding to discuss James and Conrad and novel-writing as an art. Likewise Galsworthy, in his 1924 essay 'Six Novelists in Profile', presents Maupassant as 'the prince of teachers' for literary style, praising the 'vigour of his vision, and his thought, the economy and the clarity of the expression'. Better than any other author, Galsworthy asserts, Maupassant 'has taught us what to leave out'. In short,

Maupassant represents 'the apex of the shaped story, the high mark of fiction which knows exactly what it is about', and 'fiction which knows exactly what it is about' was the aim of all these authors.

In May 1904, Joseph Conrad started work on a preface for Ada Galsworthy's translation of Maupassant (*Yvette and Other Stories*).* In introducing Maupassant to an English audience, one problem he faced was that, as he put it, 'Maupassant's renown is universal, but his popularity is restricted'. Conrad explains this by calling Maupassant 'a Frenchman of Frenchmen': 'intensely national in his logic, in his clearness, in his aesthetic and moral conceptions'. The other problem, related to this, was that Maupassant's art, like Zola's, was regarded by the English as 'immoral'. The preface begins by praising Maupassant for 'the consummate simplicity of his technique' and his 'conscientious art'. More challengingly, Conrad then goes on to praise Maupassant's realism: 'there is both a moral and an excitement to be found in a faithful rendering of life . . . Facts, and again facts, are his unique concern.' For contemporary English readers, however, this was part of the problem: quite apart from some of the facts Maupassant chose to represent, a novel based on facts did not leave room for explicit moral judgements. Conrad's insistence on the morality of observation has to be seen in this

* This was republished, shortly before Conrad's death, in *Notes on Life and Letters* (1921), and is reproduced below.

light. Conrad notes that Maupassant 'neglects to qualify his truth with the drop of facile sweetness' required by English readers and that this 'lays him open to the charges of cruelty, cynicism, hardness'. By way of answer, Conrad contends that Maupassant 'looks with an eye of profound pity' rather than cynicism; at the same time, he is courageous 'and does not turn away his head'. Conrad also praises Maupassant's commitment to the Flaubertian aesthetic of *le mot juste*: 'by a more scrupulous, prolonged and devoted attention to the aspects of the visible world', he argues, 'he discovered at last the right words as if miraculously impressed for him upon the face of things and events'. In this context Conrad mentions his own 'long and intimate acquaintance' with Maupassant's work, but he also testifies to 'the appreciation of Maupassant manifested by many women gifted with tenderness and intelligence'. These women are 'good judges of courage' and understand 'his genuine masculinity without display, his virility without a pose'.

Conrad perhaps had two particular women in mind: Ada Galsworthy, the translator of the selection of stories for which he was writing the Preface; and Ford's wife, Elsie Martindale, who had published her own translations of Maupassant the previous year. In both cases, Conrad had had some input into the translation.*

---

* For a more detailed account, see Helen Chambers, *Conrad's Reading: Space, Time, Networks* (Palgrave Macmillan, 2018), pp. 190–200.

The Translators

In November 1903 Conrad wrote to his close friend John ('Jack') Galsworthy, 'Please tell Mrs Galsworthy that I am delighted to hear of Yvette in English. Please may I have a sight of her?' Conrad was referring, of course, to the translation of 'Yvette' by Ada Galsworthy, who had been Jack's lover (*de facto* wife indeed) since 1895, although still married to his cousin Arthur Galsworthy. The unhappy marriage to the incompatible Arthur Galsworthy found echo in the depiction of the marriage of Irene and Soames in the soon-to-appear first volume of Galsworthy's *Forsyte Saga*. Ada, the adopted daughter of a Norwich doctor, was thirty-five at the time she undertook these translations, having spent her adolescence and early adult years travelling in Europe with her mother, perfecting her French and German, and mixing in musical society with Wagner and Liszt. Elegant and well-dressed, she was a talented pianist and later a composer of songs.

However, as we have seen, she was not the first English-woman to translate Maupassant's stories. Elsie Martindale, the wife of Ford Madox Ford (then known as Ford Madox Hueffer), had already begun her collection of translations the previous year. By then twenty-six years old, Elsie was tall, dark-haired, and wore amber beads and eccentric dresses sewn from curtain fabric and velvet. In her teenage years she accompanied Ford to lectures by expatriate Russian anarchists in London, and she mixed with Ford's Pre-Raphaelite artist relatives. (His grandfather was the artist Ford Madox Brown.) Ford and Elsie had first met at Pretoria House, a progressive trilingual boarding school in Folkestone, Kent. They went from being school friends to soulmates, to literary collaborators, then lovers, and eloped in 1894. Ford was twenty, and Elsie, at seventeen, still a minor. By late 1902 Elsie, with two very young daughters, was not only writing a novel about a marriage which, like her own, was under strain but, encouraged by her husband and by Conrad, at the time their friend and neighbour in Kent, started translating Maupassant.

Elsie's choice of stories was a little random. She must have used as source texts whichever of the original inexpensive French collections of the stories she could find either at home or at Conrad's house, since they were all too poor to buy new editions, nor would they, given their peripatetic lifestyles, have hoarded the old French periodicals in which the stories originally appeared. (Ada's selection may also have depended on which collections were most easily available, although the Galsworthys were far from poor.) That Conrad helped Elsie is obvious from the comments and alterations in his handwriting in the existing page proofs of the translations, which were first published in 1903 as *Stories from de Maupassant*. Ford also helped, contributing a preface, but distancing himself a little from the project. Conrad similarly collaborated actively with Ada, and, as mentioned above, wrote the preface to these translations, which were first published, in 1904, as *Yvette and Other Stories*. This volume was subsequently reissued with three stories removed and four others added. It is the text of this later edition (1914) that forms the basis of the present collection.

Women translators during the late nineteenth and very early twentieth century were often relatively invisible. Elsie was listed on the title page only as 'E. M.' (i.e. Elsie Martindale) and Ada originally as 'A. G.'. In the later editions, however, she appeared as 'Mrs John Galsworthy'. Some translations of Maupassant stories had already appeared by this time. As noted earlier, Henry James's young friend Jonathan Sturges had published some dull but worthy ones in America in 1889. Around 1903 a prestige series of very expensive American editions appeared, with unknown or anonymous translators. Maupassant's American biographer later described these translations as of 'appalling crudity', and even a casual glance readily confirms how clumsy and at times extremely inaccurate these were. Ada's and Elsie's translations broke new ground in terms of accuracy, fidelity and sensitivity. This was partly because of the innate ability of both women to interpret Maupassant's distinctive style and idiomatic speech patterns, and partly because Conrad, Galsworthy and Ford (all of whom were fluent in French) all greatly admired Maupassant for his concise, impressionistic style and were available for consultation.

The Stories

The stories included in this volume all first appeared in French periodicals between 1882 and 1890, and soon afterwards appeared in various book collections. While it is not possible to include all the stories translated by Elsie and Ada, the stories that have been selected were chosen to include a wide variety of themes and subject matter in order to represent something of the range of Maupassant's fiction. We open with Elsie's translation of the atmospheric long story 'The Field of Olives' ('Le Champ d'oliviers'), the tale that Elsie's husband much later called 'the most wonderful of all Maupassant's stories, which if the reader has not read he should read at once'. With its vividly depicted Provençal landscape, and tense, remorseless build-up to its bloody climax between the father and his unacknowledged son, it stands in stark contrast to Maupassant's stories of bourgeois sensibility and peasant humour in Normandy. The unexpected appearance of a family member is also the focus of another story translated by Elsie, 'The Return' ('Le Retour'). Stylishly and precisely translated, the setting here is Maupassant's beloved Normandy coastline, where a potential domestic drama in a fishing community is resolved in a happy ending. The raucously humorous 'A Sale' ('Une vente'), translated by Ada, was written in a slightly different register, but shares the theme of marital tangles.

The Franco-Prussian war of 1870–71, played out in provincial

France and in Paris, forms the moral landscape of the next four stories. 'Saint-Antoine' is a rural tale of cruelty and black humour, while 'Two Friends' ('Deux amis') explores simple male friendship and loyalty during the Siege of Paris in the face of Prussian brutality. 'Mademoiselle Fifi', set in a Prussian-occupied château in the Normandy countryside, highlights one of Maupassant's favourite themes, the good-hearted prostitute, here the courageous Rachel, and her revenge on the Prussian conqueror. By contrast, in 'Old Mother Savage' ('La Mère Sauvage'), the account of a woman's heroism in avenging her son's death is tempered by the narrator's empathy towards the Prussian mothers who had also lost their sons.

The unrequited loves of ageing women was another of Maupassant's abiding themes. 'The Chair-Mender' ('La Rempailleuse'), a gentle, slightly bitter tale, juxtaposes the generosity of a nomadic peasant woman with the callousness of the bourgeois object of her lifelong but misplaced passion. In contrast, 'Mademoiselle Perle', which displays a kind of winter fairy-tale quality, recounts an affluent middle-class family's kindness to a foundling, and eventually reveals a mutually undeclared but lifelong love. With 'Miss Harriet' Maupassant offers us, in an impressionistic, painterly Normandy landscape, the tragi-comic tale of the hopeless love of a stereotypical but sympathetically observed English spinster, prone to fits of religious ecstasy. 'The Holy Relic' ('La Relique') is a humorous little anti-religious piece, based on a cruel deception. English women also feature in 'The Wreck' ('L'Épave'), where we catch a fleeting glimpse of unrequited love, narrated from a male perspective. The other maritime story 'At Sea' ('En mer') recounts a dramatic and very realistic tragedy aboard a Channel trawler, vividly translated, and with recognizably authentic input from that master mariner, Joseph Conrad.

There then follow two short, beautiful, Paris-based stories: 'Minuet' ('Menuet'), an ethereal cameo about ageing, set in the Luxembourg Gardens; and the extraordinarily powerful 'Night' ('La Nuit'), whose original subtitle describes it as a nightmare ('Un Cauchemar'). This atmospheric, highly impressionistic sketch follows a man's nocturnal wanderings in Paris and his premonition of lonely death by water.

The collection closes with 'Yvette', by far the longest story in the volume, which became one of Maupassant's best-known and later much anthologized works. A charming young girl, naively flirtatious, grows up in her mother's Parisian demi-monde. Most of the action, however, takes place on the banks of the Seine near Paris – the scene of Maupassant's own youthful (and eventually lethal) sexual adventures. This setting is invoked in such a painterly manner that the reader almost finds themselves within Auguste Renoir's contemporary *Luncheon of the Boating Party* (1881). The young Yvette's psychological breakdown and recovery is delicately charted. Despite its length, the story never flags, and clearly reveals the author's sensitive appreciation of women. Although these Maupassant stories have since been re-translated several times, it was the work of two highly intelligent women – Elsie Martindale and Ada Galsworthy – that first allowed them to be appreciated by a wider anglophone readership.

Conrad's Preface (1904)

To introduce Maupassant to English readers with apologetic explanations as though his art were recondite and the tendency of his work immoral would be a gratuitous impertinence.

Maupassant's conception of his art is such as one would expect from a practical and resolute mind; but in the consummate simplicity of his technique it ceases to be perceptible. This is one of its greatest qualities, and like all the great virtues it is based primarily on self-denial.

To pronounce a judgment upon the general tendency of an author is a difficult task. One could not depend upon reason alone, nor yet trust solely to one's emotions. Used together, they would in many cases traverse each other, because emotions have their own unanswerable logic. Our capacity for emotion is limited, and the field of our intelligence is restricted. Responsiveness to every feeling, combined with the penetration of every intellectual subterfuge, would end, not in judgment, but in universal absolution. *Tout comprendre c'est tout pardonner*. And in this benevolent neutrality towards the warring errors of human nature all light would go out from art and from life.

We are at liberty then to quarrel with Maupassant's attitude towards our world in which, like the rest of us, he has that share which his senses are able to give him. But we need not quarrel with him violently. If our feelings (which are tender) happen to be hurt because his talent is not exercised for the praise and consolation of mankind, our intelligence (which is great) should let us see that he is a very splendid sinner, like all those who in this valley of compromises err by over-devotion to the truth that is in them. His determinism, barren of praise, blame, and consolation, has all the merit of his conscientious art. The worth of every conviction consists precisely in the steadfastness with which it is held.

Except for his philosophy, which in the case of so consummate an artist does not matter (unless to the solemn and naive mind), Maupassant of all writers of fiction demands least forgiveness from his readers. He does not require forgiveness because he is never dull.

The interest of a reader in a work of imagination is either ethical or that of simple curiosity. Both are perfectly legitimate, since there is both a moral and excitement to be found in a faithful rendering of life. And in Maupassant's work there is the interest of curiosity and the moral of a point of view consistently preserved and never obtruded for the end of personal gratification. The spectacle of this immense talent served by exceptional faculties triumphing over the most thankless subjects by an unswerving singleness of purpose is in itself an admirable lesson in the power of artistic honesty, one may say of artistic virtue. The inherent greatness of the man consists in this, that he will let none of the fascinations that beset a writer working in loneliness turn him away from the straight path, from the vouchsafed vision of excellence. He will not be led into perdition by the seductions of sentiment, of eloquence, of humour, of pathos; of all that splendid pageant of faults that pass between the writer and his probity on the blank sheet of paper, like the glittering cortège of deadly sins before the austere anchorite in the desert air of Thebaïde. This is not to say that Maupassant's austerity has never faltered; but the fact remains that no tempting demon has ever succeeded in hurling him down from his high, if narrow, pedestal.

It is the austerity of his talent, of course, that is in question. Let the discriminating reader, who at times may well spare a moment or two to the consideration and enjoyment of artistic excellence, be asked to reflect a little upon the texture of two stories included in this volume: 'A Piece of String', and 'A Sale'. How many openings the last offers for the gratuitous display of the author's wit or clever buffoonery, the first for an unmeasured display of sentiment. And both sentiment and buffoonery could have been made very good too, in a way accessible to the meanest intelligence, at the cost of truth and honesty. Here it is where Maupassant's austerity comes in. He refrains from setting his cleverness against the eloquence of the facts. There is humour and pathos in these stories; but such is the greatness of his talent, the refinement of his artistic conscience, that all his high qualities appear inherent in the very things of which he speaks, as if they had been altogether independent of his presentation. Facts, and again facts are his unique concern. That is why he is not always properly understood. His facts are so perfectly rendered that, like the actualities of life itself, they demand from the reader that faculty of observation which is rare, the power of appreciation which is generally wanting in most of us who are guided mainly by empty phrases requiring no effort, demanding from us no qualities except a vague susceptibility to emotion. Nobody has ever gained the vast applause of a crowd by the simple and clear exposition of vital facts. Words alone strung upon a convention have fascinated us as worthless glass beads strung on a thread have charmed at all times our brothers the unsophisticated savages of the islands. Now, Maupassant, of whom it has been said that he is the master of the *mot juste*, has never been a dealer in words. His wares have been, not glass beads, but polished gems: not the most rare and precious, perhaps, but of the very first water after their kind.

That he took trouble with his gems, taking them up in the rough and polishing each facet patiently, the publication of the two posthumous volumes of short stories proves abundantly. I think it proves also the assertion made here that he was by no means a dealer in words. On looking at the first feeble drafts from which so many perfect stories have been fashioned, one discovers that what has been matured, improved, brought to perfection by unwearied endeavour is not the diction of the tale, but the vision of its true shape and detail. Those first attempts are not faltering or uncertain in expression. It is the conception which is at fault. The subjects have not yet been adequately seen. His proceeding was not to group expressive words that mean nothing around misty and mysterious shapes dear to muddled intellects, belonging neither to earth nor to heaven. His vision by a more scrupulous, prolonged and devoted attention to the aspects of the visible world discovered at last the right words as if miraculously impressed for him upon the face of things and events. This was the particular shape taken by his inspiration; it came to him directly, honestly in the light of his day, instead of on the tortuous, dark roads of meditation. His realities came to him from a genuine source, from this universe of vain appearances wherein we men have found everything to make us proud, sorry, exalted, and humble.

Maupassant's renown is universal, but his popularity is restricted. It is not difficult to perceive why. Maupassant is an intensely national writer. He is so intensely national in his logic, in his clearness, in his æsthetic and moral conceptions that he has been accepted by his countrymen without having had to pay the tribute of flattery either to the nation as a whole, or to any class, sphere or division of the nation. The truth of his art tells with an irresistible force; and he stands excused from the duty of patriotic posturing. He is a Frenchman of Frenchmen beyond question or cavil, and with that he is simple enough to be universally comprehensible. What is wanting to his universal success is the mediocrity of an obvious and appealing tenderness. He neglects to qualify his truth with the drop of facile sweetness; he forgets to strew paper roses over the tombs. The disregard of these common decencies lays him open to the charges of cruelty, cynicism, hardness. And yet it can be safely affirmed that this man wrote from the fulness of a compassionate heart. He is merciless and yet gentle with his mankind; he does not rail at their prudent fears and their small artifices; he does not despise their labours. It seems to me that he looks with an eye of profound pity upon their troubles, deceptions, and misery. But he looks at them all. He sees – and does not turn away his head. As a matter of fact he is courageous.

Courage and justice are not popular virtues. The practice of strict justice is shocking to the multitude who always (perhaps from an obscure sense of guilt) attach to it the meaning of mercy. In the majority of us, who want to be left alone with our illusions, courage inspires a vague alarm. This is what is felt about Maupassant. His qualities, to use the charming and popular phrase, are not lovable. Courage being a force will not masquerade in the robes of affected delicacy and restraint. But if his courage is not of a chivalrous stamp, it cannot be denied that it is never brutal for the sake of effect. The writer of these few reflections, inspired by a long and intimate acquaintance with the work of the man, has been struck by the appreciation of Maupassant manifested by many women gifted with tenderness and intelligence. Their more delicate and audacious souls are good judges of courage. Their finer penetration has discovered his genuine masculinity without display, his virility without a pose. They have discerned in his faithful dealings with the world that enterprising and fearless temperament, poor in ideas, but rich in power, which appeals most to the feminine mind.

It cannot be denied that he thinks very little. In him extreme energy of perception achieves great results, as in men of action the energy of force and desire. His view of intellectual problems is perhaps more simple than their nature warrants; still a man who has written 'Yvette' cannot be accused of want of subtlety. But one cannot insist enough upon this, that his subtlety, his humour, his grimness, though no doubt they are his own, are never presented otherwise but as belonging to our life, as found in nature whose beauties and cruelties alike breathe the spirit of serene unconsciousness.

Maupassant's philosophy of life is more temperamental than rational. He expects nothing from gods or men. He trusts his senses for information and his instinct for deductions. It may seem that he has made but little use of his mind. But let me be clearly understood. His sensibility is really very great; and it is impossible to be sensible, unless one thinks vividly, unless one thinks correctly, starting from intelligible premises to an unsophisticated conclusion.

This is literary honesty. It may be remarked that it does not differ very greatly from the ideal honesty of the respectable majority, from the honesty of law-givers, of warriors, of kings, of bricklayers, of all those who express their fundamental sentiment in the ordinary course of their activities, by the work of their hands.

The work of Maupassant's hands is honest. He thinks sufficiently to concrete his fearless conclusions in illuminative instances. He renders them with that exact knowledge of the means and that absolute devotion to the aim of creating a true effect – which is art. He is the most accomplished of narrators.

It is evident that Maupassant looked upon his mankind in another spirit than those writers who make haste to submerge the difficulties of our holding place in the universe under a flood of false and sentimental assumptions. Maupassant was a true and dutiful lover of our earth. He says himself in one of his descriptive passages: '*Nous autres que séduit la terre . . .*' It was true. The earth had for him a compelling charm. He looks upon her august and furrowed face with the fierce insight of real passion. His is the power of detecting the one immutable quality that matters in the changing aspects of nature and under the ever-shifting surface of life. To say that he could not embrace in his glance all its magnificence and all its misery is only to say that he was human. He lays claim to nothing that his matchless vision has not made his own. This creative artist has the true imagination; he never condescends to invent anything; he sets up no empty pretences. And he stoops to no littleness in his art — least of all to the miserable vanity of a catching phrase.

J. Conrad

Mademoiselle Perle
and Other Stories

The Field of Olives

I

W HEN THE MEN of Garandou, a little Provençal seaport
at the end of the Bay of Pisca, between Marseilles and
Toulon, made out the Abbé Vilbois's boat returning from fishing,
they went down to the shore to help in hauling her up.

The Abbé was alone, and, in spite of his fifty-eight years, he
pulled at the oars with uncommon energy, like an able seaman.
With his sleeves rolled over his muscular arms, with his cassock
turned up and held in place by his knees, and partly unbuttoned
at the chest, with his three-cornered hat lying on the seat by his
side, and wearing instead a cork helmet covered with white cloth,
he looked like a robust and exceptional priest in a tropical land,
a man more suited for adventure than for saying mass.

From time to time he glanced behind him to make certain of
the landing point, then recommenced pulling with a rhythmical,

3

powerful, steady stroke, to show those inferior sailors of the South once more how the men of the North can handle the oars.

The boat, keeping her way to the last, ran up the shore as if she meant to climb the sands, ploughing a furrow with her keel; then she stopped short, and the five men who had been watching the Abbé's arrival, drew near, looking pleased, appreciative, and full of good-will towards their priest.

'Well,' said one, with his strong Provençal accent, 'have you had a good catch, monsieur le curé?'

The Abbé Vilbois stowed his oars, changed his helmet for the three-cornered hat, turned down his sleeves, and buttoned up his cassock; then, having resumed the appearance and bearing of a village minister, he replied proudly:

'Yes, yes, excellent – three loups, two murènes, and some girelles.'

The five fishermen went up to the boat, they leaned over the gunwale, and with the air of connoisseurs examined the dead creatures, the fat loups, the flat-headed murènes, hideous serpents of the sea, and the violet girelles, streaked with zigzag, golden, orange-coloured stripes.

One of the men said:

'I will carry them home for you, monsieur le curé.'

'Thank you, my boy.'

The priest shook hands all round and started off, followed by the one man, leaving the others occupied with his boat.

He took long, slow strides, with an air of strength and dignity.

He was still warm from having rowed with so much vigour; in passing under the light shade of the olive trees he took off his hat now and then to expose, to the sultry evening air cooled a little by a slight breeze, his square forehead, surmounted with white hair, straight and close cut, the forehead of an officer rather than of a priest. The village came into sight, on a rising knoll, in the middle of a broad open valley sloping towards the sea.

It was a July evening. The dazzling sun, nearly touching the jagged crest of the distant hills, cast the interminable shadow of the priest slantingly over the white road that was buried under a shroud of dust. An enormous three-cornered hat went along in the neighbouring field, like a large sombre blotch, that seemed to play at climbing nimbly on to all the trunks of the olive trees that it met, to fall again immediately and creep along the ground.

From under the feet of the Abbé Vilbois a cloud of fine dust, of that impalpable flour-like powder with which the Provençal roads are covered in summer, rose up like smoke around his cassock, veiled it and shaded its hem with a grey tint, which, by degrees, grew lighter and lighter. He went along, refreshed now, with his hands in his pockets and the slow and powerful gait of a mountaineer making an ascent. His tranquil eyes looked at the village, his village, where he had been priest for twenty years — the village chosen by him, obtained by great favour, and where he counted on dying. The church — his church — crowned the large cone of houses packed closely together, with its two unequal and square towers of brown stone, that raised, in this beautiful southern valley, their ancient silhouettes, more like turrets of a strong castle than belfries of a sacred edifice.

The Abbé felt pleased, for he had caught three loups, two murènes, and some girelles.

He would have this fresh little triumph amongst his parishioners — he whom they esteemed above all, perhaps because he was, in spite of his age, the most muscular man in the neighbourhood. Those slight, innocent vanities were his greatest pleasure. He could cut the stem of flowers in two with a pistol shot, he fenced sometimes with his neighbour the tobacconist, an old regimental fencing master, and he could swim better than anyone on that coast.

He had once been a man of the world, well known and very elegant — the Baron Vilbois, who had taken orders at thirty-two, after an unfortunate love affair.

Descended from an old Picardian royalist and religious family, who, for several generations, had given their sons to the army, to the bench, or to the church, he had thought at first of following his mother's advice and taking orders; then, at the instance of his father, he had decided to go simply to Paris, to take his degree and afterwards to devote himself seriously to the law.

But while he was finishing his studies, his father succumbed to pneumonia after a day's shooting in the fens, and his mother, overcome with grief, died shortly afterwards. Then, having suddenly inherited a large fortune, he gave up the idea of making any kind of career, in order to enjoy the life of a rich man.

Being a handsome youth, and intelligent, although his mind was confined by beliefs, traditions, and principles, hereditary like his muscles of the Picardian squire, he pleased people; he was a success in good society, and enjoyed the life of a high-principled, wealthy, and esteemed young man.

But it happened that, after some meetings at a friend's house, he fell in love with a young actress, quite a young pupil from the Conservatoire, who had made a brilliant début at the Odéon.

He fell in love with her with all the violence, with all the passion, of a man born to believe in absolute ideas. He fell in love with her, seeing her through the romantic part in which she had obtained her great success the first time she appeared before the public.

She was pretty, naturally perverse, with the air of a naive child, which he called the air of an angel. She knew how to conquer him completely, how to make of him one of those raving madmen, one of those lunatics that a single glance or a fluttering skirt of a woman kindles into flame on the pile of mortal passions. He took her as his mistress, made her leave the stage, and loved her, for four years, with continually increasing ardour. Certainly, in spite of his name and the honourable traditions of his family, he would have ended by marrying her, if he had not discovered one day that she had been deceiving him for a long time, with the friend who had introduced him to her.

The drama was all the more terrible in that she was enceinte, and he was awaiting the birth of the child to make up his mind about the marriage.

When he held in his hands the proofs (some letters he had discovered in a drawer), he reproached her for her unfaithfulness, her perfidy, and her ignominy, with all his half-savage brutality.

But she, impudent and audacious, as certain of the one man as of the other, a child of the people that erect barricades, braved and insulted his anger; and when he was on the point of giving way to his fury, she cried:

'Don't kill me. The child is not yours, it's his.'

This arrested him; and she, afraid at last of the death which she saw coming from the glance and terrifying gestures of that man, repeated:

'It isn't yours. It's his.'

He murmured with clenched teeth, thunderstruck:

'The child.'

'Yes.'

'You lie.'

He could not believe it. And before the persistent menace of his aspect she made a last effort to save her life.

'I tell you it is his. Think how long we have been living together! You would have been a father before now.'

This argument struck him as being like truth itself. In one of those flashes of thought, when so many arguments appear at the same time with illuminating clearness, precise, irrefutable, conclusive, and irresistible, he was convinced; he was sure that he could not be the father of that unborn, miserable offspring of a

8

prostitute; and, suddenly relieved, set free, and almost appeased, he gave up all thought of killing this infamous creature.

He said in a calmer voice:

'Get up, be off, and don't let me ever see you again.'

She obeyed. She was vanquished, and went away.

He never saw her again.

He, for his part, went away also. He went towards the south, towards the sun, and stopped in a village, in the middle of a valley, by the side of the Mediterranean. The appearance of a little inn, with a view of the sea, pleased him; he took a room in it and resolved to stay. He lived there eighteen months, in his grief, in his despair, in complete isolation. He lived there with the preying memory of the treacherous woman, of her charm, her atmosphere, her indescribable sorcery, her presence, and her caresses.

He wandered about the Provençal valleys, walking in the sunlight that fell sifting through the greyish leaves of the olive trees, haunted by his one thought, brain-sick and weary.

But his old pious ideas, his first faith (its ardour a little cooled) returned very gently to his heart in this dolorous solitude. Religion, which had appeared to him before like the abandonment of an unknown world, appeared to him now like a refuge from a life full of deceit and torture. He had preserved the habit of prayer. In his grief he took refuge in that, and he often went, in the twilight, to kneel down in the shadowy church, where the speck of light sparkled from the lamp, alone at the end of the choir, sacred guardian of the sanctuary and symbol of the divine presence.

He dared to confide his trouble to God; to his God; and he told Him of all his wretchedness. He asked Him for advice, pity, help, protection, and consolation; and each time he put more feeling into his prayers, which he repeated every day with an increasing fervour.

His bruised heart, eaten up by the love for a woman, remained open and throbbing, always desirous of tenderness; and little by little, by dint of praying, by living like a hermit with growing habits of piety, by abandoning himself to the secret communication of devout souls with the Saviour who consoles and enshrouds the wretched sinner, the mystical love for God took possession of his soul and drove away the other passion.

Then he resumed his early plans, and decided to offer to the Church a shattered life which he had been so near giving her with its purity intact.

He was ordained a priest. Using the influence of his family and his high connections, he got himself appointed to serve in this poor village parish in Provence, where chance had thrown him at first; having given away a great part of his wealth to charity, he kept only as much as would allow him to remain useful and helpful to the poor until his death; and he took refuge in a tranquil existence of pious practices and devotion to his fellow beings.

He made a worthy priest, with narrow views, a kind of

religious guide with a soldier's temperament, a guide of the Church who masterfully leads into the straight road erring, blind humanity, lost in this forest of life, where all our instincts, our tastes, our desires are tracks that direct us astray. But much of the man of another time remained alive in him. He did not lose his love of violent exercise, active sports, and fencing; and he dreaded women, all of them, with the fear of a child before a mysterious danger.

II

THE SAILOR WHO followed the priest had on the tip of his tongue all the southerner's desire to talk. He was afraid to, for the Abbé cast a spell of respect over his flock. At last he hazarded:

'Well, does your little bastide please you, monsieur le curé?'

This little place was one of those microscopic houses where the Provençals settle down in summer for a change from town and village. The Abbé had hired this tiny dwelling in a field, five minutes' walk from the vicarage (which was too small and confined), in the centre of the parish, close to the church.

He did not live in the bastide continuously even in summer, he only went there for a few days, now and again, to breathe freely in the midst of the fields and to do some pistol practice.

'Yes, my friend,' said the priest, 'I like being there.'

Built amongst trees, the low pink-painted dwelling came into sight. Striped, welted, and cut into little pieces by the branches and leaves of the olive trees, with which the unenclosed field was planted, the little place seemed to have sprung up like a Provençal mushroom.

A tall woman was to be seen passing many times before the door, preparing a little table for dinner. She laid with methodical deliberation a solitary knife and fork, a plate, a serviette, a piece of bread, a glass. She wore a little Arlésienne cap, peaked up with black silk velvet, with a mushroom-like crown of white muslin.

When the Abbé was within earshot, he called out to her:

'Hey, Marguerite!'

She paused to look up, and recognized her master.

'Té! Here you are, monsieur le curé?'

'Yes. I have brought you a good catch; go and cook this loup immediately, in butter, nothing but butter, melted butter, d'you hear?'

The servant approaching them examined, with the eye of a connoisseur, the fish which the sailor carried.

'But we have already got a boiled fowl,' she said.

'That can't be helped. Fish a day old is nothing to fish that is fresh from the water. I will have a little feast, it does not happen too often, and besides the sin is not a great one.'

The woman picked out the loup, and as she was going away carrying it, she turned back.

'Oh! A man has been here three times to see you, sir!'

He asked with indifference:

'A man! What sort of a man?'

'A fellow that's not much good.'

'What! A beggar?'

'Perhaps, yes, I can't say. I should rather think an evil-doer – a maoufatan.'

The Abbé Vilbois laughed at this Provençal word, which signified a malefactor and a tramp, for he knew of Marguerite's timid disposition; whenever she stayed in the lonely bastide, she would imagine all day long and, above all at night, that they were going to be murdered.

He gave some coppers to the fisherman, who went off; and then, having retained all the careful habits and customs of his previous life, he was saying: 'I will go and wash my face and hands,' when Marquerite from the kitchen, where she was already scraping the fish, whose scales came off a little besmeared with blood, like infinitesimal silver sequins, called out:

'Look! – here he is.'

The Abbé turned to look along the road, and saw a man, who appeared in the distance to be very poorly clad, coming slowly towards the house. He waited, still smiling over his servant's terror, and thinking: 'Really, I believe she is right, he certainly looks like a maoufatan.'

The stranger came near, without hurrying himself, with his hands in his pockets and his eyes on the priest. He was young, with a long, fair curly beard; locks of hair waved about under his soft felt hat, so dirty and knocked about that no one would have been able to guess its original colour and shape. He wore a long, maroon overcoat, a pair of trousers frayed at the ankles, and shoes of plaited grass, called espadrilles, which gave him a soft, suspicious, almost silent gait, the inaudible step of a prowler.

When a few strides away from the priest, he took off the ragged felt that screened his brow, baring to view, with rather a theatrical air, a crapulous, worn, good-looking face, a head with a bald patch on the top, a sign of privation or precocious debauch, for this man certainly did not look more than five-and-twenty.

The priest also took off his hat, feeling instinctively that this fellow was no ordinary vagabond, no casual, no labourer out of work, or habitual criminal on the tramp between two terms of imprisonment, speaking nothing but the mysterious slang of the jails.

'Good day, monsieur le curé,' said the man. The priest answered simply, 'Good day to you' – not wishing to address this suspiciously ragged person as 'Monsieur'. They looked at one another fixedly, and the Abbé Vilbois, under the gaze of this tramp, felt uneasy and agitated, as though face to face with an unknown enemy; invaded by one of those strange anxieties which creep with shudders through flesh and blood.

At last the vagabond answered:

'Well, d'you know me?'

The priest answered, very astonished:

'I? Not in the least: I don't know you in the least.'

'Ah, not in the least. Take another good look at me.'

'It's no use my looking at you, I am sure I've never seen you in my life.'

'That's true enough,' replied the other, ironically, 'but I will show you someone that you'll know better.'

He put on his hat again and unbuttoned his overcoat. His chest was bare underneath. Around his thin stomach a red belt kept his trousers up over his hips.

He took an envelope out of his pocket; one of those amazing envelopes, stained, marbled with every possible blotch; one of those envelopes produced out of the coat linings of wandering scoundrels, together with some sort of papers, either stolen or genuine, the precious upholders of liberty against any gendarme. He drew out a photograph, a carte-de-visite, an old-fashioned portrait gone yellow, rubbed and much worn, warmed in the contact with the man's flesh, and dimmed by the heat of his body.

Then, holding it up on a level with his face, he asked:

'And this one here, do you know him?'

The Abbé took two steps forward to see it better, and stood there growing pale, astounded, for it was his very own portrait given to *her* in the remote time of their love.

He said nothing, not understanding.

The vagabond repeated:

'D'you know him – this one?'

The priest stammered:

'Yes, of course.'

'Who is it?'

'It's myself.'

'Is it really you?'

'Of course.'

'Well then, look at us – look at both of us now; look at your portrait and look at me.'

He had seen it already, the wretched man. He had seen that these two beings, the one on the card and the one who grinned beside it, resembled each other like two brothers; but he did not yet understand it all, and he faltered.

'What do you want with me in any case?'

Then replied the scoundrel, in a wicked voice:

'What do I want? Why! First of all I want you to recognize me.'

'Who are you, then?'

'Who am I? Go and ask anyone on the road; ask your servant; let us go and ask the mayor if you like, and show him this, and he will fairly laugh, I can tell you! Ah! So you don't want to acknowledge me for your son, papa curé?'

Then, the old man, raising up his arms with a biblical and despairing gesture, groaned:

'It is not true.'

The young man closed up with him, face to face.

'Ah, it is not true! Ah, Abbé, there's an end to lying now – do you hear.'

His face was menacing and his hands clenched, he spoke with so violent a conviction, that the priest, gradually drawing back, was asking himself which of the two at this moment was mistaken.

However, he persisted once more:

'I have never had a child.'

The other retorted:

'Nor yet a mistress, perhaps?'

The old man uttered resolutely, one single word, a proud avowal:

'Yes.'

'And that mistress was not expecting a child when you drove her away?'

Suddenly the old anger of twenty-five years past, not really stifled, but only immured in the depths, broke through the vaultings of faith, of resigned devotion, of complete renunciation, which he had erected over his lover's heart; and, beside himself, he exclaimed:

'I cast her out because she had deceived me and because she bore the child of another – or else I should have killed her, monsieur, and you too at the same time.'

The young man hesitated, surprised in his turn by the sincere passion of the priest; then he replied slowly:

'Who told you this story, that it was someone else's child?'

'She did, she herself, she told me so, defying me.'

Then the vagabond, without disputing this assertion, concluded with the indifferent tone of a street rough, pronouncing a judgment.

'Oh well! Then it's mother who made the little mistake when she went for you, that's all.'

Regaining mastery over himself, after this outburst of fury, the Abbé inquired:

'And who was it told you that you were my son?'

'She did, when she was dying, monsieur le curé. And then – this.'

He held out the little photograph.

The old man took it in his hand; slowly, for a long time, with rising anguish, he compared this unknown prowler with his old likeness, and he could doubt no longer that this was indeed his own son.

A feeling of distress swept into his soul; an inexpressible emotion, unbearably painful, like the remorse of a former crime. He understood a little, he could guess the rest. He saw again the brutal scene of separation. It had been in order to save her own life, threatened by the outraged man, that the woman, the false and perfidious woman, had thrown out that lie at him. And the lie had been successful. A son had been born to him, had grown up, had become this mean street runner, who exhaled the scent of vice as a he-goat exhales his odour.

He murmured:

'Will you come a few steps with me, so that we may have some further talk about this?'

The other chuckled.

'Of course, parbleu! That's just what I came here for.'

They started off together, side by side, along the field of olives. The sun had disappeared. The exceeding freshness of a southern twilight spread a cold invisible mantle over the country. The Abbé shivered, and suddenly lifting his eyes with the customary movement of an officiating minister, he perceived all around him, trembling in the sky, the little greyish leafage of the sacred tree which had sheltered in its frail shadow the greatest sorrow, the only wavering of the Christ.

A short and desperate prayer rose up to his lips, formed by that internal voice, which does not pass at all through the mouth, and by which believers implore the Saviour: 'My God, help me.'

Then, turning towards his son:

'So you say your mother is dead?'

A fresh grief awoke in him while uttering the words, 'your mother is dead,' and gripped his heart; a strange misery of the flesh which has never done with remembering, and a cruel echo of the torture that he had passed through; but still more, perhaps, now that she was gone, a revival of that short, delirious happiness of youth whereof nothing remained but the wound of her recollection.

The young man replied:

'Yes, monsieur le curé, my mother is dead.'

'A long time ago?'

'Yes, these three years already.'

Another doubt occurred to the priest.

'How is it you have not come to see me before this?'

The other hesitated.

'I couldn't. I have had hindrances . . . But pardon my inter-rupting these disclosures which I will go into later as minutely as you please, in order just to mention that I have eaten nothing since yesterday morning.'

A sudden feeling of pity quite moved the old man, and holding out both his hands hastily:

'Oh, my poor child,' he said.

The young man received his large, stretched-out hands, which grasped his more slender, warm, and feverish fingers.

Then he answered with that chaffing sneer which hardly ever left his lips:

'Well, really! I begin to think we shall understand one another after all.'

The priest walked briskly.

'Let us go and dine,' he said.

He thought suddenly, with a little feeling of pleasure, instinct-ive, confused, and bizarre, of the fine fish that he had caught, which, together with the boiled fowl, would make a good meal for his miserable child.

The Arlésienne, restless and already grumbling, was waiting at the door.

'Marguerite,' called the Abbé, 'clear the table and carry it into the sitting-room. Quickly, quickly, and set two places. Quickly.'

The servant was scared at the thought of her master's going to dine with this good-for-nothing.

Then the Abbé Vilbois himself commenced to clear away and to transfer the table, laid out for him alone, into the only room on the ground floor.

Five minutes later he was seated opposite the vagabond, before a tureen full of cabbage soup, from which a little cloud of steam rose up between both their faces.

III

WHEN THE PLATES had been filled, the vagabond began to swallow his soup eagerly in rapid spoonfuls. The Abbé was no longer hungry, and he only sipped the savoury cabbage soup slowly, leaving the bread at the bottom of his plate.

Suddenly he asked:

'How do you call yourself?'

The man laughed with the satisfaction of appeased hunger.

'Father unknown,' said he. 'No other surname than my mother's, which you probably have not forgotten. To make up for that I've two Christian names, which, by-the-bye, are hardly suitable, "Philippe Auguste".'

The Abbé turned pale, and asked with a lump in his throat:

'Why did they give you those names?'

The vagabond shrugged his shoulders.

'You can easily guess. After you had gone, mother wished to make your rival believe that I was his, and he did believe it until I was about fifteen. But at that time I commenced to resemble you too much. And he disowned me, the scoundrel. You see, they had given me his two Christian names, Philippe Auguste, and if I had happened not to resemble anyone in particular, or to have been simply the son of a third rascal, who had never shown up, I should call myself today, Vicomte Philippe Auguste de Pravallon, the lately recognized son of the count of that name, senator. As for me, I have christened myself "Ill-starred".'

'How do you know all that?'

'Because they had it out before me, parbleu! – rowing each other like anything. You may guess. Ah, that's the sort of thing to open your eyes.'

Something more painful and more tormenting than all he had endured and suffered for the last half-hour oppressed the priest. It created in him a feeling of suffocation, which would grow and would end by killing him; and this came not so much from the things that he heard as from the way in which they were said, and from the vile expression of the rascal that underlined their meaning. Between this man and himself, between his son and himself, he was beginning to perceive the depths of moral turpitude, like a foul sewer, which acts like fatal poison on certain souls. Was this a son of his own? He could not yet believe it. He wished for all the proofs, all of them; to learn everything, to hear everything, to listen to everything, to suffer everything. He thought again of the olive trees that surrounded his little bastide, and murmured for the second time: 'Oh, my God, help me.'

Philippe Auguste had finished his soup. He asked: 'Isn't there anything more to eat, Abbé?'

The kitchen was outside the house, in an adjoining building, and as Marguerite could not hear her master's voice so far, he would call her by striking a Chinese gong, which hung on the wall behind him.

He took up the stick with a leather head, and struck the flat disc of metal several times. A feeble ringing sound came forth at first, then, growing louder, became an accentuated, vibrating, piercing, overpowering, ear-splitting uproar – the horrible plaint of beaten brass.

The servant appeared. She had a sour expression, and she cast furious glances at the maoufatan, as if she had a presentiment with her faithful, dog-like instinct, of the drama that had fallen on her master. In her hands she carried the grilled loup, from which wafted up a savoury odour of melted butter. The Abbé divided the fish from end to end with a spoon, and offered the fillet out of the back to the child of his youth:

'I caught it myself a little while ago,' he said, with the remains of pride that welled up in his distress.

Marguerite did not go away.

'Bring some wine – the best, the white wine of Cap Corse.'

She made almost a gesture of revolt, and he had to repeat severely:

'Go along: two bottles.' For, when he offered some wine to anyone, a rare pleasure to him, he always allowed himself a bottle of it.

Philippe Auguste, beaming, murmured:

'That's prime. It's a long time since I have had a meal like this.'

The servant came back in two minutes. They had seemed long to the Abbé, like eternity, for a desire to know everything was now burning in his blood, consuming it as with an infernal flame.

The bottles had been uncorked, but the servant stayed there with her eyes on the man.

'You may leave us,' the priest said.

She pretended not to hear.

He repeated almost roughly:

'I have told you to leave us alone.'

Then she went off.

Philippe Auguste devoured the fish with voracious haste; his father watched him, more and more surprised and tormented by all the vileness he discovered in this face which resembled his own so much. The little morsels that the Abbé lifted to his lips, that his parched throat refused to swallow, remained in his mouth, and he masticated them a long time, while he sought amongst all the questions that came into his mind, the one which he wished to be first answered.

He ended by murmuring:

'What did she die of?'

'The lungs.'

'Was she ill for a long time?'

'About eighteen months.'

'What did it come from?'

'Nobody knows.'

They became silent. The Abbé was pondering. So many things that he might have wished to know before depressed him, for since the day of parting, since the day when he had almost killed her, he had heard nothing whatever about her. Certainly, he had not wished to hear; he had cast her away resolutely into a pit of forgetfulness, her and his days of felicity; but now she was dead, there had sprung up in him an ardent desire to hear all about her, a jealous longing, almost a lover's desire.

He went on:

'She was not living alone, was she?'

'No, she was still with him.'

The old man started.

'With him, with Pravallon?'

'Why, yes!'

And the formerly betrayed man calculated that this same woman who had deceived him had lived faithfully with his rival for more than thirty years.

He stammered almost in spite of himself:

'Were they happy together?'

The young man replied, chuckling:

'Oh, yes, with up and downs. It would have been all right without me. I always spoilt everything – I did.'

'How, why?' said the priest.

'I have already told you about it. Because he believed I was his son until I was about fifteen. But he was not a fool, the old fellow; he discovered the resemblance quite of his own accord, and then there were rows. As for me, I listened at the keyholes. He accused mother of having taken him in. Mother retorted: "Is it my fault? You knew very well when you took me that I was someone else's." That someone was you.'

'Ah, then, they spoke of me sometimes?'

'Yes, but they never mentioned you before me, except at the last, just at the end, in the last days, when mother felt herself lost. They were careful enough in that way, anyhow.'

'And you, you soon learned that your mother's position was irregular?'

'Rather! I'm not a fool, I'm not, and I never have been. One guesses these things directly, as soon as one begins to know the world.'

Philippe Auguste filled himself glass after glass. His eyes brightened; he was getting drunk all the quicker for his long fast. The priest, noticing his state, was on the point of interfering, when it occurred to him that a drunken man will chatter without reserve of what is uppermost in his mind, and, taking the bottle, he filled the young man's glass again.

Marguerite brought in the boiled fowl. Having placed it on

the table, she glared at the tramp again; then she said to her master indignantly:

'But look at him, monsieur le curé – he's drunk.'

'Leave us in peace,' replied the priest, 'and go away.'

She went out, slamming the door.

He asked:

'What did your mother say about me?'

'Why, just what one always says of a man one has thrown over; that you were not easy to get on with – worrying to a woman – and would have made her life very difficult with your ideas.'

'Did she often say that?'

'Yes, sometimes in a roundabout way, so that I should not understand, but I guessed everything all the same.'

'And you, how did they treat you in that house?'

'Me? Very well at first, and afterwards very badly. When mother saw that I was spoiling her game, she kicked me out.'

'How was that?'

'How was that? Very simple. I had played a few pranks when I was about sixteen, and then those heartless swine put me into a reformatory, to get rid of me.'

He propped his elbows on the table, rested his two cheeks between his hands, and quite inebriated, the balance of his mind upset by the wine, he was suddenly seized with one of those irresistible impulses to talk of himself, which make drunkards ramble into the most fantastic bragging speeches.

He smiled prettily, with feminine grace in the curl of the lip, a perverse grace, well known to the priest. Not only did he recognize it, but he felt the hateful and endearing charm that had conquered him and had ruined his life in the past. It was the mother that the child most resembled now; he resembled her not so much in feature as in the captivating and false expression of his face, and above all, by the seduction of the deceitful smiling lips, which seemed to open the door to all the infamy inside.

Philippe Auguste related:

'Ah! Ah! Ah! I have had a life of it, I have, since the reformatory; a funny life, for which a big novelist would give a tidy price, I can tell you! Really père Dumas, in his *Monte Cristo*, has found nothing more extravagant than what I've passed through.'

He became silent, with the philosophical gravity of a drunken man who is reflecting; then, slowly:

'When one wishes a boy to turn out well, one should never send him into a reformatory, whatever he may have done, because of what he learns in there. I had played a good joke, I had, but it turned out badly. As I was fooling about with three chums, all of us a little tight, one evening, towards nine o'clock, on the highroad, near the ford across the Folac, I came across a trap full of people, all asleep. There was the driver and his family, and they were some people from Martinon returning from a dinner in town. I took hold of the horse by the bridle, I led him quietly down into the ferry-boat, and then I shoved the whole thing into the middle of the river. That made some noise: the chap who was driving wakes up, the night was dark, he sees nothing and whips up his gee-gee. Then the old crock starts off with a jump and tumbles into the river, trap and all. All drowned! My pals gave me away. They had laughed enough at first, watching my little joke. Certainly, we didn't think it would turn out so badly. We wanted to give them nothing more than a bath, something funny to laugh at.

'Since that I have done worse things to revenge myself for the first, which did not deserve the reformatory, upon my honour. But it's not worth while telling you all. I will tell you only the last, because it will please you, I'm sure. I have revenged you, papa.'

The Abbé looked at his son with terrified eyes, and he ate nothing more.

Philippe Auguste was ready to go on.

'No,' said the priest, 'not just now – presently.'

Turning round, he beat the strident gong and made it cry out.

Marguerite entered immediately.

Her master gave his orders in such a harsh voice, that she bent her head submissive and alarmed.

'Bring us the lamp and all that you have still to put on the table, then you need not come in again until you hear the gong.'

She went away, came back and put on the cloth a white porcelain lamp, covered with a green shade, a big piece of cheese, some fruit and then left them.

The Abbé said resolutely:

'Now, I am ready to listen to you.'

Philippe Auguste calmly filled his dessert plate and poured some wine into his glass. The second bottle was nearly empty, although the curé had drunk nothing at all.

The young man commenced again, stammering, his utterance made thick with food and drunkenness.

'The last, here it is. It's a good one: I had returned home . . . and I stayed there in spite of them, because they were afraid of me . . . afraid of me . . . Ah! I'm not a person to be put upon . . . I'm capable of anything when I'm roused . . . you know . . . they lived . . . not together. He had two houses – he had the house of a senator and the house of a lover. But he lived more with mother than alone, for he could not get on without her. Ah . . . she was a clever one and a fine one. She knew how to keep hold of a man, she did. She had him in her clutches, body and soul, and she kept him until the end. What fools men are. So, I returned, and I made them afraid of me. I know my way about, I do! When I am put to it, for malice, craftiness, and strength, too, I am up to any man alive. Well then, mother fell ill, and he took her to a beautiful estate near the Meulan, in the middle of a park as large as a forest. That lasted about eighteen months . . . as I have told you . . . Then we saw the end was coming. He came from Paris every day, and he grieved – certainly real grief.

'Then, one morning, they had been chattering for nearly an hour, and I was asking myself what they could find to jabber about so long, when they called me in. And mother said to me:

'"I am near dying, and there is something that I want to disclose to you in spite of the count's advice." She always called him the count in speaking of him. "It is the name of your father, who is still alive."

'I had asked her more than a hundred times . . . more than a hundred times . . . my father's name . . . more than a hundred times . . . and she had always refused to tell me.

'I believe, even, that one day I gave her a slap in the face, to make her blurt it out, but it was no good. And then, in order to get rid of me, she had told me that you had died penniless, that you were a man of not much account, anyhow – an error of her youth, a young girl's mistake, don't you see. She went about it so jolly well, that she took me in completely, took me in with that story of your death.

'Then she said to me:

'"It is your father's name."

'The other, who was seated in an armchair, said like this three times:

'"You are doing wrong, you are doing wrong, you are doing wrong, Rosette."

'Mother sat up in bed, and I see her still, with her red cheek bones and brilliant eyes; for she loved me very much, in spite of everything; and she said to him:

'"Then do something for him yourself, Philippe!"

'In speaking to him, she called him Philippe, and me she called Auguste.

'He began to shout like a madman.

'"For that drunkard, for that scamp, that liberated convict, that . . . that . . . that . . ."

'And he found as many names for me as if he had not tried for anything else all his life.

'I was getting angry, too: mother pacified me, and said to him:

'"You wish him to starve then, for I haven't anything, I haven't."

'He replied, without upsetting himself very much:

'"Rosette, I have given you thirty-five thousand francs a year for thirty years; that makes more than a million. You have lived with me a rich woman, a beloved woman, I may say a happy woman. I do not owe anything to this scoundrel, who has spoilt our last years; and he shall have nothing from me. It is useless to insist. Refer him to the other one if you like. I regret it, but I wash my hands of all this."

'Then mother turned towards me. I said to myself: "Good . . . here I am finding out my father at last . . . if he has got the tin, I am a made man . . ."

'She continued:

'"Your father, Baron Vilbois, is now called the Abbé Vilbois, curé of Garandou, near Toulon. He was my lover when I left him for this one."

'And she told me all, except that she made a fool of you about her pregnancy. But women, you know, never can speak the truth.'

He chuckled, letting out unconsciously and freely all his vileness. He drank again, and, with his face continually beaming, he continued:

'Mother died two days, two days after. We followed her coffin to the cemetery, he and I – isn't it funny . . . eh? . . . he and I . . . and three servants . . . that was all. He wept like a cow . . . we were side by side . . . one would have said the father and the father's son.

'Then we went back to the house. Only we two. I said to myself: "I suppose I must be off without a sou." I had only fifty francs. What could I do to revenge myself?

'He touched my arm, and said:

'"I want to speak to you."

'I followed him into his study. He sat down before his desk; then, slobbering and all in tears, he told me that he did not wish to be as disagreeable to me as he had told mother; he begged me not to worry you . . . This concerns us, though, you and me . . . He offered me a bank note for a thousand . . . a thousand . . . a thousand . . . What could I do with a thousand francs . . . I . . . a man like me? I saw that he had more money in his drawer, a whole lot of notes. The sight of all that paper made me itch to stick the beast. I stretched out my hand to take the note he was holding out, but instead of taking hold of his cursed dole, I spring on him, I throw him on to the ground, I grasp his throat until his eyes begin to start out of his head; then, when I saw he was pretty near gone, I gagged him, tied him up hand and foot, undressed him and turned him over . . . Ah . . . ah . . . ah . . . I revenged you . . .'

Philippe Auguste coughed, spluttered with glee, and on his lips, parted with a grin of ferocious gaiety, the Abbé Vilbois saw always the old smile of the woman who had made him lose his head.

'And then?' he asked.

'Then . . . Ah . . . ah . . . ah . . . There was a big fire in the grate . . . it was in December . . . in the cold weather . . . that she died . . . mother . . . a large fire of coal . . . I took the poker . . . I made it red hot . . . and then . . . I burned some crosses with it, on his back, eight, ten, I don't know how many . . . Wasn't that a lark, eh? papa. That's the way they used to brand the convicts. He writhed like an eel . . . but I had gagged him well . . . he couldn't shout. Then I took the notes . . . twelve – with mine that made thirteen (they brought me no luck). And then I bolted, telling the servants not to disturb the count until dinner time, as he was asleep.

'I really thought he would say nothing for fear of the scandal, seeing that he is a senator. I made a mistake. Four days after I was nabbed in a restaurant in Paris. I had three years in chokey. That is why I have not been able to come to see you sooner.'

He drank again, and stammering so that he could hardly pronounce his words:

'Now . . . papa . . . papa curé! . . . It's funny to have a priest for a father! Ah . . . ah . . . you must be nice, very nice with

34

bibi, because bibi is not of the common sort . . . and because he played a good joke . . . is it not true . . . a good one . . . on the old fellow . . .'

The same anger which formerly had maddened the Abbé Vilbois against his treacherous mistress roused him now against this abominable man.

He, who had pardoned so much in God's name, the infamous secrets whispered in the mystery of the confessional, felt without pity, without mercy in his own name, and now he no longer called to his aid the God of succour and of pity, for he understood that no protection, celestial or earthly, can save those here below upon whom fall such misfortunes.

All the ardour of his passionate heart and violent blood, extinguished by his sacred office, awoke with irresistible revolt against this scoundrel who was his son, against this resemblance to himself and also to the mother, the infamous mother who had formed him like her, and against the fate which riveted this wretch to his paternity as a cannon-ball is riveted to the foot of a galley slave.

He saw, he foresaw everything in the sudden clearness, awakened by this shock from the twenty-five years of pious sleep and tranquillity.

Suddenly, convinced that he must speak strongly to be feared by this malefactor, and to terrify him from the first, he said, his teeth clenched in fury, and no longer thinking of the man's drunkenness:

'Now that you have told me all, listen to me. You shall go away tomorrow morning. I'll tell you where you are to live. You shall never leave the place without my permission. I will make you an allowance which will be sufficient for your necessities, but it will be small, because I have no money. If you disobey me once, all will be at an end, and you'll have to reckon with me.'

Although besotted with the wine he had drunk, Philippe Auguste understood the threat. The criminal in him surged up suddenly. He spat out words mingled with hiccoughs.

'Ah, papa, you mustn't try it on with me . . . You are a curé . . . I have you . . . and you will have to cave in . . . you too . . . like the rest.'

The Abbé started up; and there was twitching in his muscles of an old Hercules an invincible impulse to seize this monster, to bend him like a twig, and to show him that he must yield to his will.

He shouted, shaking the table with both his hands against the other's chest.

'Ah! take care, take care . . . you'll find that I'm not afraid of anyone . . .'

The drunken man, losing his balance, swayed in his chair. Feeling that he was going to fall, and that he was in the priest's power, he stretched out his hand, with a murderous look, towards one of the knives on the cloth. The Abbé Vilbois saw the movement, and gave a violent push to the table, overturning his son headlong on to his back. He lay sprawling on the floor. The lamp rolled over and went out.

For a few seconds a delicate tinkle of glasses, ringing against each other, sounded in the darkness; then there was the thud of a soft body falling, then nothing more.

With the shattering of the lamp the sudden night was shed over them – a night so swift, unexpected, and profound, that they were amazed by it, as though by some frightful event. The drunken man, cowering against the wall, did not move any more; and the priest remained on his chair, immersed in the deep gloom which had swallowed up his anger. This sombre veil cast over him, arresting his passion, stilled also the furious impetuosity of his soul, and other thoughts came to him, as black and sad as the darkness.

Silence fell, the heavy silence of a closed tomb, where nothing seemed to live or breathe any more. No sound came from outside, no rumbling of wheels in the distance, no barking of a dog, no rustle in the branches or along the walls of a faint breath of wind.

This lasted a long time, a very long time, perhaps for a whole hour. Then suddenly the gong rang out! It rang out under a single blow, hard, sharp, and strong, after which came a strange noise of something falling heavily and of a chair overturning.

Marguerite, still on the alert, came running to the room; but as soon as she had opened the door she drew back amazed at the impenetrable darkness within. Then, trembling, with a beating heart, and in a gasping, low voice, she called out:

'M'sieu l'curé, m'sieu l'curé!'

No one answered, nothing stirred.

'Good Lord, good Lord,' she thought, 'what have they done? What has happened?'

She did not dare to advance, she did not dare to go back to get a light; a wild impulse to run away, to escape, and to shriek out took hold of her, although she felt her legs tremble as if she were going to drop.

She repeated:

'M'sieu l'curé . . . m'sieu l'curé, it's me — Marguerite.'

But suddenly, in spite of her fear, an instinctive desire to help her master, and one of those audacities of women which come to them in heroic moments, filled her soul with terrified boldness. She ran to the kitchen and brought her little lamp.

She stopped at the door of the room. At first she observed the vagabond stretched out against the wall asleep, or seeming to be asleep, then the broken lamp, then, under the table, the two black feet and black stockinged legs of the Abbé Vilbois, who, stretched on his back must have struck the gong with his head as he fell.

She panted with fright, her hands trembled. She repeated:

'My God! my God! what is this?'

And approaching nearer, slowly, with short steps, she slipped on something greasy, and very nearly fell down.

Then, stooping low, she noticed that on the red floor a liquid equally red was running, spreading around her feet, and flowing quickly towards the door. She guessed that it was blood!

Nearly out of her mind, she flung away her light in order not to see any more, and took to flight; she flew across the dark land towards the village, stumbling headlong against the trees, with her eyes fixed on the distant lights of the houses, and shrieking as she ran.

Her piercing voice swept out into the night like the sinister cry of a screech owl, and it yelled without ceasing: 'The maoufatan! . . . the maoufatan! . . . the maoufatan!'

When she reached the first houses, a number of excited men ran out and surrounded her, but she only struggled amongst them without answering, for she had very nearly lost her senses.

In the end they understood that there was something very wrong in the Abbé's bastide out in the fields, and snatching up whatever came to hand, a number of them ran in a body to offer assistance.

The little pink-tinted cottage in the middle of the field of olives had become invisible and black in the dark and silent night. Ever since the only light of its bright window had been extinguished like an eye that is closed, it had stood immersed, lost in the darkness, undiscoverable for anyone not a native of the place.

Soon some lights appeared running along close to the ground, amongst the trees. They ran over the parched grass with long yellow beams; and, struck by their wandering flashes, the twisted branches of the olive trees showed fitfully like monsters, like serpents from hell entwined and writhing. The reflections falling afar brought out of the darkness something pale and indistinct at first; then the low square wall of the little dwelling became pink again in the light of the lanterns. Some villagers who carried them were escorting two gendarmes, revolvers in hand, the garde-champêtre, the mayor, and Marguerite, who was being assisted by some men. She was in a half-fainting condition.

Before the door that remained alarmingly open, there was a moment of hesitation. But the brigadier seized a lantern, went in first, and was followed by the others.

The old woman had spoken the truth. The blood, congealed now, covered the tiles like a carpet. It had reached the vagabond, where he lay with one of his feet and one of his hands in the red pool.

The father and the son were both sleeping, the one with his throat cut, in the sleep everlasting, and the other plunged in a drunkard's slumber.

The two gendarmes rushed upon him, and before he was well awake he had the handcuffs on his wrists. He rubbed his eyes in besotted amazement, muddled with the wine; and when he saw the dead body of the priest, his face took on an expression of bewildered terror.

'How is it he didn't clear out?' the mayor wondered.

'He was too drunk,' replied the brigadier.

And they all agreed with him; for the idea would never have occurred to anyone, that, perhaps, the Abbé Vilbois had taken his own life.

The Return

THE SEA CHAFES the shore with short, monotonous waves. Little white clouds pass quickly across the wide blue sky, driven like birds by the strong wind; and the village, basking in the sun, nestles in the fold of a dale which slants down to the ocean.

Alone, at the entrance to the hamlet, by the side of the road, stands the house of the Martin-Lévesques. It is a fisherman's cottage, with clay walls and a thatched roof bedecked with tufts of blue irises. A few onions, cabbages, parsley, and chervil sprout up in a kitchen garden, that is no larger than a pocket-handkerchief; it forms a square before the door; a hedge separates it from the high road.

The husband has gone out fishing, and in front of the hut the wife is mending a great brown net, which hangs spread out over the wall like an immense spider's web. At the entrance to the garden, a girl of fourteen is sitting on a rush-bottomed chair, tilted against the post of the gate. She is mending some linen under-garments – clothes of poor people, that have been patched and darned already. Another girl, a year younger, is nursing a very small baby, as yet too young for speech or gesture; and, squatting down face to face, a couple of mites of two and three grub about in the dust with clumsy hands, throwing handfuls of dirt at each other.

No one speaks a word. Only the baby, which is being hushed to sleep, cries continually with a small, sharp, frail voice. A cat dozes on the window-sill, and a number of bees make a great hum over the thick white border of pinks that bloom at the foot of the wall.

The girl, sewing at the gate, calls out suddenly:

'Mother!'

The woman answers:

'What's the matter now?'

'Here he is again.'

They have been made uneasy all the morning by a man roaming round the house, an old man who looks like a beggar. They had noticed him first when they went out to see the father off in his boat. He had been sitting then by the roadside, in front of the cottage. On their return from the shore, they had found him there still, staring at their house.

He looked ill and very wretched. For more than an hour he had not stirred; then, seeing that he was suspected of hanging around for no good, he rose and walked away, trailing his feet wearily.

But before long they had seen him coming back with his slow, tired gait; and he had sat himself down once more, a little further off this time, as if he were bent on watching them.

The mother and the girls felt afraid, the mother especially. She kept on worrying, for she was of a timid nature, and her husband, Lévesque, would not return from sea till after nightfall.

Her husband was called Lévesque; she had kept the name of Martin; and they, the couple, were known as the Martin-Lévesques.

It came about in this way: she had been married first to a sailor called Martin, who went every summer to the Newfoundland fisheries.

Within the two years of married life she had had one daughter, and she was expecting another child when the vessel in which her husband sailed, a barque from Dieppe, called the *Deux Sœurs*, disappeared, without leaving a trace.

No news of her ever came, none of the crew returned, and she was considered lost with all hands.

La Martin waited ten years for her man; she had reared her two children with great difficulty; then, as she was considered a worthy, hard-working woman, Lévesque, a fisherman of the village, a widower with a boy of his own, had asked her to be his wife. She married him, and again had two children within the next three years.

They had a hard struggle to live. Bread alone was dear enough, and meat was almost unknown in the household.

Sometimes, in winter, during the stormy months, they ran into debt with the baker. Nevertheless, the little ones throve well enough. People would say:

'They are a worthy couple, these Martin-Lévesques. La Martin is a good one for work, and as for Lévesque, the fellow hasn't his equal in a fishing boat.'

The girl at the gate spoke again:

'You'd think he knows us. It may be he's some beggar coming from Épreville or Auzebosc.'

But the mother wouldn't hear of it. No – no – she was perfectly sure that this could be no one from the neighbourhood.

As he remained motionless, like a post, with his eyes fixed obstinately on their dwelling, La Martin became furious, and her fear making her brave, she seized the fire shovel and came out of the door.

'What are you doing there?' she shouted at the tramp.

He replied in a hoarse voice:

'Why – I am just taking a breath of air. What harm am I doing you?'

She retorted:

'Why are you spying like this around my house?'

The man rejoined:

'I'm not doing anyone any harm. Mayn't a man sit down by the road?'

Finding nothing to say in reply, La Martin went in again.

The day wore on slowly. About noon the man disappeared.

Towards five o'clock he passed by again. He was not seen any more that evening.

Lévesque came home after dark. He listened to the whole story, and concluded:

'I dare say he's only a loafer or some other good-for-nothing.'

And he went to bed quite undisturbed, whilst the woman by his side, was haunted by the image of the prowler who had looked at her with such strange eyes.

At daybreak there was a strong wind blowing, and the seaman, unable to go out that day, settled down to help his wife with her net-mending.

Towards nine o'clock, the eldest girl, a Martin, who had been sent out to fetch the bread, came running home, with a scared face, and called out:

'Oh, mother – here he is again!'

The woman felt a sudden emotion, and, turning round, said to her man:

'Do go and speak to him, Lévesque: make him leave off watching us like this. It upsets me.'

Lévesque, a tall fisherman, with a brick-dust complexion, a thick red beard, with light blue eyes, pierced with black specks, and a thick neck, always wrapped up in a woollen muffler against the wind and the rain, walked out with tranquillity and approached the tramp.

They fell to talking.

The mother and the children, anxious and excited, watched them from a distance.

Suddenly the stranger rose and went with Lévesque towards the house.

La Martin drew back in agitation. Her husband addressed her:

'Give him a bit of bread and a glass of cider. He's not had a bite since the day before yesterday.'

They entered the hut together, followed by the woman and the children. The tramp sat down and began to eat, hanging his head, while they all stared at him.

The mother stood still, scanning his face; the elder girls, the two Martins, with their backs to the door, one of them holding the baby, never took their eyes off him for a moment; and the two mites also, sitting amongst the ashes on the hearth, stopped playing with the black saucepan, as if lost in wonder at the sight of the stranger.

Lévesque, after having sat down, asked:

'So, you've come a long way?'

'I come from Cette.'

'Tramping – like this?'

'Yes, tramping. One must when one hasn't a penny.'

'Where are you going, then?'

'I was coming here.'

'You know someone here?'

'May be I do.'

They ceased. He ate slowly, although he was famished, and he took a sip of cider after each mouthful of bread. His face was worn, wrinkled, and hollowed. He seemed to have undergone great hardships.

Lévesque inquired, brusquely:

'What's your name?'

He replied, without raising his head:

'My name's Martin.'

A strange shudder ran through the woman. She made one step forward, as if to look closer at the vagabond, then faced him, with her arms hanging down, and her mouth open. No one spoke.

At last Lévesque began again:

'Are you from these parts?'

He replied:

'Yes, I am.'

And he at last looked up at the woman; their glances met, remained fixed, mingled together, as if they had been linked to each other by their eyes.

She exclaimed, suddenly, in an altered, trembling, low voice:

'Is it you – my man?'

He pronounced, slowly:

'Yes – it's me.'

He did not move, however, and went on masticating his bread.

Lévesque, more surprised than disturbed, stammered:

'It's you, Martin?'

The other said, simply:

'Yes – it's me.'

The second husband asked:

'But where have you been all this time?'

'On the coast of Africa. We foundered after running on a sand bank. Three of us swam ashore. Picard, Vatinel, and me. And then we got captured by some savages, who kept us for twelve years. Picard and Vatinel died; an English traveller, passing through the country, took me with him, and landed me in Cette. And here I am.'

The woman had begun to cry, hiding her face in her apron.

Lévesque uttered:

'What on earth are we to do now?'

Martin asked:

'Are you her husband?'

Lévesque replied:

'Yes, I am.'

They looked at one another, and became silent. Then Martin, after gazing around at all the children in turn, nodded towards the two girls.

'Are these two mine?'

Lévesque said:

'Yes. They're yours.'

He did not get up, he did not offer to embrace them, he simply remarked:

'Good Lord! Aren't they tall!'

Lévesque repeated:

'What on earth are we to do?'

Martin, perplexed, could find nothing to say at first. Then, with an effort, he made up his mind.

'As for me, I will do what you think best. I don't want to do you any harm. It's a nuisance, all the same, seeing that there's the house here. I have two children, you have three – each must look after his own. Then, there's the mother – what about her? Is she yours or mine? I am ready to agree to anything you like; but the house is my own – seeing that my father left it to me, that I was born in it, and that she knows that the papers are with the lawyer.'

La Martin wept continually, with short sobs, her face hidden in her blue linen apron. The two girls had come nearer, and were watching their father uneasily.

He had done eating by then; and, in his turn, he put the question:

'What are we to do?'

Lévesque had an idea:

'We had better go to the priest – let him settle it.'

Martin got up, and as he moved towards his wife, she flung herself on his breast, sobbing out:

'My man! My man! – Oh, my Martin – my poor Martin – is it you?'

She held him clasped in her arms, swayed by this breath of her past, overcome by the rush of memories, reminding her of her youth and of her first embrace.

Martin, also giving way to emotion, kept on kissing her cap. The two children on the hearth, hearing their mother cry, began to howl both together; the last-born, held in the arms of the second Martin girl, screamed out piercingly, like a shrill fife.

Lévesque stood by, waiting.

'Come,' he said, at last, 'we must go and have this thing settled.'

Martin released his wife. His eye rested on the two girls, and the mother said to them:

'Aren't you going to kiss your father – you two?'

They approached him, together, with dry eyes, surprised and intimidated; and he gave each a loud smacking kiss on both cheeks. Beholding this unknown person so close, the little baby screamed so violently as to go off nearly into a fit.

Then the two men started off side by side.

As they happened to be passing by the Café du Commerce, Lévesque suggested:

'We might just as well go in and have a drink.'

'I don't mind if I do,' Martin said.

They entered the café, and sat down in a room, which, at this early hour, was quite empty.

'Hey, there, Chicot – a round of your best! Here's Martin turned up; Martin, you know, my wife's Martin; you remember Martin of the *Deux Sœurs* that was lost.'

And the corpulent, red-faced, bloated inn-keeper, holding three glasses in one hand, and a small decanter in the other, came up to them and observed with the utmost tranquillity:

'Well – well! So you've turned up then, Martin?'

Martin answered:

'Yes. I have turned up . . .'

A Sale

The PARTIES, Brument (Cæsar Isidor) and Cornu (Prosper Napoleon), were appearing before the Lower Seine Assize Court on a charge of attempting to murder the woman Brument, lawful wife of the first named, by drowning.

The two accused are seated side by side on the time-honoured bench. They are both peasants. The first is little and fat, with short arms, short legs, and a round, red, pimply head planted direct upon the trunk, which is also round and short, and devoid of any appearance of neck.

He is a pig-breeder, living at Cacheville-la-Goupil, in the district of Criquetot.

Cornu (Prosper Napoleon) is thin, of medium height, with enormously long arms. His head is askew, his jaw twisted, and he has a squint. A blue blouse as long as a shirt falls to his knees, and his thin, yellow hair, plastered down on his skull, gives his face a worn-out, dirty, fallen-in kind of look, that is really frightful. He bears the nickname of 'the parson' because he can imitate Church chanting to perfection, and even the tones of the serpent.* He is an innkeeper at Criquetot, and this talent of his attracts to the inn plenty of customers who prefer 'mass à la Cornu' to mass proper. Mme Brument, seated in the witness-box, is a thin country-woman who looks half asleep throughout the proceedings. She sits motionless, her hands crossed on her knees, with a fixed stare and stolid expression.

The magistrate continues his inquiry. 'So, Mme Brument, they came into your house and threw you into a barrel full of water. Now, tell us the facts in detail. Stand up.'

She stands up, looking as tall as a ship's mast, her cap topping her head with white. She makes her statement in a droning voice:

'I was shellin' beans. They comes in. I says to myself: "What's the matter with 'em? They look funny ; they're up to something." They kept watchin' me sideways, like this – 'specially Cornu, 'cos, you see, he squints. I never likes to see them two together; they're never up to any good when they're together. I says to 'em: "What d'you want with me?" They didn't give no answer, and I felt sort o' frightened like . . .'

The prisoner Brument here suddenly interrupts the statement by exclaiming:

'I was tight.'

---

* An out-of-date musical instrument, used in church.

Whereupon Cornu, turning to his accomplice, pronounced, in a voice as deep as the bass note of an organ:

'If ye said we were both tight, ye wouldn't be far wrong.'

The magistrate (severely): 'You mean to say that you were drunk?'

Brument: 'That's about it.'

Cornu: ''T might happen to anyone.'

The magistrate (to the victim): 'Go on with your statement, Mme Brument.'

'Well,' she resumed, 'Brument, he says to me, "Would ye like to earn a crown?"

'"Yes," says I, "seein' ye don't pick a crown-piece off the road every day."

'"Well, look sharp, then," he says to me, "and do what I tell ye"; and off he goes to fetch the big open barrel that's underneath the gutter in the corner. Then he turns 'er over, then he gets 'er into my kitchen, and he stands 'er up on end in the middle o' the room, and he says to me, "You go an' fetch water," he says, "an' keep on pourin' it in till she's full."

'So off I goes to the pond with two buckets, and I keeps on fetchin' water, an' more water, an' more water, for a good hour. That old barrel's as big as a vat, savin' your worship's presence.

'All that time Brument and Cornu they was havin' drinks, first one, and then another, and then another. They was just gettin' their back teeth under, both of 'em, and I says to 'em: "It's you that's full up, that's what you are — fuller than that there barrel."

'So Brument he gives it me back: "Don't you worry yourself," says he; "go on wi' your work, your time's comin' – everyone mind his own business." But I didn't take no notice, he bein' tight.

'When the barrel was full to the brim, I says: "There you are." And Cornu he gives me a crown-piece.'Twasn't Brument, 'twas Cornu that giv' it to me.

'And Brument he says to me: "D'ye want to earn another?"

'"Yes,' says I, "seein' I'm not used to gettin' presents so easy."

'"Well," he says, "undress yourself!"

'"Undress!" says I.

'"Yes," says he. "If ye feel it awkward-like," he says, "ye can keep yer shift on," he says; "we don't mind that."

'A crown's a crown, so I undresses; but it was clean against the grain, you understand, doin' it before them two good-for-nothin's. I takes off my cap, and then my bodice, an' then my skirt, and then my shoes.

'Brument, he says: "You can keep yer stockin's on too; we're a good sort, we are."

'An' Cornu, he says: "Yes! we're a good sort, we are."

'So there I was, pretty near like our Mother Eve. Then up they get, an' they could hardly stand, they was that tight, savin' your worship's presence.

'I says to myself: "Now, whatever are they up to?"

'And Brument he says: "Are ye ready?"

'And Cornu he says: "Ready! aye, ready!"

'An' if they didn't catch hold o' me, Brument by the head and Cornu by the heels, like a bundle o' linen for the wash, as ye might say. And didn't I just scream! An' Brument he says: "Hold your noise, ye cat!"

'An' they hoists me up over their heads and pops me into that there barrel full o' water, an' it just turned my blood cold, and froze the marrow in my bones.

'An' Brument says, "Will that do?"

'An' Cornu says, "Aye! That'll do."

'An' Brument says, "The head an't in. That counts!"

'An' Cornu says, "In wi' the head."

'Then Brument he pushes my head right under, just as if he meant drownin' me, and the water runs up me nose, and I begins to see Paradise, an' then he gives me another shove, an' down I goes.

'Well, then, he must ha' got scared. He pulls me out, and says, "Take an' dry yourself quick, ye scarecrow!"

'An' off I makes as hard as I can run to the parson, and he lends me a skirt belonging to his servant, seein' I was pretty nigh naked, an' he goes an' fetches M. Chicot the keeper; an' he goes off to Criquetot to fetch the police, and they all come to my house with me.

'And there we find Brument an' Cornu goin' for each other like two rams.

'Brument, he shouts, "It's a lie, I tell ye, there's a cubic metre, for sure. That's not the way to measure."

'Cornu, he howls, "Four bucketsful, 'tisn't hardly *half* a cubic metre. Hold your tongue, I say it's all right."

'The brigadier claps his hands on 'em. That's all.'

She sits down. There was some laughter in court. The jurymen looked at one another in astonishment. The magistrate pronounced, 'Prisoner Cornu, you seem to have been the instigator of this infamous plot. What have you to say?'

Cornu gets up in his turn.

'Your worship, we were tight.'

The magistrate replied gravely, 'That I know. Go on.'

'I *am* going on. Well, Brument comes to my place about nine o'clock an' calls for two drinks, an' says to me, "There's one for you, Cornu." So I sit down opposite him, and I take my drink, an' out o' politeness, I stand him one in return. Then he stands me one again, and I stand him another, and so we go on nippin' and nippin' till, about midday, we were properly fuddled.

'Then Brument he begins to cry, and that touches my heart, that does, an' I ask him what's the matter.

'He says to me, "I must have forty pound by Thursday." But that chills me off at once, ye understand. And then he proposes to me, point blank, "I'll sell ye my wife."

'I was tight, and I'm a widower. It stirred up my feelin's, I can tell ye. I didn't know her at all, his wife, but a woman's a woman, anyhow, an't she? So I ask him, "How much d'ye want for her?"

'He thought a bit, or he pretended to. When ye're tight ye're not so very clear in the head, and then he answers, "I'll sell her to ye by the cubic metre."

'Well, that didn't surprise me, for I was as tight as he was, and as for the cubic metre, I knew all about that in my trade. It means a thousand litres, and it just suited me properly.

'Only there was still the price to settle. *That* all depends on the quality. I said to him, "How much the cubic metre?"

'"Eighty pound," he says.

'That made me jump like a rabbit, but then it struck me that a woman couldn't be equal to more than three hundred litres. All the same I said, "It's too dear!"

'"Can't do it under," says he. "I should lose by it."

'You an't a pig-dealer for nothing, you understand – he knows his trade. But if he's a bit sharp at selling lumps o' fat, I'm a bit sharper at selling drops o' liquor. Ha! ha! ha! So I said to him, "If she was new goods, I don't say, but ye've had your wear and tear, she's second-hand. I'll give ye sixty pound the cubic metre, not a ha'penny more. Is it a deal?"

'"Right," he says, "done with ye."

'I said, "Done," too, and off we go, arm in arm. Must help each other along, y' know, in this life.

'But it came into my head uneasy-like, "However are ye goin' to measure her without makin' her into liquid?"

'Then he explains me his notion, and 'twasn't so easy for him, seeing he was tight. "I take a barrel," he says to me, "I fill it to the brim with water; I put her in, and I measure all the water that runs over; that'll do the trick."

'I said to him, "That's all very well, that is, but the water that runs over 'll run away. How are ye goin' to get it up?"

'And then he laughed at me for a softy, an' explained how there was nothing to do but to fill up the barrel again, once his wife was out of it. As much water as ye put in again is the measure of what's to pay. Suppose there's ten bucketsful, that'll be one cubic metre. He an't so stupid after all when he *is* tight, the varmint!

'To cut it short, we got to his place, and I had a look at the female party. As far as beauty goes, she an't no beauty, ye can see that for yourselves, for there she sits. I said to myself, "Never mind, 't all counts; I'm getting a new start in life, and good-looking or plain, they all answer the same purpose, eh, your worship?" An' then I noticed she was as thin as a lath, and I said to myself, "Why, she won't make four hundred litres!" I know something about it, being in the liquor trade.

'As to the doing, she's told ye about that. I even let her keep her shift and her stockin's on, which was all to the bad for me.

'When it was done, if she didn't fly out of the place. "Look out, Brument," I says, "she's off!"

'"Don't ye worry yourself," he says, "*we* shall get her back all right. She'll have to come home to sleep. Let's measure what ye've got to pay me."

'I measured. Not four bucketsful! Ha! ah! ah! ah!'

The prisoner gives way to such persistent laughter that a gendarme is obliged to slap him on the back. Regaining his composure, he goes on: 'To cut it short, Brument he declares, "The bargain's off; it an't enough!" I bawl at him, he bawls at me, I bawl louder, he dots me one, I give 'im one better. It looked like lasting till the day o' judgment, seeing we were both tight.

'In come the gendarmes, and begin swearing at us, an' they put *handcuffs* on us and take us off to prison. I ask for damages.'

He sits down.

Brument declares his accomplice's confession to be true in every detail. The astounded jury retire to consider their verdict.

They came back in an hour's time, and acquitted the prisoners, but added a severe rider, pointing out the sanctity of marriage, and laying down the exact limits proper to commercial transactions.

Brument set out for the conjugal abode in company with his wife.

Cornu returned to his business.

Saint-Antoine

H<small>E HAD BEEN</small> nicknamed 'Saint-Antoine', because his name was Antoine, and also, perhaps, because he was a good fellow, merry, jovial, a mighty eater, and a great drinker, and still vigorously enterprising with his servant girls, although he was more than sixty years old.

He was a big peasant landowner of the Caux district, florid in complexion, with a vast girth of chest and stomach, and perched on long legs, which seemed too thin for his corpulent trunk.

Being a widower, he lived alone on his farm, with his maid-servant and his two labourers. He managed his property with astuteness and knowledge, careful of the main-chance in business, and with great skill in the care of his stock and the cultivation of his land. His two sons and three daughters had all married well; they lived in the neighbourhood, and came over once every month to dine with their father. His bodily strength was famous in all the surrounding parishes; it was a current saying about anyone exceptionally powerful: 'He is as strong as our Saint-Antoine.'

When the Franco-German war began, Saint-Antoine swore uproariously, in the village taproom, that he was ready to eat an army of Prussians; for he was a braggart, like a real Normandy peasant – a little craven at bottom, and boastful withal. He would bring down his fist on the wooden table, making the coffee cups and little glasses dance; and, fiery red in the face, with uneasy eyes, he would yell with the affected fury of an easy-going jolly toper: 'I shall have to eat some of them yet, as true as there is a God above us!' In reality, he never expected the Prussians to come as far as Tanneville; but, when he heard that they were already at Rautôt, he shut himself up in his house and kept a perpetual watch out of the little kitchen window, expecting every moment to see the points of bayonets appear on the road.

One morning, as he sat at table, taking his soup with his servants, the door flew open, and the mayor of the commune, Maître Chicot, entered, followed by a soldier, who was wearing a black helmet with a brass spike on the top. Saint-Antoine bounded to his feet, and his people looked on thunderstruck, expecting every moment to see him tear the Prussian to pieces; but he only shook hands with the mayor, who said to him: 'Here's one of them for you, Saint-Antoine. They got here last night. Above all, don't you try any of your foolish tricks; they threaten to kill, burn, and destroy for the least little offence. Now, I've warned you. Give him something to eat; there's no harm in the fellow. Good day. I must be off. There's enough of them for everybody!' And he went out.

Saint-Antoine had turned pale; he looked at his Prussian. He was a stout young fellow, with a pink-and-white skin, blue eyes, fair hair, bearded up to the cheek bones, with an air of innocence, timidity, and good nature. The malicious Norman judged his man at a glance, and, taking heart, invited him, by signs, to sit down. He asked: 'Will you have some soup?' The foreigner did not understand. Antoine then, with growing audacity, pushed a plate filled to the brim right under his nose. 'There! you swallow that, you fat pig.'

The soldier answered, 'Ja,' and forthwith fell to voraciously, while the farmer, triumphant, feeling his character retrieved in a measure, winked at his servants, who were grimacing strangely, being very afraid, and wanting to laugh at the same time.

When the Prussian had gulped down his plateful, Saint-Antoine helped him to another, which disappeared in the same way; but he drew back, refusing the third, which the farmer tried to force upon him, repeating: 'Come on. Get outside this lot too. You must put on fat, or I'll know the reason why, you pig!'

And the soldier, understanding only that he was desired to eat his fill, laughed good-humouredly, trying to explain by signs that he was satisfied.

Then Saint-Antoine, becoming quite familiar, struck him lightly on the stomach with the back of his hand, shouting: 'He has a full paunch, my pig has! You just see if he hasn't.'

Suddenly he writhed with joy, grew crimson, unable to speak, as though he were going to have an apoplectic fit. An idea had come to him, which made him choke with laughter: 'That's it, that's the very thing, "Saint Anthony and his pig." Here look at my pig.' And the three servants also went off into roars of laughter.

The old man was so pleased with himself, that he ordered up a bottle of cognac of the best sort – the sort that makes your hair curl – and offered it all round. They touched glasses with the Prussian, who smacked his lips to make himself agreeable, and to show them that he thought it famous stuff. Saint-Antoine shouted at him, under his very nose: 'Hey, here's something good! You don't get liquor like this to drink at home! Do you, my pig?'

After this, Father Antoine was never seen abroad without his Prussian. He had found what he wanted in that joke; it was his revenge for everything – the vengeance of a big, fat, malicious buffoon. The whole countryside that was ready to die with fear, laughed and squirmed behind the backs of the conquerors at this prime joke of their Saint-Antoine. Really, the beggar had not his equal anywhere for a bit of fun. He alone was capable of such a farcical set-out. There was nobody like him in the world. 'Cré coquin, va!'

Every afternoon he would start off to visit the neighbours, arm in arm with his German, whom he introduced jovially with a slap on the shoulder: 'Here, this is my own pig; only look how fat he's getting, the beast.'

And the peasants grinned with delight. – Wasn't he comical, that beggar, Saint-Antoine?

'I will sell him to you, Césaire, for three pistoles!'

'Done. That's a bargain, Antoine, and I shall invite you to come and eat the black pudding.'

'What I should like best is his trotters.'

'Just feel round his stomach, there's nothing but fat there.'

They exchanged stealthy winks, without laughing too openly, however, for fear the Prussian should guess that he was being made fun of. Only Antoine himself, growing bolder every day, ventured to pinch his thighs now and then, yelling: 'Here's fat for you,' or slapped him behind, howling: 'All that is pure lard.' He would take him up in his arms of an old colossus capable of lifting a blacksmith's anvil, and shout: 'He weighs six hundred clear, and there's not a pound of waste in the whole carcass.'

He had made it a practice to get people to give his pig something to eat wherever they went calling together. This was the cream of the joke, the great daily diversion – 'Give him what you like, he can swallow anything.' And they pressed upon the man bread, butter, potatoes, cold stew, all sorts of food, and pork sausages too, with a sly remark: 'Of your own, and really prime.'

The soldier, simple-minded and gentle, would eat out of civility, pleased at being shown so much attention, and would even make himself ill rather than refuse; and he really was growing fat, uncomfortably buttoned up in his uniform, which was getting too tight for him. This delighted Saint-Antoine, who would often say: 'I say, my pig, we shall have to make you a bigger cage presently.'

They had become the best of friends meantime, and when the old man went anywhere on business in the neighbourhood, the Prussian would offer to go with him for the pleasure of being in his company.

The weather was terribly severe; everything was frozen hard; the awful winter of 1870 seemed like another plague added to the misfortunes of France.

Father Antoine liked to be beforehand with his work, and knew how to seize every opportunity. He foresaw that he would be short of manure in the spring, and bought some from a neighbour, who was in pressing need of money; and it was arranged that he should come every evening, at his convenience, to fetch away a load.

Every day then, before nightfall, he would start off with his cart, always accompanied by his pig, for the farm of the Haules, a couple of miles away. And each day there was the fun of feeding the animal. The whole countryside could be seen wending its way there, as people go to church on a Sunday to hear mass.

The soldier, however, was evidently beginning to suspect something, and when the laughter around him grew too uproarious, he would roll his eyes about, his uneasy eyes which flashed with anger now and then.

One evening, when he had eaten his fill, he refused to have any more, and attempted to get up to go away. But Saint-Antoine stopped him with a turn of the wrist, and putting both his powerful hands upon his shoulders, pushed him back into his seat with such force that the chair gave way under the man.

A tempestuous gaiety broke out, and Antoine, radiant, picking up his pig, pretended to look to some imaginary wounds. He declared: 'If you don't want to eat any more, you shall be made to drink, by God!' And a supply of cognac was sent for to the inn.

The soldier darted vicious glances, but he consented to drink, nevertheless; he was ready to take as much as they wanted him to; and Saint-Antoine set himself to drink against him, to the great joy of the onlookers.

The Norman, fiery eyed, and as red as a tomato, tilted the bottle, clinked the glass, bawling out, 'To you!' – and the Prussian tossed the spirits down his throat, time after time, without uttering a word.

It was a struggle, a battle, a revenge. Which would drink the other under the table? The excitement was intense. By the time the bottle had been emptied, both had about as much as they could carry; but neither of them had the better of the other. They went away quits, as it were, and that was all. They must have a deciding bout next day.

They went out staggering, and started for home, by the side of the dung cart, loaded with manure, which rolled slowly along the road, drawn by two heavy horses.

The snow had begun to fall again, and the moonless night

was lighted mournfully by the dead whiteness of the plains. The great cold took hold of the two men and increased their intoxication. Saint-Antoine, dissatisfied with himself for not having done better in the contest, found his solace in continually shouldering up against his pig, in the hope of making him tumble headlong into the ditch. The other avoided his pushes by stepping back; and every time he would mutter a few words in German, in an irritated tone, which provoked a burst of laughter from the peasant. At last, the Prussian got exasperated, and, as Antoine was trying to give him another shove, he met it by a heavy blow from the shoulder, which made the colossus stagger.

Inflamed with drink, the old fellow seized the man, put his arms around his body, lifted him up, shook him as though he had been no bigger than a child, and flung him away clear over to the other side of the road. Then, pleased with this feat of strength, he folded his arms, and burst out into laughter again.

But the soldier picked himself up swiftly, bare-headed, for his helmet had rolled away, and, unsheathing his sword-bayonet, rushed upon Father Antoine.

When he saw him coming, the peasant seized hold of the stock of his whip by the middle — his long carter's whip of holly, straight, strong, and supple like the sinew of an ox.

The Prussian charged, headlong, with the point of his weapon forward, and certain of killing his man. But the old fellow fearlessly caught the blade, which was ready to rip him open, with his bare hand, flung it aside, and, with a sharp blow on the temple from the butt end of his whip, struck down his enemy, who fell senseless at his feet.

Terrified and stupid with astonishment, he surveyed the body, at first shaken with convulsive jerks, then remaining motionless, face downwards in the snow. He stooped over it, turned it on its back, and contemplated it for some time. The man's eyes were closed, and a trickle of blood ran from a cut on the side of the forehead. In the dimness of the night Saint-Antoine could see the brown stain of blood on the snow.

He remained standing still, with his head in a whirl, while the loaded cart went on steadily behind the slow pacing horses.

What should he do now? They would shoot him, burn down his farm, and devastate the whole district. What could be done? What could be done? How would he manage to hide the body, conceal this death, and deceive the Prussians? A sound of voices reached him from afar, across the great silence of the snows; then, almost mad with apprehension, he picked up the helmet, forced it on to the head of his victim, laid hold of the body, raised it up in his arms, ran along, caught up the cart, and flung his inanimate burden on to the top of the load. There would be time when he got home to think what must be done next.

He walked slowly, racking his brains, and finding no issue. He saw his ruin, he felt himself lost. He followed the cart into the stable yard. A light shone from a garret window, his servant girl was not asleep yet. He backed his team quickly to the edge of the dung hole. He thought that the body lying on the top of the load would soon be underneath the manure, and he made the cart tip backwards.

The soldier disappeared, and was buried, as he had foreseen. Antoine levelled the whole with his fork, and stuck it into the ground near by. He called up his man, ordered him to take the horses out, and went upstairs to his room.

He went to bed, thinking continually of what he had better do next; but not a single idea illuminated his sombre perplexity. He grew more and more terrified lying there, quite still, in his bed. He would certainly be shot! He sweated all over with fear; his teeth chattered, he got up shivering, he felt it impossible to lie quietly under his blankets any longer.

Then he went down into the kitchen, took a bottle of cognac out of the cupboard, and climbed up the stairs again. He gulped down two big drinks, one after the other; it brought the excitement of fresh intoxication upon the remaining fumes of the old, without being able to calm the anguish of his soul. He had done a fine stroke of work there, by God, the confounded imbecile fool that he was!

He paced wildly to and fro, seeking for some stratagem, inventing explanations, calling up all his cunning; and from time to time he would swallow a mouthful of spirits, to keep his pecker up, anyhow.

But he could think of nothing to save himself. Nothing whatever.

Towards midnight, his watch-dog, a wolf-like brute, which he had named 'Dévorant', began, as the saying is, to howl at Death.

69

Father Antoine felt a tremor in the very marrow of his bones; and each time the animal took up its lugubrious and prolonged moan a shudder of fear ran from head to foot through the old man's flesh.

He had dropped limply into a chair, his legs having given way under him, stupefied, incapable of doing anything; he waited anxiously for Dévorant to recommence his howling plaint, quivering all over with sudden starts which an abiding sense of terror sets up in the vibrating tenseness of our nerves.

The clock downstairs struck five. The dog would not stop his howling, and the old peasant felt himself on the verge of madness. He got up to let the brute loose, so as not to hear any more of this noise. He went down, opened the door, and stepped out into the night air.

It was still snowing hard. Everything around was white. The farm buildings stood out in great black masses. The man went up to the kennel. The dog was straining at his chain. He let him loose; then Dévorant made one great bound, and stopped short, his coat bristling up, his fore-paws rigid, his fangs bared, his nose pointed to the heap of manure.

Saint-Antoine trembled in every limb; he stammered out: 'What's the matter with you now, you dirty cur?' and moved forward a few steps; he scanned the pale obscurity, the undefined, dim shadows of the yard.

At last he made out an indistinct form, the form of something like a man sitting on the manure heap.

He gazed at it, paralysed and gasping with horror. But suddenly he noticed near him the handle of his manure fork, stuck upright there in the ground; he tore it out violently, and in one of those gusts of desperate fear, which drive the greatest cowards to acts of courage, he rushed forward, resolved to see what this thing could be.

It was he – his Prussian, who had emerged, all miry, from his bed of filth, the warmth of which had called him back to life. He had sunk almost unconscious into a sitting position, and remained there, under the powdery fall of snow, covered with filth and gore, soiled, besotted with drink, half stunned from the blow, exhausted by the loss of blood from his wound.

He perceived Antoine, and as yet too dazed to understand anything, made a movement as if to get up. But the old man, as soon as he had recognized him, flew into a transport of brutal rage.

He stuttered, foaming at the mouth: 'Ah, you pig! You pig! You aren't dead yet! You are going to split on me, are you? You wait . . . you wait!'

He rushed upon the German, thrust forward the manure fork, poised like a spear, and with his whole strength drove the four iron prongs right up to the handle, into the man's breast.

The soldier fell backwards and expired with a long death sigh, while the old peasant, withdrawing his weapon from the wounds, drove it down again and again, blow after blow, into the stomach, into the throat, into the chest. He struck the palpitating body like a madman; he stabbed holes in it, from head to foot, and the blood gushed out in great bubbles.

At last, exhausted by the violence of his exertions, he stopped; he drew deep breaths, swallowing the fresh air by mouthfuls, feeling appeased by the murder he had committed.

Then, as the cocks were beginning to crow in the farm-yard, and the first streak of daylight appeared in the sky, he set to work to bury the corpse.

He dug down, right through the layers of manure, struck the earth underneath, went on digging still deeper, went on working with headstrong ardour, with a passionate display of strength, with furious movements of his arms and of his whole body.

When the trench appeared deep enough, he rolled the corpse into it with the four-pronged fork, shovelled the earth back again, stamped it down thoroughly, piled up the heap of manure over it. And he smiled at the thick snowfall, which completed his work, hiding every trace with its white veil.

Then he planted his fork into the dung heap, and went indoors. The cognac bottle, still nearly half full, was standing on the table. He gulped down the lot without once pausing for breath, flung himself on to his bed, and fell fast asleep.

He woke up, sober, calm, and feeling well, with his head clear, capable of thinking coolly over the matter, and ready to meet any emergency.

In less than an hour he was running all over the neighbourhood, inquiring everywhere for the missing soldier. He even went so far as to address himself to the officers, wishing to know, he said, why his man should have been taken away from him like this.

As the fact of their friendship was notorious, no shadow of guilt ever fell on him; he even volunteered his help in the search that was made, and asserted that the Prussian used to go out late every evening to run after petticoats.

An old retired gendarme, who kept an inn in a neighbouring village, and who happened to have a pretty daughter, was taken upon suspicion, and shot.

Two Friends

PARIS WAS BLOCKADED, famished, at the last gasp. Sparrows were scarce on the roofs, and the sewers depleted of their rats. Every mortal thing was being eaten.

Strolling sadly along the outer boulevard on a fine January morning, with his hands in the pockets of his military trousers, and his stomach empty, M. Morissot, a watchmaker by profession, and a man of his ease when he had the chance, caught sight of a friend, and stopped. This was M. Sauvage, an acquaintance he had made out fishing.

For before the war Morissot had been in the habit of starting out at dawn every Sunday, rod in hand, and a tin box on his back. He would take the train to Argenteuil, get out at Colombes, then go on foot as far as the Island of Marante. The moment he reached this Elysium of his dreams he would begin to fish, and fish till night. Every Sunday he met there a little round and jovial man, this M. Sauvage, a haberdasher of Rue Notre Dame de Lorette, also a perfect fanatic at fishing. They would often pass half the day side by side, rod in hand, feet dangling above the stream, and in this manner had become fast friends. Some days they did not talk, other days they did. But they understood each other admirably without words, for their tastes and feelings were identical.

On spring mornings, about ten o'clock, when the young sun was raising a faint mist above the quiet-flowing river, and blessing the backs of those two passionate fishermen with a pleasant warmth, Morissot would murmur to his neighbour: 'I say, isn't it heavenly?' and M. Sauvage would reply: 'Couldn't be jollier!' It was quite enough to make them understand and like each other.

Or in autumn, towards sunset, when the blood-red sky and crimson clouds were reflected in the water, the whole river stained with colour, the horizon flaming, when our two friends looked as red as fire, and the trees, already russet and shivering at the touch of winter, were turned to gold, M. Sauvage would look smilingly at Morissot, and remark: 'What a sight!' and Morissot, not taking his eyes off his float, would reply ecstatically: 'Bit better than it is in town, eh?'

Having made sure of each other, they shook hands heartily, quite moved at meeting again in such different circumstances. M. Sauvage, heaving a sigh, murmured: 'Nice state of things!' Morissot, very gloomy, quavered out: 'And what weather! Today's the first fine day this year!'

The sky was indeed quite blue and full of light.

They moved on, side by side, ruminative, sad. Morissot pursued his thought: 'And fishing, eh? What jolly times we used to have!'

'Ah!' muttered M. Sauvage. 'When shall we go fishing again?'

They entered a little café, took an absinthe together, and started off once more, strolling along the pavement.

Suddenly Morissot halted: 'Another nip?' he said.

'Right-o!' responded M. Sauvage. And in they went to another wine-shop. They came out rather light-headed, affected by so much alcohol on their starving stomachs. The day was mild, and a soft breeze caressed their faces.

M. Sauvage, to whose light-headedness this warmth was putting the finishing touch, stopped short: 'I say – suppose we go!'

'What d'you mean?'

'Fishing!'

'Where?'

'Why, at our island. The French outposts are close to Colombes. I know Colonel Dumoulin; he'll be sure to let us pass.'

Morissot answered, quivering with eagerness: 'All right; I'm on!' And they parted, to get their fishing gear.

An hour later they were marching along the highroad. They came presently to the villa occupied by the Colonel, who, much amused by their whim, gave them leave. And furnished with his permit, they set off again.

They soon passed the outposts, and, traversing the abandoned village of Colombes, found themselves at the edge of the little vineyard fields that run down to the Seine. It was about eleven o'clock.

The village of Argenteuil, opposite, seemed quite deserted. The heights of Orgemont and Sannois commanded the whole countryside; the great plain stretching to Nanterre was empty, utterly empty of all but its naked cherry trees and its grey earth.

M. Sauvage jerking his thumb towards the heights, muttered: 'The Prussians are up there!' And disquietude stole into the hearts of the two friends, looking at that deserted land. The Prussians! They had never seen any, but they had felt them there for months, all round Paris, bringing ruin to France, bringing famine; pillaging, massacring; invisible, yet invincible. And a sort of superstitious terror went surging through their hatred for this unknown and victorious race.

Morissot stammered: 'I say – suppose we were to meet some?'

With that Parisian jocularity which nothing can repress M. Sauvage replied: 'We'd give 'em some fried fish.'

Nonetheless, daunted by the silence all round, they hesitated to go further.

At last M. Sauvage took the plunge. 'Come on! But we must keep our eyes skinned!'

They got down into a vineyard, where they crept along, all eyes and ears, bent double, taking cover behind every bush.

There was still a strip of open ground to cross before they could get to the river-side; they took it at the double, and the moment they reached the bank plumped down amongst some osiers.

Morissot glued his ear to the ground for any sound of footsteps. Nothing! They were alone, utterly alone.

They plucked up spirit again, and began to fish.

In front of them the Island of Marante, uninhabited, hid them from the far bank. The little island restaurant was closed, and looked as if it had been abandoned for years.

M. Sauvage caught the first gudgeon, Morissot the second, and every minute they kept pulling in their lines with a little silvery creature wriggling at the end. Truly a miraculous draught of fishes!

They placed their spoil carefully in a very fine-meshed net suspended in the water at their feet, and were filled by the delicious joy that visits those who know once more a pleasure of which they have been deprived too long.

The good sun warmed their shoulders; they heard nothing, thought of nothing, were lost to the world. They fished.

But suddenly a dull boom, which seemed to come from underground, made the earth tremble. The bombardment had begun again.

Morissot turned his head. Away above the bank he could see on the left the great silhouette of Mont Valerien, showing a white plume high up – an ashy puff just belched forth. Then a second spurt of smoke shot up from the fort's summit, and some seconds afterwards was heard the roar of the gun.

Then more and more. Every minute the hill shot forth its deadly breath, sighed out milky vapours that rose slowly to the calm heaven, and made a crown of cloud.

M. Sauvage shrugged his shoulders. 'At it again!' he said.

Morissot, who was anxiously watching the bobbing of his float, was seized with the sudden fury of a man of peace against these maniacs battering at each other, and he growled out: 'Idiots I call them, killing each other like that!'

'Worse than the beasts!' said M. Sauvage. And Morissot. busy with a fish, added: 'It'll always be like that, in my opinion, so long as we have governments.'

M. Sauvage cut him short. 'The Republic would never have declared war—'

Morissot broke in: 'Under a monarchy you get war against your neighbours; under a republic – war amongst yourselves.'

And they began tranquilly discussing and unravelling momentous political problems with the common sense of two gentle, narrow creatures, who agreed at any rate on this one point, that Man would never be free.

And Mont Valerien thundered without ceasing, shattering with its shells the homes of France, pounding out life, crushing human beings, putting an end to many a dream, to many a longed-for joy, to many a hoped-for happiness; opening everywhere, too, in the hearts of wives, of girls, of mothers, wounds that would never heal.

'That's life!' declared M. Sauvage.

'I should call it death,' said Morissot, and laughed.

They both gave a sudden start; there was surely someone coming up behind them. Turning their eyes they saw, standing close to their very elbows, four men, four big bearded men, dressed in a sort of servant's livery, with flat caps on their heads, pointing rifles at them.

The rods fell from their hands and floated off down-stream.

In a few seconds they were seized, bound, thrown into a boat, and taken over to the island.

Behind the house that they had thought deserted they perceived some twenty German soldiers.

A sort of hairy giant, smoking a great porcelain pipe, and sitting astride of a chair, said in excellent French: 'Well, gentlemen, what luck fishing?'

Whereupon a soldier laid at his officer's feet the net full of fish, which he had carefully brought along.

The Prussian smiled. 'I see – not bad. But we've other fish to fry. Now listen to me, and keep cool. I regard you two as spies sent to watch me. I take you, and I shoot you. You were pretending to fish, the better to disguise your plans. You've fallen into my hands; so much the worse for you. That's war. But, seeing that you passed through your outposts, you must assuredly have been given the password to get back again. Give it me, and I'll let you go.'

Livid, side by side, the two friends were silent, but their hands kept jerking with little nervous movements.

The officer continued: 'No one will ever know; it will be all right; you can go home quite easy in your minds. If you refuse, it's death – instant death. Choose.'

They remained motionless, without a word.

The Prussian, calm as ever, stretched out his hand towards the water, and said: 'Think! In five minutes you'll be at the bottom of that river. In five minutes. You've got families, I suppose?'

Mont Valerien went on thundering. The two fishermen stood there silent.

The German gave an order in his own language. Then he moved his chair so as not to be too near his prisoners. Twelve men came forward, took their stand twenty paces away, and grounded arms.

The officer said: 'I give you one minute; not a second more.'

And, getting up abruptly, he approached the two Frenchmen, took Morissot by the arm, and, drawing him aside, whispered: 'Quick, that password. Your friend need never know. It will only look as if I'd relented.' Morissot made no answer.

Then the Prussian took M. Sauvage apart, and asked him the same question.

M. Sauvage did not reply.

Once again they were side by side. The officer gave a word of command. The soldiers raised their rifles.

At that moment Morissot's glance lighted on the net full of gudgeons lying on the grass a few paces from him. The sunshine was falling on that glittering heap of fishes, still full of life. His spirit sank. In spite of all effort his eyes filled with tears.

'Adieu, M. Sauvage!' he stammered out.

M. Sauvage answered: 'Adieu, M. Morissot.'

They grasped each other's hands, shaken from head to foot by a trembling that they could not control.

'Fire!' cried the officer.

Twelve shots rang out as one.

M. Sauvage fell forward like a log. Morissot, the taller, wavered, spun round, and came down across his comrade, his face upturned to the sky; blood spurted from his tunic, torn across the chest.

The German gave another order. His men dispersed. They came back with ropes and stones, which they fastened to the feet of the two dead friends, whom they carried to the riverbank. And Mont Valerien never ceased rumbling, crowned now with piled-up clouds of smoke.

Two of the soldiers took Morissot by the head and heels, two others laid hold of M. Sauvage. The bodies, swung violently to and fro, were hurled forward, described a curve, then plunged upright into the river, where the stones dragged them down feet first.

The water splashed up, bubbled, wrinkled, then fell calm again, and tiny waves rippled out towards the banks.

A few bloodstains floated away out there.

The officer, calm as ever, said quietly: 'It's the fish who've got the luck now!' and went back towards the house.

But suddenly catching sight of the net full of gudgeons on

the grass, he took it up, looked it over, smiled, and called out: 'Wilhelm!'

A soldier in a white apron came running up. The Prussian threw him the spoil of the two dead fishermen.

'Get these little affairs fried at once while they're still alive. First-rate like that!'

And he went back to his pipe.

Mademoiselle Fifi

MAJOR COUNT FARLSBERG, the Prussian Commandant, was just finishing the contents of his post-bag. His back was screwed deep into a big tapestry armchair, and his booted feet rested on the elegant marble mantelpiece, where his spurs, during a three months' occupation of the chateau d'Uville, had made two deep ruts, growing a little deeper every day.

A cup of coffee was steaming on a little marqueterie table, spotted with the cigar-burns, liqueur-stains, and pen-knife cuts left by this conquering hero, who, following the dictates of idle fancy, would sometimes stop sharpening a pencil to cut in a quaint design or perhaps a row of figures on the rich wood.

When he had finished his letters and gone through the German newspapers that his orderly had just brought in, he got up, threw on the fire some three or four immense green logs – for these gentlemen were gradually cutting down the park for their firewood – and went towards the window.

It was pouring with rain, that Normandy rain which always seems as if hurled down by a furious hand, a slanting rain, thick as a curtain, or a diagonally striped wall; a lashing, splashing rain, drowning everything, a regular rain of Rouen, that wash-pot of all France.

The commandant looked long at the sopping lawns, then at the swollen Andelle, overflowing its banks down there below them; and while he gazed he drummed a Rhineland waltz on the window-pane. Turning, at a sound behind him, he saw his second in command, Baron Kelweingstein, now holding the rank of captain.

The major was a broad-shouldered giant, beautified by a long beard that spread fan-shaped on his chest; the whole of his tall person made one think of a peacock, a military peacock, carrying his tail unfurled from his chin. His eyes were blue, cold, and mild; and one cheek had been slashed across by a sabre in the war with Austria. He had the reputation of being a good sort and a brave soldier.

The captain, a little rubicund fellow with a big, tight-belted stomach, was not too clean-shaven, and the traces of his fiery beard and moustache, under certain conditions of light, made his face look as if it had been rubbed with phosphorus. Two teeth, lost one festive night (he never quite remembered how), made his speech thick and queer, so that he was not always to be understood. He was bald on the top of the head only, tonsured like a priest, with a crop of short, reddish, glistening hair round that circle of bare skull.

The commandant shook hands with him, and, swallowing at a gulp his sixth cup of coffee since the morning, listened to his junior's report of the day. Then they both went back to the window, with the remark that 'things were not too lively'. The major, a quiet man with a wife at home, put up with the situation well enough; but the captain, a regular rake, frequenter of night clubs and of women, raged continually at being shut up for months together in the celibacy of this desolate outpost.

At a knock on the door the commandant cried, 'Come in!' and a drilled puppet of a soldier appeared in the gap, announcing by his mere presence that lunch was served.

In the dining-room they found their three junior officers, Lieutenant Otto von Grössling, Second Lieutenants Fritz Scheunaburg, and the Marquis Wilhelm von Eyrik, a little blond cock-sparrow, haughty and harsh of manner, merciless towards the conquered, and as explosive as a pistol.

Since their arrival in France his comrades never called him anything but Mademoiselle Fifi, a nickname suggested by his smart appearance, his slender figure which looked as if he wore corsets, his pale face where the budding moustache hardly showed at all, and also by reason of his new habit of continually using the French phrase, 'Fi, fi donc!' pronounced with a slight hiss, to express his sovereign contempt for things and people.

The dining-room in the chateau d'Uville was a long, majestic apartment, whose mirrors of old crystal, now starred by pistol-shots, and high-hung Flemish tapestries, slashed by sabre-cuts till they drooped here and there, bore witness to the prowess of Mlle Fifi in his hours of ease.

On the walls three family portraits – a warrior in armour, a cardinal, and a president – had long porcelain-bowled pipes thrust into their mouths, while in her ancient, faded-gold frame a noble dame, very tight-laced, sported with an air of arrogance a huge pair of blacked-on moustaches.

In this mutilated room, darkened by the storm outside, with its mournful look of defeat, and its old oak parquet floor hard now as that of a tavern, the officers lunched almost in silence.

Not till they had finished eating, and had come to spirits and tobacco, did they begin their daily lamentation on their boredom. Passing the liqueurs from hand to hand, they leaned back and sipped away, without removing from the corners of their mouths those long curved pipe-stems, with egg-shaped china bowls daubed with little pictures in a style that could appeal only to a Hottentot.

As soon as a glass was empty it was wearily refilled. But Mlle Fifi made a point of breaking his each time, and an orderly would at once bring him another.

Enveloped in a fog of pungent smoke, they seemed to be steeping themselves in a dreary, drowsy drunkenness, the gloomy soaking of men with nothing else to do.

But suddenly the baron, in a spasm of revolt, pulled himself together and ejaculated: 'By gad! We simply can't go on like this. We must damn well invent something!'

Lieutenant Otto and Second Lieutenant Fritz, both types of the stodgy, solemn-faced young German, answered as one man: 'Yes; only — what?'

The baron reflected a moment: 'Well, we must get up a spree, if the colonel will let us.'

The major took his pipe out of his mouth: 'How do you mean — a spree?'

The baron came across to him: 'You leave it all to me, sir. I'll send Old Automaton to Rouen to bring some girls out here. I know where they're to be found. We'll give 'em a supper; we can do it in great style, and we'll have a jolly good evening, for once.'

Count Farlsberg smiled, and said, with a shrug of his shoulders: 'You're cracked, my dear fellow.'

But all the young men had got up, and came crowding round the commandant, adding their entreaties. 'Oh, do let him, sir! It's so infernally dull here.'

'All right!' said the major, giving in at last. And at once the baron sent for Old Automaton — a veteran who had never been seen to smile, but who could be relied on to carry out fanatically any order given by his officers. This veritable ramrod of a man received the baron's instructions without moving a muscle of his face, and left the room. Five minutes later a military waggon, with a hooped canvas cover, went rattling off through the furious rain behind four horses at full gallop.

And at once a thrill of reviving animation went stealing

through their spirits; they lounged no more, their faces brightened, and conversation flowed.

Although the rain continued to come down with unabated fury, the major swore that the clouds were not so heavy, and Lieutenant Otto affirmed that it was certainly going to clear. As for Mlle Fifi, he simply could not keep still, fidgeting up and down, and searching with his clear hard eyes for something to break. They lighted suddenly on the moustachioed lady. Drawing out his revolver, the blond young beast remarked: '*You're* not going to look on, though!' and, without getting up, he fired, putting out the portrait's eyes with two consecutive shots.

Then he called out: 'Let's play the mine game!' And instantly all conversation ceased, under the spell of this new and powerful attraction. The mine game was entirely Mlle Fifi's invention, his pet amusement for gratifying his genius for destruction.

The owner of the chateau, Count Fernand d'Amoys d'Uville, had left in too great haste to be able to take away or hide anything except the silver, which had been stowed away in a hole in the wall. The great salon, opening into the dining-room, of this very rich and lordly person, had, up to the moment of his precipitate flight, presented the appearance of a museum gallery.

The walls of the vast room were garnished with pictures, drawings, and valuable watercolours. On the tables, shelves, and in elegant cabinets a thousand knick-knacks were arranged – Chinese vases, statuettes, Dresden shepherds, oriental monsters, old ivories, and Venetian glass – a perfect medley of rare and precious stuff.

There was little left of it all by now. Not that there had been any looting. Major Count Farlsberg would by no means have permitted that, but from time to time Mlle Fifi played the mine game, and on such occasions at any rate all the officers were thoroughly amused for full five minutes.

The little marquis went off to the salon for what he needed, and came back with a very charming little porcelain teapot, Famille Rose. Filling it with gunpowder, he delicately inserted down the spout a long piece of tinder, lighted it, and ran back with his infernal machine into the next room.

He returned with remarkable celerity, and shut the door. And all the Germans waited, stiff with expectation and curious childlike smiles. The moment the explosion came off, shaking the whole chateau, they all darted together into the salon.

Mlle Fifi, the first in, was clapping his hands ecstatically before a terra-cotta Venus, whose head had been blown off at last. They all proceeded to pick up fragments of porcelain, admiring the strange lacework of the splinters, examining the latest havoc, and disclaiming for today certain ravages undoubtedly done in the previous explosion; while the major, with a fatherly air, contemplated the splendid room thus spiflicated by that Neronic bomb, and sanded with the smithereens of Art. He was the first to retire, remarking genially: 'It was a great success, this time!'

But such a smother of smoke had got into the dining-room,

mingling with the tobacco fumes, that it was impossible to breathe. The commandant opened the window, and all the officers, who had returned for a last liqueur of brandy, gathered round it.

The damp air drew in, with its scent of flooded country; a powdering of rain pearled their beards. They could see the great trees bending under the storm, the broad valley half hidden beneath a mist of dark, low-hanging clouds, and in the far distance the belfry of the church, a grey point piercing the downpour.

Since their coming its bell had never rung. This was the sole resistance the invaders had met with in those parts – this of the church bell. The priest had not refused to billet Prussian soldiers, had even accepted invitations to drink beer or wine with the hostile commandant, who often made use of him as a friendly intermediary; but it was no good asking him to have the church bell rung; he would sooner have let himself be shot. It was his way of protesting against the invasion, a peaceful, silent protest, the only one that in his view befitted a priest, a man of peace, not war; and everybody, for ten miles round, lauded the steady heroism of the Abbé Chantavoine, who dared thus to proclaim the national grief by the stubborn muteness of his church bell. The whole village, fired by this resistance, were ready to back up their pastor through thick and thin, to face anything, considering that by this tacit protest they held the national honour safe. It seemed to the peasants that they had deserved better of their country than Belfort or Strasbourg, that they had shown as fine an example, that the name of their hamlet was earning immortality. Apart from this, they refused nothing to their Prussian conquerors.

The commandant and his junior officers had many a laugh over this harmless courage, and since the whole countryside showed itself obliging and submissive, they tolerated that mute exhibition of patriotism quite cheerfully.

The little Marquis Wilhelm, alone, wanted badly to make the church bell ring. The politic condescension of his chief towards the priest enraged him, and every day he besought the commandant to let him make 'Ding-don-don' just once, only once, just for a joke. And he would put a feline grace into his begging, and use the dulcet tones of some wheedling minx crazy for the gratification of her whim. But Count Farlsberg was adamant, and Mlle Fifi had to console himself by playing the mine game in the Chateau d'Uville.

The five men stayed some minutes at the window, inhaling the damp air, till Lieutenant Fritz said, with a thick laugh: 'These young ladies haven't much of a day for their outing.'

On that they separated, going to their various duties, the captain having a lot to do in preparation for the dinner.

When they met again at dusk they all burst out laughing, so smart and glossy were they all, so perfumed and pomaded, as if just starting off to a review. The commandant's hair seemed less grey than in the morning; the captain had shaved, keeping only his moustache — a veritable flame beneath his nose.

In spite of the rain they left the window open, and every now and then one of them would go and listen. At ten minutes past six the baron announced a distant rumbling; they all rushed to the door. Very soon the waggon came dashing up, with its four horses still at a gallop, muddied up to their eyes, blown, and steaming.

Five ladies alighted at the front-door, five good-looking damsels, carefully picked out by a friend of the captain, to whom Old Automaton had taken a private note from the baron.

Not that the ladies had made any bones about it, sure of good terms, and having three months' experience now of the Prussians. They had to take men and things as they found them. 'It's all in the day's work,' they said to each other during the drive, by way of stilling any remaining pricks of conscience.

They all went at once into the dining-room. Lighted up it looked more lugubrious than ever in its pitiful dilapidation, and the table, loaded with viands and the fine dinner service, as well as the silver rescued from that wall where the owner had hidden it, made one think of a brigand's supper, set after a successful raid. The captain, in his element, took charge of the ladies, past master of the art as he was, scrutinizing and appraising their charms; and when the three younger men showed signs of pairing off, he jumped on them at once, undertaking the work of partition himself, so that the strict demands of hierarchy might be properly fulfilled.

In order to avoid all discussion, dispute, suspicion of partiality, he lined the ladies up according to their height, and, addressing the tallest in the tone of a colonel on parade, asked: 'Your name?'

'Pamela,' she answered, making her voice as manly as she could.

'Number one, name of Pamela, allotted to the commandant.'

Having kissed Blondine, the second, in token of proprietorship, he assigned the chubby Amanda to Lieutenant Otto, the auburn-haired Eva to Second Lieutenant Fritz, and the shortest of all, Rachel, a dark and very young Jewess with eyes as black as ink (whose upturned nose proved the rule, among her race, of turned-down noses), he gave to the youngest officer, the little Marquis Wilhelm von Eyrik.

All, moreover, were plump and pretty, though without much distinction of feature, being reduced to somewhat the same pattern in style and complexion by the conditions of their life.

The three young men were for taking their ladies to have a wash and brush-up, but the captain, in his wisdom, was against that. They did not need it, in his opinion, and it would certainly lead to confusion. His ruling as a man of great experience was adopted. So there was only a certain amount of osculation.

All of a sudden Rachel began choking, and coughing till the tears came into her eyes, and the smoke out of her nostrils. The marquis, under pretext of a kiss, had puffed tobacco-smoke into her mouth. She showed no temper, and did not say a word, but she fixed her dark eyes on that young man; in the depths of them anger had begun to glow.

They sat down to dinner. Even the commandant appeared enraptured; he had on his right Pamela, and on his left Blondine. As he unfolded his napkin, he remarked: 'Really a splendid idea of yours, Captain!'

Lieutenants Otto and Fritz, as polite as if to women of their own class, were a little alarming to their neighbours; but Baron Kelweingstein, at the top of his form, was positively sparkling and bubbling with jokes, while his red head seemed to be in flames. He made himself extremely gallant in French as spoken on the Rhine, and his coarse compliments, hurled through the gap left by the departure of those two teeth, reached the ladies amid volleys of saliva. They were far from understanding a word of what he said, and only became animated as his talk became more gross, full of allusions, murdered by his vile accent. Then, indeed, they went into fits of laughter, leaning across their neighbours and repeating to each other lubricities that the baron now purposely mispronounced for the pleasure of hearing them respoken. The wine had not been long in going to the girls' heads, and they were soon behaving after their kind, playing with the moustaches to right and left, squeezing the men's arms, drinking out of everyone's glass, singing French ditties and tags of German songs learned in their daily encounters with the enemy.

Soon the men, too, began to play the fool, shouting and smashing the crockery, while the soldier servants behind their backs, perfectly impassive, went on serving.

The commandant alone maintained a certain dignity.

Mlle Fifi had taken Rachel on his knee, and with a sort of cold fury began to kiss the little dark hairs curling on her neck, and to breathe her in luxuriously. Then he would pinch her through her thin dress hard enough to make her cry out; for he was perpetually driven by a longing to hurt something. Once in the middle of a long kiss he suddenly bit her lip so severely that blood trickled down her chin on to her bodice.

Again she looked at him fixedly, and murmured, as she dabbed the wound: 'You'll have to pay for that!'

'All right,' he said, with a harsh laugh, 'I'll pay!'

They were at dessert by now, and champagne was being served. The commandant rose, and in a tone he might have used for proposing the health of the Empress Augusta, called out: 'I give you – the health of the ladies!'

After that came a stream of tipsy toasts, jocular and gross, and all the worse for the bad French in which they were proposed. One after another the young men got up, trying to be funny; while the ladies, very far gone by now, with vacant eyes and loosened mouths, applauded wildly. Then the captain, in a supreme effort to be gallant, raised his glass once more, and said: 'To our conquests of the fair!'

At that Lieutenant Otto, a regular Black Forest bear, drew himself up, and in a sudden heat of tipsy patriotism, cried: 'To our conquest of France!'

Intoxicated though they were, the girls were suddenly

silent; but Rachel, turning to him, stammered out in her rage: 'You – you – I know some Frenchmen you wouldn't dare say that to!'

The little marquis, who still held her on his knee, began to laugh. 'Ha! Ha! I've never seen a Frenchman. As soon as we show ourselves they cut and run!'

'You beast! You liar!' the infuriated girl shouted in his face.

He looked at her for a second much as he had looked at the portraits before putting their eyes out with his bullets, then said mockingly: 'Well, that's a brilliant thing to say! Should we be here if they were any good?' And with sudden exultation he shouted out: 'We're their masters. France is ours!'

She jerked herself off his knee back on to her own chair. And he got up, stretching out his wine-glass over the table, and shouted again: 'France is ours, and the French; and the woods, and the fields, and the homes of France!'

And all the others, in a burst of drunken brutal ardour, lifted their glasses, and shouting, 'Prussia for ever!' emptied them at a gulp.

Dumbed with a sudden fear the girls made no protest; even Rachel was silent.

The little marquis filled up his glass, and placing it on her dark head, went on: 'And ours, too, every woman of France!'

She started up; the glass, tilting over, baptized her black hair with its golden wine, and broke on the floor. Her lips trembled, her eyes defied his mocking eyes, and in a voice choking with rage she stammered out: 'That's — that's not true! You'll never have the women of France!'

He laughed so that he fell back into his chair. And aping as best he could the true Parisian accent, he said: 'She's killing, she really is! What have you come here for, then, my dear?'

She was silent a moment, too wildly upset to take in these last words. Then, suddenly catching on to his meaning, she flung out furiously: 'I! I! I'm not a woman, I'm only a — a — slut! That's good enough for a Prussian!'

Before she had finished he caught her a swinging box on the ear; but just as he was raising his hand again, blind with rage, she seized a little silver dessert-knife from the table, and, so quickly that no one saw it done, drove the point right into his throat just where it joined the chest.

The word he was saying was cut in half within his windpipe; his mouth fell open, his eyes gave one horrified look.

In confusion everyone jumped up, shouting; but, hurling her chair at the legs of Lieutenant Otto, who fell over it full-length, she flew to the window, threw it open, and, before anyone could reach her, vanished into the darkness and the rain that was still falling.

In two minutes Mlle Fifi was dead. Fritz and Otto drew their swords and were for massacring the women, who were clinging round their knees. With difficulty the major prevented this butchery, and getting the four terrified girls into another room, put a guard of two soldiers over them. Then, as if marshalling his forces for a battle, he organized the pursuit of the fugitive, quite certain of recapturing her.

Fifty men, spurred on by threats, were set to scour the park, two hundred more to search the woods and every house in the valley.

The table, cleared in a second, was now serving for a death-bed, and the four officers, stern and sobered, with the rigid faces of soldiers on duty, posted themselves at the windows, and peered forth into the night.

Torrents of rain were still coming down. An unending clamour filled the darkness, the whispering hiss of falling water and flowing water, of water trickling down, and water splashing up from the ground.

Suddenly a shot rang out, then another, very distant; and from time to time, for full four hours, they kept hearing shots, now near, now far, and voices hailing, and calling out queer guttural words.

At dawn the soldiers came back. Two had been killed, three others wounded by their comrades in the ardour of the chase and the scared confusion of that night pursuit. But they had not caught Rachel.

From that time on the inhabitants were terrorized, their houses turned upside down, the whole valley quartered, and searched again and again. The Jewess seemed to have left not a trace of her flight.

The general, who had to be told, ordered the whole affair to be hushed up, so as not to set a bad example to the army, and he severely dropped on the commandant, who in turn took it out of his juniors. 'We don't make war,' the general had said, 'for the pleasure of kissing courtesans.' And Count Farlsberg, in exasperation, resolved to avenge himself upon the countryside.

Thinking out a plausible pretext for severity, he sent for the priest, and ordered him to toll the church bell for the funeral of the Marquis von Eyrik.

Contrary to all expectation, the priest promised, with the utmost docility, to comply. And when the body of Mlle Fifi, carried by soldiers, preceded, surrounded, and followed by soldiers with loaded rifles, set out from the Chateau d'Uville, on its way to the cemetery, the bell at last regained its voice, tolling out a funeral knell, but with a certain mirth, as if some loving hand were stroking it.

It rang again in the evening, and the next day, and every day; it chimed as often as heart could wish. Sometimes even during the night it began of itself just shaking out into the darkness two or three silvery gay notes inexplicably. The peasants of the neighbourhood declared it was bewitched, and none but the priest and the sacristan would now go near the belfry.

In truth, a poor girl was living up there, lonely and anxious, secretly looked after by those two men.

So she stayed, till the German troops departed. Then one evening, the priest, having borrowed the baker's char-à-banc, himself drove his prisoner to the gate of Rouen. When he had embraced her, she jumped out and made her way quickly to the house she belonged to, where they had long given her up for dead.

Some time afterwards a patriot, who had no prejudices, took her away from there; he loved her first for her fine deed, but later for herself. And marrying her, he made of her a Lady as good as many another.

Old Mother Savage

I HADN'T BEEN TO Virelogne for fifteen years. But I found myself there again in the autumn, for some shooting with my friend Serval, who had at last rebuilt his chateau, destroyed by the Prussians.

I was always in love with that part of the country. There are certain delicious places in this world that have a really sensuous charm about them; one loves them as one loves a woman. Those of us whom Nature moves like that have a store of tender memories of – here a spring, and there a wood, a pool, a hill, often revisited, and never failing to emotionalize us in just such a way as will some joyful event. Occasionally one's thoughts will return to a nook in a coppice, a bit of riverbank, an orchard in blossom, seen but once under a radiant sky, yet graven in one's heart like the memory of some fair unknown, met in the street on a spring morning, who, passing in her light, filmy dress, has left in one's soul and in one's body an unsatisfied longing, unforgettable – the sensation as of happiness having fluttered by, and vanished.

I loved every bit of the country at Virelogne, its little woods, and little streams coursing through the earth like veins, carrying life-blood to the soil. There were crayfish to be caught there, and trout, and eels. Splendid! Here and there were pools one could bathe in, and often a snipe would rise from the tall reeds that border those little water-courses.

I was going along, light as a bird, watching my two dogs hunting ahead, and Serval, twenty yards away on my right, was walking up a clover-field, when, turning by the bushes at the end of the Saudres woods, I caught sight of a ruined cottage.

And suddenly I remembered it as I had seen it last, in 1869 – clean, covered with greenery, fowls in front of the door. Is there anything more mournful than a deserted home, or, rather, its sinister, shattered skeleton, still standing?

I recollected, too, that the good woman of the house had offered me a glass of wine, one day when I was very tired, and that Serval had told me all about the people who belonged there. The father, an old poacher, had been shot by gendarmes. The son, whom I remembered having seen, was a tall, lean fellow, who also had the reputation of a tremendous poacher. They were called the Savages, I wondered whether it was their real name, or merely a nickname.

I hailed Serval, and when he came up, with that long, loping stride of his, I asked: 'What's become of the people here?' Whereupon he told me this story:

When war was declared, the younger Savage, who was then about thirty-three, enlisted, leaving his mother alone at home. The old lady was not over-much pitied, for she was known to be well off.

So she was left to stay all by herself in that lonely house, far from the village, on the edge of the wood. She was not at all timid about it, being of the same type as her men-folk, a formidable old woman, tall and gaunt, neither given to joking nor to being joked with. Indeed, countrywomen hardly ever laugh; that's the men's business! Sad and narrow are the good wives' souls, to match their dull and mournful lives. The men-folk come in for a little fun at the inn, but the women are always very staid, with an unchanging severity of mien. The muscles of their faces have never learned how to stretch in laughter.

Old Mother Savage pursued her ordinary life at the cottage, where the snow soon lay all around. She would go to the village once a week, to buy herself bread and a little meat; then get back home at once. There was talk of wolves being about, and she would take a gun with her, her son's, a rusty gun, whose stock was worn and polished by much use. It was weird to see her, tall, a little bent, striding slowly through the snow, the barrel of the gun showing above the black head-dress that tightly bound her head and imprisoned the grey hair, which no one had ever seen.

One day the Prussians came. They were billeted on the inhabitants, according to the latter's means and accommodation. The old lady, known to be well off, had four – big fellows, with fair skins, fair beards, blue eyes, and still fleshy, in spite of all the fatigue they had been going through; well-behaved enough, too, for all that they were in a conquered land. They showed much consideration for their lonely old hostess, and spared her all the fatigue and expense they could. The four were often to be seen, in shirt-sleeves, making their toilette round the well, dashing the ice-cold water, those raw, snowy days, over their pink and white Northern skins, while 'old Mother Savage' passed backwards and forwards, getting the soup ready. Then they would clean up the kitchen, scrub the flagstones, chop wood, peel potatoes, wash the house-linen – do, in fact, all the housework, as four good sons might do for their mother.

But the old woman was always thinking of her own son – her tall son, with his aquiline nose and his brown eyes, and his thick moustache like a brush of black hair on his lip. And she was always asking one or other of her soldier guests:

'Do you know where the 23rd infantry regiment – French, I mean – is now? My son's in that.'

They would reply:

'No, not know; not know at all.'

And, understanding her anxiety and distress, they, who had mothers of their own at home, redoubled their little attentions to her. Yes, and she grew quite to like them, enemies though they were. Simple folk don't go in for the luxuries of patriotic hatred; that's the special prerogative of the superior classes. The poor and lowly, who pay the heaviest price, since each fresh burden presses desperately on their poverty, who in their masses are killed off wholesale, true food for cannon, who suffer by far the most from the atrocious misery of war, because they are the feeblest and least resistant among us, such as these scarcely understand the meaning of our bellicose ardour, our touchy points of honour, our sacred political obligations, as they are called, which in six months can exhaust two nations, victor no less than vanquished.

The folk round about there, speaking of old Mother Savage's four Germans, would say: 'Those four have fallen on their feet, and that's a fact!'

Well, one fine morning when the old woman was at home, alone, she caught sight of a man in the distance coming across the fields towards her cottage, and presently made him out to be the postman. He handed her a folded paper. Drawing out of their case the spectacles she used for sewing she read:

MRS SAVAGE –

This same has got a bit of bad news to bring you. Your boy Victor was killed yesterday by a cannon-ball, which cut him in two, as you might say. I was close by, because we was next each other in the same company, and he'd been talking to me about letting you know at once if anything happened to him. So I took his watch out of his pocket, to bring it along to you when the war gets over.

With kind regards,

CAESAR RIVOT,

Soldier of the 2nd class in the 23rd Infantry.

The letter was dated three weeks back.

She did not cry, but stood motionless, so stricken, so stupefied, that for the moment she did not suffer. 'There's Victor killed now!' she thought. Then slowly the tears came into her eyes, and suffering flooded her heart. Thoughts came to her one by one, dreadful torturing thoughts. She would never hold him in her arms again – her boy, her big boy, never again! The gendarmes had killed the father, the Prussians had killed the son . . . Cut in two by a cannon-ball. She seemed to see the whole horrible thing; his head falling, his eyes wide open, and his teeth gnawing the end of his big moustache, as he was wont to do when he was angry.

What had they done with his body afterwards? If only they had given her back her boy, as they had given her back her husband, with the bullet wound in the middle of his forehead!

But suddenly she heard the sounds of voices. Her Prussians were returning from the village. She hid the letter very quickly in her pocket, and met them with an unmoved face, having had time even to wipe her eyes carefully.

They were all four laughing, in excellent spirits, having got hold of a fine rabbit, poached, no doubt, and they signalled to the old lady the jolly prospect of something tasty. At once she set about getting ready the midday meal; but when it came to killing the rabbit, her courage suddenly failed – not that it was by any means an unaccustomed task! So one of the soldiers gave it a sharp knock behind the ears.

Now that the creature was dead, she drew its red carcass out from the fur; but the sight of the blood covering her hands, the warm blood that she could feel getting cold and clotted, made her tremble from head to foot; all the time she was seeing her boy, her great tall son, cut in two, all red, like this creature still almost a-quiver.

She sat down to table with the Prussians, but not a single mouthful could she eat. They devoured the rabbit without paying any attention to her. And she gazed at them sidelong, silent, maturing a plan, her face so unmoved that they noticed nothing.

Suddenly she said:

'I don't even know your names, and it's a month now we've been here together.'

They could just make out what she wanted, and told her their names. But that was not enough for her; she insisted on it all being written down, with their home addresses. Settling her spectacles on her large nose, she scrutinized this incomprehensible writing, then, folding the paper, put it in her pocket, above the letter which had told her of her son's death.

When the meal was finished, she said to the men:

'I'm going to do something for you.' And she began carrying hay up into the granary where they slept.

When they expressed surprise at the trouble she was taking, she explained that it would make it warmer for them; so they helped her. Piling the trusses up to the thatched roof, they made a kind of big room with the four walls of forage, warm and sweet-smelling, where they would sleep like tops.

At dinner, one of them expressed concern at seeing her again not eating. She said she had got the cramp, and lighted a good fire, to get warm all through. The four Germans went up to their bedroom by the ladder which served them for staircase every night.

As soon as the trap-door was shut after them, she removed the ladder, then noiselessly reopened the outer door and went out to fetch more trusses of straw, which she stacked in the kitchen. She went bare-foot in the snow, so softly that nothing could be heard. From time to time she would stop and listen to the loud, uneven snoring of her four sleeping soldiers.

When she considered her preparations complete, she threw one of the trusses on the fire, and as soon as it was well alight, scattered it all over the others. Then she went outside to watch.

Within a few seconds a strong glare lighted up the whole interior of the cottage, that soon became a frightful brazier, a gigantic glowing oven, whose light streamed out through the little window in a brilliant ray on to the snow.

Suddenly a loud cry sounded from the top of the house, then a clamour of human shrieks, the most awful screams of anguish and terror. Then, the trap-door falling to the ground, a tornado of flame shot up into the granary, pierced the thatched roof, leaped up against the sky like an immense torch, and the whole cottage became a blazing mass.

Nothing could now be heard from within but the crackling of the fire, and the splitting of the walls, and the noise of the beams falling. All at once the roof fell in; and from the glowing shell of the cottage a great plume of sparks shot high into the air, red against a pall of smoke.

And the snow-covered earth, illumined by the fire, shone like a silvery sheet, dyed crimson.

A clock in the distance began to strike.

Old Mother Savage stood there in front of her ruined home, armed with the gun – her son's gun – for fear that one of the soldiers might yet escape.

When she saw that all was over, she threw her weapon into that furnace, and there was the sound of a shot as it went off.

People had begun to assemble now, peasants and Prussians.

They found her tranquilly sitting on a tree-trunk, appeased by her revenge.

A German officer who spoke French perfectly asked her:

'Where are your soldiers?'

She raised a thin arm, pointed towards the shapeless ruin, no longer blazing, and replied in a loud voice:

'In there!'

Everyone crowded round her. And the Prussian asked:

'How did the fire come about?'

She said:

'I lighted it, myself.'

No one believed her, thinking that the disaster had driven her mad. Thereupon she told her story from beginning to end to the listening crowd, from the arrival of the letter to the last cry of the men burned within her house; she left untold not a single detail of what she had felt or done.

When she had finished, she took the two papers from her pocket, and, the better to distinguish them, put on her spectacles, for the light from the fire was getting dim. Then, holding up one, she said:

'That's about Victor's death.'

Nodding towards the glowing ruin, she showed them the other, and added:

'That's their names, so that you can write to their homes.'

Then, calmly holding out the white sheet of paper to the officer, who had seized her by the shoulders, she continued:

'Tell them how it happened, and tell them it was I who did it, Victoire Simon, that they call the Savage. Don't forget.'

The officer shouted an order in German. They seized her, and hurled her against the red-hot cottage walls. Twelve soldiers quickly took up position twenty paces away. She did not stir. She had understood, and waited.

A command rang out, followed at once by the long rattle of a volley. Then one shot, by itself.

The old woman did not fall. She seemed rather to sink down, as if her legs had been cut off.

The Prussian officer went up to her. She was cut almost in two, and in her clenched fist she held her letter, covered with blood.

My friend Serval added: 'The Germans burned down my chateau, just by way of reprisal.'

But I was thinking of the mothers of those four good fellows burnt in there; and of the atrocious heroism of that other mother, propped against the wall, and shot.

And I picked up a little stone, still blackened by the fire.

The Chair-Mender

THE FIRST DINNER of the shooting season at the Marquis of Bertran's was drawing to a close. Eleven sportsmen, eight young women, and the local doctor were seated around the large brilliantly lighted table, which was covered with fruit and flowers.

They had been talking of love, and a great discussion arose, the eternal discussion as to whether we are capable of loving truly more than once in our lives. They cited instances of people who had never had more than one serious love affair; they also mentioned others where people had fallen violently in love more than once. Most of the men maintained that the passion of love, like an illness, may attack the same person several times; and that it may bring him even to death's door, if an insurmountable obstacle opposes its course. Although this manner of looking at it seemed incontestable, the women, whose opinions were based rather upon poetic imaginings than upon observed facts, affirmed that love, true and great love, can only be an unique experience to us mortals; that it is like a stroke of lightning, and that a heart touched by this kind of love remains empty, ravaged, and burnt up so completely that it is for ever after sterile to strong sentiment, and even to tender dreams.

The Marquis, who had loved many times, opposed this belief vigorously.

'I can tell you that a man can love more than once with his whole heart and soul. You bring up cases of people who've killed themselves for love, as a proof of the impossibility of a second passion. I can answer this by assuring you that, if they had not been fools enough to commit suicide, which took away all chance of a relapse, they would have been cured; and they would have recommenced, and kept it on for the natural term of their lives. It's the same with lovers as with drunkards. He who has drunk will drink again – he who has loved will continue to love. It's a matter of temperament. That's all it is.'

They made the doctor umpire in the dispute. He was an old Parisian, who had retired into the country. They begged him to give his opinion.

He had none to give, as it happened.

'As the Marquis has said, it is a matter of temperament: however, I have a personal knowledge of a passion which lasted for fifty-five years, without a day's respite, and ended only with death.'

The Marquise clapped her hands.

'Isn't that beautiful! And what a thing to be loved like that. What happiness, to live fifty-five years quite enveloped by an intense and penetrating devotion! How blessed and happy he must have been in a love like that!'

The doctor smiled.

'Indeed, madame, you are not mistaken on the point; the object of that love was a man. You know him well; it is M. Chouquet, the chemist of our market town. As for her, the woman, you knew her too; she was the old chair-mender who called at the castle on her rounds every year. Perhaps you will let me try to explain it to you.'

This calmed the women's enthusiasm, and their disgusted expressions seemed to imply that the transports of love were exclusively the privilege of the refined and distinguished beings, who alone seem worthy of interest to people of their world.

The doctor went on:

'Three months ago I was called to this old woman's death-bed. She had arrived here the night before, in the rickety caravan that was her home, drawn by the wretched old horse you may have seen, and accompanied by the two big black dogs, her protectors and her friends. The priest was there already. She made us the executors of her will, and, in order to disclose the motives of her last wishes, she told us the whole story of her life. I do not know anything more curious, or more poignant.

'Her father and mother were travelling chair-menders. She had never slept in a dwelling fixed permanently in the ground.

'When quite little, she ran about in rags, covered with vermin and sordidly dirty. They would pull up on the outskirts of villages, close to the ditch; the horse, unharnessed, browsed by the roadside, the dog slept, with his nose between his paws, and the little girl rolled about in the grass, while the father and mother, in the shade of the elm trees, would set themselves to mend the seats of all the old chairs in the parish. There wasn't much talking in this wandering home. After the few necessary words to settle who should make the round of the houses, uttering the well-known cry: "Chairs to mend!" they would go to work, face to face, or side by side, twisting the rushes in silence. When the child had wandered off too far in her play, or tried to scrape up acquaintance with some ragamuffin from the village, the father's angry voice would call after her: "Will you come back here – you crapule!" They were the only expressions of tenderness she ever heard.

'When she grew bigger, they used to send her to gather in the harvest of worn-out chairs. She got to know the street boys in various places; but the parents of her new friends would call back their offspring brutally: "Come here at once, you rascal. Don't you let me see you playing about again with dirty barefooted brats."

'The little urchins often threw stones at her.

'Once some kind ladies gave her a few coppers: she treasured them up carefully.

'One day – she was eleven years old – they were passing

through our district when she met the little Chouquet boy, behind the wall of the cemetery. He was crying bitterly, because a playmate had taken two farthings from him. Those tears of a little well-to-do child, of one of those children whose lot she had pictured in her outcast's little brain as being always fortunate and happy, completely upset all her notions. She approached him, and when she had learned the cause of his sorrow, she put all her savings into his hands, seven sous, which he took as a matter of course, and dried his tears. Then, quivering with joy, she had the audacity to give him a kiss. He was absorbed in the contemplation of the money, and did not think of objecting. Finding herself neither repulsed nor beaten, she renewed her caresses, she hugged and embraced him to her heart's content. Then she ran away.

'What was it that took place in that miserable little head? Did she become attached to this boy because she had sacrificed her tiny fortune to him, or because she had given him her first tender kiss? The mystery is the same, whether we are little or big.

'For months she dreamt of that corner of the cemetery and of that boy. In the expectation of seeing him again, she purloined from her parents, filched one sou here, another there, either from the money paid for the mending of a chair or from what she was given when sent on an errand to buy provisions.

'When she came this way again she had two francs in her pocket, but she could only catch sight of the chemist's son, with a very clean face, behind the windows of the paternal shop, between a large red carboy and a glass jar, containing a tapeworm preserved in spirit.

'She only loved him all the more, seduced, moved, entranced by this glory of coloured water, this apotheosis of brilliant crystals.

'She kept his memory indelible, and when she met him the following year, at the back of the schoolhouse, playing marbles with other boys, she rushed to him, seized hold of him and kissed him with so much violence that he began to howl with fright. Then, to appease him, she gave him all her money – three francs, twenty centimes – a real hoard, which he looked at with wide-open eyes.

'He took it, and let her caress him as much as she wanted.

'For four years, she continued to pour all her savings into his hands. He pocketed them conscientiously in exchange for the kisses he permitted her to give. Once it was thirty sous, on another occasion two francs, once only twelve sous (she cried about it, with grief and humiliation, but the year had been a bad one), and the last time she handed over five francs, a big round coin, which made him laugh with sheer satisfaction.

'She thought of nothing in the world but that boy; and he awaited her return with some impatience; he would start running towards her as soon as she appeared in sight, and the girl's heart would leap up at this.

Then he disappeared. He had been sent away to school. She found this out from skilful inquiries, and she used infinite diplomacy to induce her parents to change their round, so as to pass through here during the holiday months. She succeeded in effecting her object after a year of wily plotting. It was two years since she had seen him, and he was hardly recognizable, he was so changed, grown so tall, improved in appearance, and quite imposing in his school tunic, with its row of gilt buttons. He pretended not to see her, and passed proudly by.

She wept over this for two whole days; and ever since that time she suffered endlessly.

'Each year she came back, passed by him without daring to greet him, and without his deigning to give even one glance in her direction. She loved him desperately. She said to me, "He is the only man that I have seen on earth, *monsieur le médecin*. I don't even know if there are any others in existence."

'Her parents died. She went on alone; but she took two big dogs along with the caravan instead of only one – two terrible watch-dogs, that nobody would have cared to tackle.

'One day, returning to the village, where her heart had always stayed, she saw a young woman come out of Chouquet's shop, arm in arm with her beloved. It was his wife. He had got married.

'The same evening she threw herself into the horse-pond, near the town hall. Some belated tippler fished her out again, and carried her into the pharmacy. Chouquet, the younger, came down in his dressing gown to attend to the case, and after bringing her round, and without appearing to recognize her at all, he said, in a harsh voice: "You must be mad! Don't be up to these silly tricks again."

'That was enough to cure her. He had spoken to her! She felt happy for a long time afterwards.

'He refused to accept anything for his services, although she insisted obstinately on paying him.

'And her whole life went on in this way. She mended chairs while thinking of Chouquet. Every year, she saw him behind the plate-glass windows. She got into the habit of buying trifles from him, supplies of drugs. In this way she could look at him closely, and could speak to him, and still give him her money.

'As I have already told you, she died this spring. After having related all this sad story, she ended by begging me to deliver to the man she loved so patiently the savings of her whole life; for she had worked only for him, she said, often depriving herself even of food, in order to put by some money and make sure that he would think of her, at least once more, when she was dead.

'She put two thousand, three hundred, and twenty-seven francs then into my hands. I left the twenty-seven francs with M. le Curé to pay for the burial, and I took away the rest, after she had breathed her last.

'Next day I went to the Chouquets. They sat finishing their lunch, facing each other, both fat and red, redolent of pharmaceutical products, pompous and self-satisfied.

'They made me sit down; they offered me a glass of liqueur, which I accepted, and I commenced my tale in an unsteady voice, feeling certain that they would be moved to tears.

'As soon as he understood that he had been loved by this

wandering mender of chairs, by this disreputable tramp, Chouquet jumped up, fuming with indignation, as if she had stolen from him his reputation, the esteem of all respectable people, his intimate honour, something tender and delicate, that was more dear to him than life.

'His wife, quite as exasperated as he, repeated continually: "That beggarwoman! That beggarwoman!" unable to find anything else to say.

'Chouquet walked to and fro, with long strides, behind the table, his embroidered smoking cap hung sideways over one ear. He stammered: "Can you understand it, Doctor? It's something too horrible to happen to one! What's to be done? Oh, if I had only known it in her lifetime, I should have had her arrested by the police and thrown into prison. And she would not have come out of it soon, I can tell you."

'I remained astounded at the result of my pious errand. I did not know what to say or what to do. But I had to carry out my mission to the end. I went on again: "She has charged me to give over to you all her savings, which amount to the sum of two thousand, three hundred francs. As the information seems to be so painfully shocking to you, perhaps the best thing would be to devote this money to some charitable object."

'They looked at me, the man and the woman, petrified by the news.

'I pulled the money out of my pocket, the wretched money, from different countries, and of all coinages – gold, silver, and copper intermixed. Then I asked: "Well — what do you want to do?"

'Mme Chouquet spoke first: "Of course, as it was that woman's last wish, it seems to me, really, that it will be very difficult for us to refuse."

'The husband, vaguely confused, struck in: "We could always buy something for the children with it."

'I said drily: "As you please!"

'He replied: "You may as well hand it over, since she has charged you with it. We shall easily be able to find means of using it for some good work."

'I delivered the money, bowed, and went away.

'The next day Chouquet called upon me and said brusquely: "By the bye, hasn't she left her caravan here, that . . . that woman? What do you propose doing with the old thing?"

'"Nothing: you may take it if you like."

'"First-rate; that will just suit me; I will turn it into a tool shed for my kitchen garden."

'He was going off, but I called him back, "She has also left her old horse and her two dogs. Will you have them too?" He stopped, greatly surprised: "Why, no! Bless me! What should I do with them? Dispose of them as you please." He laughed, and reached out his open hand, which I took. What would you have? It does not do for the doctor and the chemist in the same district to be on bad terms.

'I have kept the dogs. The curé, who has a large paddock, has taken charge of the old horse. The cart serves as a tool shed for Chouquet; and he has bought five railway shares with the money.

'That is the only instance of deep love I have ever come across in my life.'

The doctor remained silent.

Then the Marquise, whose eyes were full of tears, sighed out: 'Decidedly, it is women alone who know how to love.'

Mademoiselle Perle

I

IT WAS REALLY a curious idea I had that evening to choose Mlle Perle as 'queen'.

I go every year to keep the Jour des Rois, with my old friends, the Chantals. Chantal was the most intimate friend of my father, who took me there first as quite a small boy. I have continued, and doubtless I shall continue, to visit them as long as I live, and as long as there is a Chantal in this world.

The Chantals, it must be said, lead a peculiar existence; they live in Paris as as though they were living in some small provincial town, in Grasse, or Yvetot, or Pont-à-Mousson.

Their house stands near the Observatory, in a little garden, and they live in that quiet neighbourhood as though buried in the country. They know nothing, they have no notion of the great Paris, of the real Paris; they are so remote, they seem to live far, far away. Sometimes, however, they make a momentous excursion into it, an arduous expedition. Mme Chantal goes forth to 'provision the household'.

Mlle Perle, who has the keys of the store cupboards (for the linen presses are looked after by the mistress of the house) – Mlle Perle, I say, announces that the sugar is almost at an end, that the store of preserves is getting low, and that there is very little raw coffee left at the bottom of the sack.

Thus warned against the approach of famine, Mme Chantal makes a thorough inspection of what remains, and takes notes in a little book.

When she has done jotting down a multitude of figures, she plunges into long calculations, and then holds an animated discussion with Mlle Perle. They end after a time by agreeing together as to the quantity of each article which is to last them for the next three months; sugar, rice, dried plums, coffee, preserves, tins of green peas, of haricots, of lobster, of fish, salt and smoked, etc., etc.

After which the day is fixed, and the two set forth in a fiacre, a sort of brougham with a gallery, for the establishment of a first-class grocer, who lives 'beyond the bridges', as the saying is, in the new quarter of the capital.

Mme Chantal and Mlle Perle make this journey together, mysteriously, and return about dinner time, still excited, but tired out with the jolting of the cab, whose roof is piled up with packages and bags, of all sorts, as if it were a country cart.

For the Chantals, the whole part of Paris on the other side of the Seine is comprised in the name of the 'new quarters'; they look upon them as inhabited by an extravagant, noisy, not very honourable population, whose days are wasted in dissipation, who spend the nights in feasting, and fling their money into the gutter. Nevertheless, the young ladies are taken to the theatre over there, from time to time, to the Opéra Comique, for instance, or to the Français, when the play which fills the bill has been reported on favourably by M. Chantal's daily newspaper.

These girls must be now nineteen and seventeen respectively; they are fine girls, tall and fresh, very well brought up; too well brought up; so exceedingly well, that they pass unperceived like two pretty dolls. The idea if paying marked attention to one of the Chantal young ladies would never enter my head. Indeed, one hardly dares to speak to them; they seem so absolutely immaculate that one is inclined to doubt the propriety of addressing them in the common forms of greeting.

As for the father, he is a charming man, very intelligent, very open, very cordial; but he likes repose, calmness, and tranquillity above everything else. He had had a great share in bringing about the fossilized state of his family, so that he can live according to his taste in a stagnant immobility. He reads much, likes to talk, and is very impressionable. He has never rubbed shoulders with mankind at large, and this absence of all contact with the rough world has made his epidermis, his moral epidermis, very sensitive and delicate. The least unusual event moves him, agitates him, and makes him suffer.

The Chantals have friends, however, but they are restricted to a few carefully chosen families in the neighbourhood. In the course of each year they also exchange two or three visits with some relations who live far away.

As for myself, I dine with them invariably on the 15th of August, and on the Jour des Rois. It seems to be a sort of imperative duty, as the religious observances of Easter are for all good Catholics.

On the 15th of August, they invite other friends besides myself, but on the Jour des Rois I am the only guest.

II

WELL, THIS YEAR, as in other years, I had been dining with the Chantals, on the Jour des Rois.

According to custom, I embraced M. Chantal, gave a kiss to Mme Chantal and Mlle Perle, and made a low bow to Mlles Louise and Pauline. I was at once beset with questions about a thousand things, about the events of the boulevards, about politics, about the public opinion on the affairs in Tonkin, and about the doings of our representatives in both Chambers. Mme Chantal — a big lady, whose ideas always give me the impression of being square, like blocks of cut stone — has the habit of ending every political discussion by the following pronouncement: 'All that is bad seed for the future.' Why is it that I always picture to myself Mme Chantal's ideas as being square? I don't know in the least; yet everything she says takes that shape in my mind; it is like a square, a large square, with four symmetrical angles. There are other people, whose ideas always seem to me to be quite round and rolling, like a lot of hoops. As soon as these people begin to utter the first sentence about anything whatever, it seems to revolve, and it goes on, it proceeds on in ten, twenty, fifty round ideas, large and small, which I seem to see running one after the other, rolling to the end of the horizon. Other people, again, have ideas that seem pointed . . . However – that doesn't matter.

We sat down to table as usual, and the dinner came to an end without anything that I can remember being said.

With the dessert they brought on to the table the traditional cake of the Jour des Rois. Hitherto M. Chantal had happened to be 'King' every year. Whether it was the result of continuous luck, or of pious fraud on the part of his family, I am unable to say, but the fact is that he invariably found the bean in his slice of cake; and, of course, he would proclaim Mme Chantal as 'Queen'. Consequently, my astonishment was very great when I felt something extremely hard in a mouthful of cake I was eating, and on which I nearly broke my teeth. I took the thing quietly out of my mouth, and I discovered it was a little china doll, no bigger than a white bean. In my surprise, I said:

'Ah!' Everybody looked at me and Chantal shouted, clapping his hands: 'Gaston has got it! It's Gaston! Long live the King! Long live the King!'

Everyone answered in chorus: 'Long live the King!' I blushed up to my ears, as one often blushes, without reason, when one is in a rather foolish situation. I remained, with my eyes lowered, holding this bit of china with the tips of my fingers, trying to laugh, and not knowing what to say or do next, when Chantal exclaimed: 'Come! You must choose a queen now.'

Then I was struck dumb. In a second a thousand thoughts, a thousand surmises crossed my mind. Did they intend me to select one of the Chantal young ladies? Was it a scheme for making me name the one I liked best? Was it a gentle, delicate, soft thrust of the parental hand, impelling me towards a possible marriage? The idea of marriage is always floating in the air of all houses where there are grown-up daughters; it takes on all sorts of forms, all sorts of disguises, it penetrates all sorts of situations. An atrocious fear of compromising my independence invaded me, and also an extreme timidity, before the so obstinately impenetrable attitude of the Mlles Louise and Pauline. To name one of them in preference to the other seemed as difficult as to choose between two drops of water; and then, the fear of being drawn into making a venture, by which I might be led to a marriage in spite of myself, quite placidly, by proceedings as discreet, as imperceptible, and as well contrived as this insignificant royalty, troubled me horribly.

But suddenly I had a lucky inspiration, and I offered the symbolical doll to Mlle Perle. Everyone was surprised at first, then – appreciating, doubtless, my good feeling and my discretion – they applauded furiously. They cried: 'Long live the Queen! Long live the Queen.'

As for her, the poor old maid, she was quite abashed; she was scared, trembled, and stammered: 'No . . . no . . . not me . . . I beg you . . . not me . . . I beg you . . .'

Then, for the first time in my life, I may say, I looked at Mlle Perle, and I wondered who she was.

I had been accustomed to see her in that house as one sees old tapestry armchairs, on which one has sat from one's childhood, without having ever taken any notice of them; till one day, one doesn't know why, because, perhaps, a ray of sun has fallen across the seat, one says to oneself, suddenly: 'Hullo, that's a curious piece of furniture,' and thereupon one discovers that the wood has been carved by an artist, and that the cover is of remarkably fine stuff. I had never taken any special notice of Mlle Perle.

She was a member of the Chantal household, that was all I knew; but on what grounds? In what relation? She was a tall, thin person, who endeavoured to remain unperceived, but who was not insignificant. She was treated with perfect friendliness; better than a housekeeper, not so well as a near relation. I became conscious now of a good many gradations of shades, of which I had taken no account before. Mme Chantal addressed her as

'Perle'; the girls said 'Mlle Perle'; and Chantal himself called her only 'Mademoiselle', with a marked reverence in his tone, it seemed.

I began to observe her. How old was she? Forty? Yes, forty. She was not old, this woman. She was trying to look old. I was suddenly struck by that discovery. The manner in which she did her hair, the style of her dress, were ridiculous, and yet, in spite of the way she decked herself out, she appeared by no means ridiculous, because she had so much simple, natural grace, a grace that was veiled and concealed with care. Really, she was a remarkable creature. How was it that I had never noticed this? She arranged her hair in a grotesque combination of little old-fashioned curls, in a quite absurd way; and under this hair of a well-preserved old maid, one saw a large, calm forehead, marked by two deep folds, two lines of enduring sadness, then two blue eyes, large and soft, so timid, so apprehensive, so humble; two beautiful eyes remaining so naive, full of the astonishments of girlhood, of youthful sensations, and also of grief, which had passed behind them, softening without dimming their glance.

The whole face was fine and reserved, one of those faces whose radiance has been extinguished, but which yet remain unfaded, unmarked by the weariness and the great emotions of life.

What a pretty mouth she had, what pretty teeth! But one would think she never dared to smile!

And, suddenly, I could not help comparing her with Mme Chantal! Certainly, Mlle Perle was better looking, a hundred times better looking, more refined, more noble, more proud.

I was astounded by my observations. Meantime, the champagne was being poured out, and I raised my glass to the 'Queen'; drinking her health with a neatly turned compliment. At first she had a mind, as I could see very well, to hide her face in her serviette; then, as her lips touched the light-coloured wine, everyone cried out: 'The Queen drinks! The Queen drinks!' She turned quite red and choked. We were all laughing heartily, but I could see plainly that she was much loved by everyone in that house.

III

DINNER OVER, M. Chantal took me by the arm. It was his time for smoking his evening cigar – a sacred hour. When he was alone, he went out into the street; when he had someone to dinner he would take his guests up to the billiard room, where he could have his game while he smoked. This evening a fire had been lit in the room, because of the festive occasion, and my old friend took his cue, a cue with a very fine tip, which he proceeded to chalk over most carefully. Then he said:

'You begin, my boy!'

Having known me from a child, he used to treat me with great familiarity, though I was five-and-twenty.

I commenced the game; I made some good strokes, I missed a few others; but as the thought of Mlle Perle haunted my mind, I asked suddenly:

'Tell me, Monsieur Chantal, is Mlle Perle related to you in any way?'

He stopped, much astonished, and looked at me.

'What? Don't you know? Haven't you heard Mlle Perle's story?'

'No.'

'Your father never told you?'

'No.'

'Well, well, that's funny! Ah! Upon my word, that is funny! Oh, but it is quite an adventure.'

He was silent, then commenced again:

'And if you knew how strange it is that you should ask me such a question today, on the Jour des Rois.'

'Why?'

'Ah, why! Listen! It is forty-one years ago. Just forty-one years ago. Just forty-one years today. We lived then in Roüy le Tors, on the ramparts; but I must first describe the situation of the house, that you may better understand. Roüy is built on a hill or rather on a sort of mound, dominating a great flat expanse of meadowland. We had a house there, with a beautiful garden, held up, supported high by the old fortifications. The house itself was in the town, you understand – in a street – whilst the garden at the back commanded a view of the plain. There was a door opening out of the garden right into the country, at the bottom of a secret staircase, which went down hidden in the thickness of the walls, as one reads in romances. A public road passed along the wall in front of that door, which was supplied with a bell-pull outside, for the peasants, who, in order to avoid the long way round, brought what produce they had to sell straight in that way.

'You see the locality, don't you? Well, that year, on the Jour des Rois, it had snowed for a week. People talked of the end of the world. When we came out on to the ramparts, and looked down at the plain, it chilled one's very spirit to see that immense white country, quite white, frozen, dead, and glistening, as if with a coat of varnish. It seemed as though the Lord God had wrapped up the old earth like this to put it away in the storehouse of worn-out worlds. I assure you that it was very depressing.

'It was a family gathering; there were many of us, very many: my father, my mother, my uncle and my aunt, my two brothers, and my four cousins, they were nice girls. I married the youngest afterwards. Of all that company there are only three of us left today: my wife, myself, and my sister-in-law, who lives in Marseilles. Sacristi! how a big family can waste away. It makes me shudder to think of it! I was fifteen then, since I am fifty-six now.

'Well, we were celebrating the festival of the Jour des Rois, and we were very merry, very merry! We were all assembled in the drawing-room, waiting for dinner, when my eldest brother, Jacques, said: "I've heard a dog howling in the meadows for the last ten minutes; it must have got lost, the poor beast."

'He had not finished speaking before the bell of the garden door rang out. It had a deep sound, like a church bell, and made you think of the dead. It sent a chill through everybody. My father rang for the servant, and told him to go down and see what it could be. We waited in perfect silence, thinking of the snow that covered the whole earth. The man returned, and assured us that there was nothing to be seen. The dog was still howling, unceasingly, and his voice had not altered its position.

'We sat down to table; but we were a little uneasy, especially the younger ones. All went well until the roast course came on, and then the bell was heard to ring three times, in three loud strokes, which seemed to vibrate into our very finger-tips, and made us catch our breath. We remained looking at each other, with our forks in our hands, listening for more, and seized by a sort of supernatural fear.

'It was my mother who spoke at last: "It's astonishing that they should have waited so long before coming back. Don't go alone, Baptiste, one of the gentlemen will go with you."

'My uncle François got up. He was a sort of Hercules, very proud of his strength, and perfectly fearless. My father said: "Take a gun with you. One never knows . . ."

'But my uncle only took a stick, and went out immediately with the servant.

'We remained trembling and anxious, without eating, without speaking. My father tried to reassure us: "You will see that it is some beggar, or someone who has lost his way in the snow.

After having rung once, seeing that we did not open the door directly, he has attempted to find his way again, then, not being able to discover it, he has returned to our gate."

'My uncle's absence seemed to last an hour. He came back furious, swearing: "Nothing, nom de nom! It's a practical joke. There's only that confounded dog out there, howling, about a hundred yards away from the walls. If I had had my gun with me I would have shot the brute."

'We went on with our dinner, but everyone remained anxious. We felt that this was not over yet, that something was going to happen, that the bell would presently ring again.

'And it did ring, just at the moment that the cake was being cut. My uncle François, who had drunk some champagne, declared that he was going out to kill that joker, with so much fury that my mother and my aunt rushed to him and clung to his arms. My father, although very calm (he was a little crippled – he had remained lame after a fall from his horse), declared his intention to find out what this meant. He would go himself. My brothers, one eighteen and the other twenty, ran to fetch their guns, and, as nobody paid any attention to me, I got a rook rifle and prepared to follow the expedition.

'We started off immediately. My father and my uncle walked in front, with Baptiste, who carried a lantern. My brothers Jacques and Paul came next, and I went after them, in spite of my mother's entreaties. She remained with her sister and my cousins on the doorstep of the house.

'For the last hour the snow had been falling thickly, and the trees were laden with it. The firs, bent down with this heavy livid clothing, stood like white pyramids, like enormous sugar-loaves; and one could hardly perceive through the grey veil of minute and hurrying flakes, the more frail bushes quite pallid in the darkness.

'The snow fell so thickly, that one could only see ten feet around one. But the lantern threw out a great light in front of us. When we commenced to go down the winding staircase in the wall I felt really afraid. It seemed as though someone were walking behind me, that someone was going to grasp me by the shoulders and carry me off. I would have gone back, but I did not dare to, because I should have had to cross the whole garden by myself.

'I heard them opening the door that gave out on to the fields; then my uncle began to swear again: "*Nom d'un nom!* the fellow's cleared off again. If I could only catch sight of his shadow I wouldn't miss the beggar, I promise you."

'It was sinister to see the plain, or rather to feel it, before us, for one could not see it under the endless cover of snow above, below, in front, to the right, to the left – everywhere.

'My uncle exclaimed: "Stay, there's that howling dog, though, I will show him how I can shoot. It will be something done, anyhow."

'But my father, who was a humane man, objected: "We had much better fetch the poor animal in, it's howling with hunger. It's barking for help, the poor wretch. He calls like a man in distress. Let us go out there."

'We started forward through the curtain, through the thick,

continuous fall of snow, through the soft, dense, mossy whirl of flakes which filled the night and the air, which stirred, floated, fell and froze while it melted on one's flesh. It froze one as though it were burning, with a sharp, rapid pain at each touch of the little white flakes upon the skin of one's face.

'We sank up to our knees in the soft, cold mass, and we had to lift our feet very high. As we advanced, the dog's voice became clearer, stronger. My uncle shouted: "Here he is!" We stopped to look at him as one would stop before an enemy at night.

'I myself saw nothing, till I caught up with the others, and then I made out the dog that was looking alarming and fantastic, a big black animal, a shepherd's dog with a rough coat and a head like a wolf, standing up on its four paws, right at the end of a long ray of light cast by the lantern on to the snow. He didn't move. He had become quiet and was watching us.

'My uncle said: "It's funny he doesn't come on or run away. I've a good mind to settle him with a shot."

'My father replied firmly: "No, we must take him with us."

'Then my brother Jacques added: "But he isn't alone, there's something else there."

'Indeed, there was something near the dog; something grey, and impossible to distinguish. We moved on again cautiously.

'On seeing us approach, the dog sat down. He did not look vicious. He seemed pleased to see us coming.

'My father went up fearlessly, and patted his head. The dog began to lick his hand; and we found out that he was tied up to the wheel of a little cart, a sort of toy waggon, quite enveloped in three or four soft blankets. We lifted up these wrappings carefully, and as Baptiste lowered his lantern to the opening of the queer conveyance, which resembled a dog kennel on wheels, we saw a tiny baby inside, fast asleep.

'We were so astonished that we could not say a word. My father was the first to speak, and as he was large-hearted and of a rather exalted sensibility, he stretched out his hand over the roof of the cart, and said: "Poor little forsaken thing, you shall be one of us!" And he ordered my brother Jacques to wheel our discovery in front of us.

'My father recommenced, as though thinking aloud:

'"Some love child, whose poor mother came ringing at my door on this night, in remembrance of the Infant Christ!"

'He stopped again, and shouted out with all his might four times into the night, towards the four corners of heaven: "We have rescued the child!" Then, laying his hand on his brother's shoulder, he murmured: "Supposing you had fired at the dog, François!"

'My uncle did not reply, but he made, in the darkness, a large sign of the cross, for he was very pious in spite of his blustering ways.

'The dog, now let loose, followed us home.

'Ah, indeed, it was charming to see our return. We had great difficulty at first in getting the cart up the steps of the rampart. We succeeded, however, and wheeled it along into the hall.

'How funny, happy, and fluttered my mother was! And my four little cousins (the youngest was six), they were like four little hens around a chick. The child, still sleeping, was taken out of its cart at last. It was a girl, about six weeks old. And they found ten thousand francs in gold, yes, ten thousand francs amongst its clothes! My father kept them for her dowry. She was not, it seems, a child of poor people . . . but, perhaps, the child of some nobleman, and of some middle-class woman in the town . . . or else . . . We made a thousand conjectures, but we never got to know anything . . . nothing . . . nothing. No one knew the dog either. He was a stranger in the district. In any case, he or she, who had come and rung three times at our gate, knew the character of my parents well, to have chosen them for this work of charity.

'This is how Mlle Perle, at six weeks old, entered the Chantal household.

'But she was only called Mlle Perle, later on. She was baptized at first: "Marie Simonne Claire"; Claire being intended for her surname.

'I assure you that the return to the dining-room was droll, with the little mite, awake, looking around her at those people and those lights with her vague, blue, and perplexed eyes.

'We sat down again, and the cake was divided. I was "King", and I took Mlle Perle for "Queen", as you did just now.

'The child was adopted and brought up in the family. She grew big; years passed by. She was pretty, tender, and obedient.

Everyone loved her, and she would have been abominably spoilt if my mother had not put her foot down.

'My mother was a woman who had a great idea of order and social distinctions. She consented to treat little Claire as a child of her own, but she would have it, nevertheless, that the distance which separated us should be properly marked, and the situation kept well in mind.

'And so, as soon as the girl could take it in, she told her her story, and let it penetrate quite gently, tenderly even, into the mind of the little thing, that, for the Chantals, she was an adopted child, accepted, but actually an outsider.

'Claire understood her position with singular intelligence, with surprising intuition, and she knew how to take and to keep the place which was made for her, with so much tact, with so much grace and gentleness, that she often moved my father to tears.

'My mother herself was so much touched by the passionate gratitude and the slightly timorous devotion of this frail and tender being, that she came to call her "my daughter". Sometimes, when the little thing had done something good and delicate, my mother would push her spectacles up on to her forehead (an act which always indicated that she was moved), and would exclaim: "But she is a pearl, a perfect pearl, this child!" – In this way the little Claire acquired that name which she has kept. She became and remained for us all "Mademoiselle Perle".'

IV

M. CHANTAL STOPPED speaking. He had seated himself on the billiard table, and he was fidgetting with a billiard ball in his left hand, whilst with his right he was flicking about the cloth which served to rub out the scores from the marking board, and which we called the chalk-cloth. Slightly red in the face, his voice lowered, he was speaking for himself alone, by this time; lost amongst his memories, wandering tranquilly through these ancient things, old happenings, which were taking shape in his thoughts, as one goes sauntering in an old home-garden where one has been brought up, and where each tree, each path, each plant, the pointed holly trees, the sweet-scented bay, the yews whose red glutinous berry bursts between the fingers, call up at each step a little fact of our past life, one of those little facts, insignificant and delicious, which form the very ground, the texture of our existence.

As for me, I remained opposite him, leaning back against the wall, my hands resting upon my idle cue.

He began again after a minute: 'Cristi! how pretty she was at eighteen . . . and graceful . . . and perfect . . . Ah! the pretty . . . pretty . . . pretty and good . . . good . . . charming girl . . . She had such eyes . . . so blue . . . transparent . . . I have never seen any like them . . . never . . . !'

He stopped speaking again. I asked:

'How is it she did not get married?'

He answered, speaking not to me, but to this passing word, 'married'.

'Why? Why? She didn't wish to . . . didn't wish to. Still she had a dowry of thirty thousand francs, and she had several offers . . . She didn't wish to! She seemed sad about that time. It was when I married my cousin, little Charlotte, now my wife, to whom I had been engaged for six years.'

I raised my eyes to M. Chantal, and it seemed to me that I could see right into his mind, that I was looking suddenly into one of those humble and cruel dramas of honest hearts, of simple hearts, of hearts without reproach; into the depths of one of those unconfessed, unexplored hearts that no one has penetrated, not even those who are their mute and resigned victims.

And a bold curiosity suddenly impelled me: I pronounced:

'You ought to have married her yourself, M. Chantal?'

He started, looked up at me, and said:

'I! Marry whom?'

'Mlle Perle.'

'What for?'

'Because you loved her more than the cousin you did marry.'

He looked at me with strange, round, frightened eyes, then stammered out:

'I loved her . . . I? . . . What? What's put that into your head?'

'Of course! It speaks for itself . . . and it's just because you loved Mlle Perle, that you were so long about marrying your cousin, who had to wait six years for you.'

He dropped the billiard ball which he was holding in his left hand, caught hold of the chalk-cloth, covered his face with it and began to sob. He shed tears in a disconsolate and ridiculous way, trickling like a squeezed sponge; he wept from his eyes, from his nostrils, and his lips all at once. He coughed, sputtered, blew his nose in the chalk-cloth, dried his eyes, sneezed, began again to drip at all the openings of his face, with a noise that reminded one of gargling.

I was scared, ashamed, I wanted to run away, and I did not know what to say, to do, or even attempt to do.

Suddenly Mme Chantal's voice resounded on the staircase: 'Will you be soon done with your smoking, up there?'

I opened the door and called out:

'Yes, madame, we are coming down directly.'

Then I hurried back to her husband, and seizing him by the elbows: 'Monsieur Chantal, dear friend, listen to me; your wife is calling you, pull yourself together, pull yourself together quickly, we must go downstairs.'

He stuttered: 'Yes . . . yes . . . downstairs . . . poor girl . . . I am coming . . . tell her I am coming.'

He began to wipe his face conscientiously with the cloth which, for the last two or three years, had been used to rub the chalk marks off the board; then he uncovered his face, smudged all over, half white and half red, his forehead, his nose, his cheeks, and his chin besmeared with chalk, and his swollen eyes still full of tears.

I took hold of his hands and drew him into his room,

murmuring: 'I beg your pardon, I really beg your pardon, M. Chantal, for having caused you so much pain . . . but . . . I did not know . . . you understand.'

He pressed my hand: 'Yes . . . yes . . . there are in life . . . difficult moments . . .'

Then he plunged his face into his wash-hand basin. When he emerged from it he did not yet look quite presentable, but a slight artifice occurred to me. As, on looking in the glass, he appeared uneasy, I suggested: 'It would be a good thing to say downstairs that you've got a bit of chalk in your eye, and then you may cry openly as much as you like.'

He adopted this expedient, and went down, rubbing his eyes with his handkerchief. Everybody was concerned at the accident, and they all wanted to be allowed to look for the piece of chalk, which could not be found, of course; and they related instances of the kind in which it had become necessary to send for the doctor.

As for me, I sat down close to Mlle Perle, and I watched her, tormented by a burning curiosity, a curiosity which became a torture. She must indeed have been exceedingly pretty, with her soft eyes so large, so tranquil, and so wide open that they looked as if she never closed them as other human beings do. Her costume was rather ridiculous, quite the get-up of an old maid, and it disfigured her, without making her look awkward.

It seemed to me that I saw into her, as I had seen into M. Chantal's soul, just now; that I could see there, from one end to the other, that humble, simple, and devoted life; but a desire seemed

145

to force my lips, a harassing desire to ask her, to find out whether she also had loved him; whether she had, like him, endured the trial of secret and acute suffering, that one does not see, that one does not know, that one does not divine, but which envelops us at night in the solitude of a room without light. I watched her, I saw her heart beat under the lace trimming of her dress, and I asked myself whether that sweet open face had sighed every evening buried in the moist softness of the pillow, whether she had lain at night with her body shaken by sobs, and burning with the fever of a sleepless couch.

I said, in a stealthy manner, as children do who break a toy just to see what is inside: 'If you had seen M. Chantal weeping, a little while ago, you would have pitied him.'

She trembled: 'What do you say? Has he been crying?'

'Oh, yes, he has been crying.'

'And what for?'

She seemed to be much distressed. I answered:

'It was on your account.'

'On my account?'

'Yes. He has been telling me how much he was in love with you in the past, and what an effort it had cost him to marry his cousin instead of you.'

Her pale face seemed to grow a little longer, her steady wide-open eyes, her quiet eyes, shut suddenly and so quickly that they seemed to have closed for ever. She slipped down from her chair to the floor, sinking softly, slowly, as a silken scarf would fall.

I called out: 'Help! Help! Mlle Perle has fainted!'

Mme Chantal and her daughters were round us at once, and while they were rushing to fetch water, smelling salts, vinegar, and so on, I snatched up my hat and escaped.

I walked away quickly, with my heart beating fast, and my mind full of remorse and regret. But now and then I felt pleased with myself. It occurred to me that what I had done was a praiseworthy and necessary action.

I asked myself: Was I wrong. Was I right? They had carried that love within their souls as one may retain a bullet in a closed wound. Would they not be more happy now? It was too late, I thought, for their suffering to begin again, and yet early enough for them to think tenderly of the cruel past.

And, perhaps, one evening in the coming spring, moved by a ray of moonlight filtering through the branches and shining on the grass at their feet, they will hold one another's hands, thinking of all that hidden and cruel suffering; and, perhaps, while that short contact sends a thrill of resuscitated passion through their veins, they will feel at last a little of that emotion they had never before known; and it will bring to them, in a second, the rapid and divine sensation of that intoxication, of that delirium, which gives to lovers more felicity in one quivering moment than other people can gather in all their lives.

Miss Harriet

WE WERE A PARTY of seven in the waggonette, four ladies and three men, one on the box beside the coachman; and our horses were slowly mounting the road that wound up the steep hillside. We had started from Étretat at daybreak, to visit the ruins of Tancarville, and, bemused by the sharpness of the morning air, were still half asleep. The ladies especially, little accustomed to these early hours, kept continually closing their eyes, nodding their heads, and even yawning, quite insensible to emotions aroused by the dawn.

It was autumn, and on both sides of the road stretched bare fields, yellow with the stubble of oats or wheat, covering the soil like a badly shaven beard. The mist rose like smoke from the earth. Larks were singing in the sky, and many birds piping in the bushes. The sun rose at last before our eyes, all red on the edge of the horizon; and, as he climbed, brighter and brighter each minute, the country seemed to awake, to smile, and stir itself, throwing off, like a girl rising from bed, its white, misty garment.

The Comte d'Etrailles, on the box seat, suddenly cried, 'Mark hare!' and pointed to a patch of clover on the left. There was the creature, slipping away, nearly hidden by the crop, and showing only his great ears; he doubled across a ploughed field, stopped, and set off again wildly; changed his mind and stopped again, uneasy, scenting danger near, undecided as to his route; then off he went, with great leaps and bounds of the hind-quarters, and disappeared in a broad square of beetroot. The men all woke up to watch the creature's flight.

'We don't seem to be making ourselves over-agreeable this morning,' said Réné Lemanoir, and looking at his neighbour, the little Baroness Serennes, who was struggling to keep awake, he said in a low voice: 'Thinking of your husband, Baroness? Don't worry! he won't be back till Saturday. You've still got four days.'

'How silly you are!' she answered, with a sleepy smile; then shaking off her torpor, added: 'Come now, tell us something to make us laugh. Monsieur Chenal, you've the reputation of having had more love affairs than the Duc de Richelieu, now do tell us a love story of your own, whichever one you like.'

Léon Chenal, an old painter, who in his prime had been a very handsome, powerfully built man, proud of his physique, and a great favourite with women, ran his hand through his long white beard and smiled; after a few minutes' thought, he suddenly became grave.

'This won't be amusing, ladies; I'm going to tell you the most tragic love affair of my life — I hope no friend of mine may ever inspire a love like that . . .

I

'I WAS FIVE-AND-TWENTY at the time, and scouring the country all along the Normandy coast. "Scouring the country", as I call it, is to idle along with a knapsack from inn to inn, on the pretext of making landscape studies from Nature. I know nothing pleasanter than that wandering, heedless life. You are perfectly free, without ties or cares or plans of any sort, without even a thought of the morrow. You go tramping along the pleasantest-looking road, just as the fancy takes you, with no object but to satisfy the eye. You stop here because a stream fascinates you, there because you catch an appetizing whiff of fried potatoes at the door of some hostelry. Or, it's a scent of clematis that brings you to a standstill, or perhaps a naive challenge from the eyes of some country wench in an inn. Never despise those simple hearts! Girls like that have plenty of soul and passion too, their cheeks are firm, and their lips are sweet, their kisses are full and hearty, as delicious as wild raspberries. Love has always a value, no matter where it springs from. A heart that beats when you come near, eyes that weep when you go away, are things so rare and sweet and precious, that they should never be despised. I can remember meetings in ditches full of primroses, behind stables where the cows were asleep, on the straw in granaries still warm from the day's sun. I have memories of coarse homespun, and strong, supple bodies, and, I can tell you, they were good, those naive, free kisses; more delicate in their frank animality than all the subtle caresses you get from charming and distinguished ladies.

'But the real heart of this happy-go-lucky wandering is the country itself, the woods, the sunrise, the dusk, the moonlight. For us painters they are regular honeymoon journeys with Nature. You are alone and quite close to her in those long, tranquil meetings. Stretched out in some meadow amongst daisies and poppies, you fix your eyes, under the clear fall of the sunlight, on a little village in the distance with a pointed church steeple, whose clock is striking noon. Or perhaps by some spring bubbling up at the foot of an oak tree, in the midst of a tangle of tall, frail grasses, glistening with life, you kneel and lean over to drink the cold, clear water that wets your nose and moustache; you drink with sheer physical delight, as if you were kissing the very lips of the spring. Sometimes in the course of these narrow streamlets, you come across a pool and plunge in, naked, and you feel on your skin from head to foot the quiver of the rapid nimble current, just like a delicious icy caress.

'You are gay up on the hills; melancholy down beside the ponds; and when the sun drowns himself in an ocean of crimson clouds and throws a ruddy glare on the river, your spirit goes soaring. Then again in the evening, under a moon sailing across the furthest heights of the sky, you muse over a thousand strange things that would never come into your head in the full blaze of daylight.

'Well, as I was wandering like this through the very country we're in now, I arrived one evening at the little village of Bénouville, on the cliffs between Yport and Étretat – I had come from Fécamp along the coast, which, about there, is as high and straight as a wall, with jutting chalky rocks that fall perpendicularly into the sea. I had walked the whole day on that short turf, as fine and yielding as a carpet, which springs up all along the edge of the cliff under the salt sea-wind.

'Striding along, singing at the top of my voice, looking up at the slow circling flight of a sea-gull, with its curved wings against the blue sky, or down at the brown sail of a fishing boat on the green sea, I had spent as happy and careless and free a day as anyone could wish. Somebody pointed out to me a little farm where they put up travellers, a sort of inn kept by a peasant woman, in the middle of the usual Normandy yard, surrounded by a double row of beeches.

'So leaving the cliff, I dropped down to this little homestead shut in by its big trees, and presented myself to Mme Lecacheur.

'She was a wrinkled, stern-looking old country-woman, who seemed to be in the habit of receiving her customers with obvious reluctance, not to say distrust. It was May, and the apple trees in full blossom spanned the yard with a roof of fragrant flowers showering down a never-ceasing rain of slow-falling pink petals on people's shoulders, and on the grass.

'"Well, Mme Lecacheur," I began, "have you got a room for me?"

'"That's as may be," she replied, astonished at my knowing her name; "everything's let; but we might see what we can do, perhaps."

'In five minutes we had come to terms, and I had deposited my knapsack on the bare earth floor of a rural apartment furnished with a bed, two chairs, a table, and a wash-stand. It looked into the great smoke-dried kitchen, where the guests took their meals in company with the farm hands and the hostess, who was a widow.

'I washed my hands and went out again. The old lady had set about fricasseeing me a chicken for dinner at the huge fire-place wherein hung a smoke-blackened jack.

'"So you've got some visitors just now?" said I.

'"There's one lady," she replied in her discontented way, "an Englishwoman, middlin' old. She's got the other room."

'By paying an extra twopence ha'penny a day I secured the right to have my meals in the yard when it was fine; so they set my table in front of the door, and I proceeded to devour the lean, tough joints of a Normandy fowl, drinking pale cider the while, and munching at a huge white loaf, four days old, but exceedingly good for all that.

'All at once the wooden gate into the road was thrown

open, and a strange person came towards the house. She was very thin, very tall, and so wrapped up in a plaid shawl with red checks, that one would certainly have thought she had no arms, if a long hand had not emerged at the level of her hips, holding the white umbrella sacred to tourists. Her mummy-like face, framed in tight-rolled curls of grey hair, bobbing up and down at every step, made me think, heavens knows why, of a red herring in curl papers. She passed me quickly, with lowered eyes, and plunged into the cottage.

'I was greatly diverted by this singular apparition, who was doubtless my neighbour, the "middlin' old" Englishwoman of whom my hostess had spoken.

'I did not see her again that day; but the following day, after I had settled myself down to paint in the depths of that charming valley which comes out at Étretat – you know the one I mean – happening to raise my eyes suddenly, I saw something peculiar reared up on the crest of the hill, something like a hop-pole, draped. It was she. On seeing me she vanished.

'I went in at midday for lunch and took my place at the public table, for the express purpose of making the acquaintance of this original old party. But she by no means responded to my politeness, remaining insensible even to such little attentions as pouring out water for her assiduously, and diligently passing her the dishes. A slight movement of the head, almost imperceptible, and an English word mumbled so that I could not hear what it was, were the only thanks I got.

'I ceased trying to make myself agreeable, but she still continued to occupy my thoughts.

'At the end of three days I knew all that Mme Lecacheur knew about her.

'Her name was Miss Harriet. In searching apparently for some quiet village wherein to spend the summer, she had lighted on Bénouville six weeks ago, and seemed by no means inclined to leave it. She never spoke at table, and ate quickly, reading away all the time at some pious little book of the strongest Protestant tendency. She distributed these tracts to everybody. The parish priest himself had received four, brought by one of the village urchins who had been given a penny for the errand. Sometimes without anything having led up to it, she would suddenly say to our hostess:

'"Je aimé le Seigneur plus que tout; je le admiré dans toute son création, je le adoré dans toute son nature; je le pôrté toujours dans mon coeur."* And she would instantly hand the amazed peasant woman one of her tracts for the conversion of the universe.

'She was not liked in the village. The schoolmaster had said that she was an atheist, and a sort of cloud rested upon her. The

---

* Miss Harriet's French, too precious to be lost, is given in the original. Its probable meaning is appended in footnotes.

'I love the Lord more than anything; I admire Him in the whole of His creation; I adore Him in all His nature; I carry Him always in my heart.'
[Ed. This and subsequent footnotes are from original translator]

parson on being consulted by Mme Lecacheur had replied: "Yes, she's a heretic, but God graciously spares the life of the sinner, and I believe her to be a person of irreproachable morals."

'These words, "Atheist – Heretic", of which the meanings were not precisely understood, threw a doubt into every mind. It was supposed that the Englishwoman was rich and had spent her life travelling all over the world, because her family had driven her from home. Why had her family driven her from home? Well, naturally, because of her impiety.

'She was, in truth, one of those highly principled, enthusiastic, headstrong Puritans, whom England produces in shoals; one of those excellent and unendurable old maids who haunt every *table d'hôte* in Europe, spoil Italy, poison Switzerland, render the charming towns along the Mediterranean quite uninhabitable, carrying about with them everywhere their bizarre hobbies, the manners of petrified vestals, indescribable toilettes, and a certain smell of indiarubber, which fosters the theory that at night they must be slipped into "hold-alls".

'Whenever I used to see one in an hotel, I would take flight like a bird that sights a scarecrow in a field.

'This one, however, seemed so extremely peculiar that she was really far from displeasing to me.

'Mme Lecacheur, instinctively hostile to all that was not of her own class, felt a sort of hatred in her narrow soul for the old maid's mystic transports. She had found a word to describe her, a decidedly contumelious word, that sounded very odd on her lips, whereto it must have come after God knows what mysterious spiritual labour.

'"She's a demoniac," she said. And this word, applied to that austere and sentimental being, struck me as so irresistibly comic, that I myself took to calling her "the demoniac", experiencing a quaint pleasure in pronouncing the word out loud whenever I caught sight of her.

'I would ask Mme Lecacheur: "Well, what's our 'demoniac' doing today?"

'And the good lady would reply with a scandalized air:

'"Would you believe it, sir, she's picked up a toad, whose leg's got crushed somehow, and she's taken it to her room, and she's put it in the wash-basin, and she's puttin' on a dressin' like yo' might on a man. If that ain't profanity!"

'Another time, during a walk at the foot of the cliff, she had bought a big fish, that had just been caught, for no other purpose than to throw it back into the sea. And the fisherman, though handsomely paid, had begun abusing her profusely, more really exasperated than if she had stolen money out of his pocket. For a month afterwards he could not speak of the affair without getting into a rage and swearing horribly.

'"Oh yes! Miss Harriet was assuredly a 'demoniac'!"

'Mme Lecacheur had had an inspiration of genius in so baptizing her.

'The stable-man, who was called Sapeur, because in his youth he had served in Africa, was of quite a different opinion:

'"The old un's been a rare rip in her time!" he said slyly.

'Ah! if the poor old maid had only known!

'The servant girl, Céleste, never took to the idea of waiting on her, nor could I understand why. Perhaps only because she was a foreigner, of a different race, tongue, religion. In short, she was a "demoniac"!

'She spent her time wandering about the country, seeking and adoring her God as manifested in Nature. I found her, one evening, on her knees in a thicket. Catching sight of something red among the leaves, I thrust aside the branches, and there was Miss Harriet, who scrambled up in confusion at being seen like that, and fastened on me a pair of eyes as wild-looking as the eyes of a night-jar surprised by daylight.

'Sometimes when I was working down among the rocks, I would suddenly catch sight of her on the top of the cliff, looking like a semaphore. She would be gazing passionately at the vast sea, all golden in the sun, and the wide expanse of sky deep-coloured with the heat. Sometimes I would make her out in the depths of a valley, walking quickly, with her springy English step; and I would go to meet her, attracted, heaven knows why! – solely to see her ecstatic face, that dry ineffable visage, lit up with a deep, inward joy. Often, too, I would come on her in some nook down by a farm, seated on the grass, under the shade of an apple tree, with her little pious book open on her knees, and her gaze wandering far away.

'For I too stayed on and on, bound to this peaceful countryside by a thousand ties of love for its broad, gentle landscapes — I felt so happy down in this obscure farm, far from the world, and close to the earth, the good, sane, beautiful green earth that we ourselves shall help to nourish with our bodies some day. And perhaps I ought to admit, too, that a spark of curiosity had a little to do with keeping me at Mme Lecacheur's. I wanted to get to know something of that queer Miss Harriet, to know something of what goes on in the lonely souls of these wandering old maids of England.

II

'WE STRUCK UP an acquaintance at last in rather an odd way.

'I had just finished a study which seemed to me first-rate; and so it was. It sold for four hundred pounds fifteen years later. It was as simple as "two and two make four", but clean away from the academic. The whole right side of my canvas represented a rock, an enormous rugged rock covered with seaweed, brown and yellow and red, over which the sunshine streamed like oil.

'The light from the sun, invisible behind me, fell on the stone, turning it to fiery gold. That was the whole thing. A foreground dazzlingly bright, and flaming, and superb. On the left the sea, not the blue, nor the slate-coloured sea, but of jade-green, milky and hard under the deep blue of the sky.

'I was so pleased with my work that I danced along, taking

it back to the inn. I should have liked the whole world to see it at that moment — I remember I showed it to a cow close by the path, and shouted to her:

'"Look at that, old girl! You won't see a thing like that every day!"

'Arrived at the house, I called to Mme Lecacheur at the top of my voice:

'"Hi! Missis! hi! Come out and look at this!"

'The good lady appeared, and ruminated over my sketch with her stupid unseeing eyes that obviously made out nothing, not even whether the thing was meant for an ox or a house.

'Miss Harriet was on her way in, and passed behind me just as I was holding my canvas at arm's length to show it to Mme Lecacheur. The "demoniac" could not help seeing, for I took care to turn the canvas so that it should not escape her glance. She stopped short, in petrified amazement. It was her own rock, it appeared, the one she was wont to climb, that she might indulge in reveries at her ease.

'She murmured so marked and flattering a British 'Aoh!' that I turned towards her smiling:

'"This is my latest study, Mademoiselle," I said.

'She muttered in an ecstasy both comic and touching:

'"Oh! Monsieur, vô comprené le nature d'une fâçon palpitante!"*

---

* 'Oh! sir, you've got the breath of life into it!'

'I blushed, yes, I blushed, more moved by that compliment than if I had received one from a queen. I was seduced, vanquished, overcome. I give you my word, I could have kissed her. I sat down to table beside her, as usual. For the first time she spoke, following up her thoughts out loud:

'"Oh! j'aimé tant le nature!"*

'I passed her the bread, the water, the wine. She accepted them now with a little mummy-like smile; and I began to talk "landscape" to her. After the meal, we rose at the same moment, and going out, strolled about the yard; then, attracted doubtless by the wonderful blaze the sunset was lighting up over the sea, I opened the gate, and off we went towards the cliffs side by side, as happy as two people who have just come to understand, and see into, each other's minds.

'It was a warm, soft evening, one of those happy evenings when body and soul feel at rest. All is beauty and charm. The warm, fragrant air is full of the scent of grasses and seaweeds, and comes sane and fresh to the nostril; it caresses the palate with the savour of the sea, and soothes the soul with its penetrating sweetness. We were walking now on the edge of the cliff above the vast ocean, with its little waves rolling in, a hundred yards below. And taking deep breaths through our open lips, we drank in the fresh breeze, which had come so far across the sea, and, salt from the long kiss of the waves, slid lingering over our

---

* 'Oh! I do so love Nature!'

faces. Swathed in her plaid shawl, with an inspired face, and with teeth bared to the wind, the Englishwoman gazed at the great sun as it sank toward the sea. Before us, far below, and far away as the eye could distinguish, a three-masted ship with all sail set showed her silhouette against the flaming sky; closer in, a steamer passed, unfurling a scroll of smoke, that left behind an endless streak of cloud across the whole horizon.

'Slowly, slowly, the red orb went down. Soon it touched the water, just behind the quiet sailing-ship, which appeared as in a frame of fire, in the centre of the blazing globe. Little by little, conquered by the ocean, the sun sank. We saw it merge, lessen, disappear. It was all over. Alone, the little vessel still showed its clear-cut profile against the golden background of the furthest sky.

'With passionate eyes Miss Harriet gazed at the flaming end of the day. I felt certain she was possessed by an intense longing to embrace the sky, the sea, the whole horizon.

'She murmured: "Aoh! j'aimé, J'aimé, j'aimé!"

'I saw the tears standing in her eyes. She went on:

'"Je vôdré étre une petite oiseau pour m'envolé dans le firmament!"*

'She remained standing, as I had often seen her, bolt upright on the edge of the cliff, with a face as glowing as her crimson shawl. I longed to put her in my sketchbook – title: "Caricature of Ecstasy"; and I turned away to hide a smile.

---

* 'Oh! how I love it! I wish I were a little bird, and could fly away into that sky!'

'Then I began talking to her about painting, as I might have talked to a chum, discussing tone, and values, and strengths, in fact, all the technical terms. She listened attentively and intelligently, trying to penetrate my thoughts and divine the obscurer meaning behind my words; from time to time she exclaimed:

'"Oh! je comprené, je comprené. C'été très palpitante!"*

'We went indoors.

'The next day she came up the moment she saw me, and held out her hand. We were friends from that minute. She was a good creature, whose soul was, as it were, on springs, leaping with startling suddenness into enthusiasms. She lacked balance, like nearly all women who reach the age of fifty without marrying. She seemed as though preserved in a sort of innocence gone sour; but in her heart she had kept something of youth, of extreme youth, and that was always taking fire. She loved nature and animals with a feverish love, fermented like liquor kept too long, with the sensual love that she had never given to man.

'I am certain that the sight of a mother dog suckling her puppies, or a mare running in a meadow with her foal at heel, or a bird's nest full of enormous-headed naked-bodied little squeakers, made her quiver all over with a passion of feeling. Poor solitary souls, sad wanderers of the *table d'hôte*, poor, lamentable, ridiculous beings – since knowing her, I have loved you all.

---

* 'Oh! I understand, I understand. It's got the breath of life!'

'I soon perceived that she had something to say to me, but dared not say it, and I was amused at her timidity.

'When I set off in the morning with my painting-gear on my back, she would go with me as far as the end of the village, silent, visibly troubled, trying to find words to begin. Then, all at once, she would leave me, and march briskly off with her skipping step.

'At last one day she plucked up courage:

'"Je vôdré voir vô comment vô faites le peinture? Volé vô? J'été trés curieux."* And she blushed as if she had said something extremely bold.

'I took her off to the bottom of the Petit-Val, where I was beginning a large study.

'She stood just behind me, following all my movements with the strictest attention.

'Then suddenly, afraid perhaps that she might be bothering me, she said:

'"Thank you!" and went away.

'But after a little she became more at ease, and used to come with me every day with obvious pleasure. She would take her camp-stool under her arm, never allowing me to carry it for her, and sit herself down at my side; she would stay there for hours, motionless and silent, following with her eyes every movement of my brush. When with a blot of colour stuck roughly on with

---

* I should like to watch you paint. May I? I'm so interested!'

the knife I succeeded in producing some true and unforeseen effect, she would utter, in spite of herself, a little "Aoh!" of astonishment, joy, and admiration. She had a feeling of tender respect for my canvases, of almost religious reverence for the reproduction by human means of a part of the Divine work. My studies evidently were to her in a way sacred pictures; and she would sometimes talk to me of God, and try to convert me. Ah! he was a queer sort of person, that God of hers, a kind of village philosopher, without much ability or power, for she always imagined him heart-broken at the injustice that went on under his eyes – as if he had not been able to prevent it.

'She was, moreover, on excellent terms with him, and seemed to be the confidante of all his secrets and dislikes. She would say, "God wishes," or "God doesn't wish," like a sergeant who tells a recruit that the colonel "has given orders". From the bottom of her heart she lamented my ignorance of the Divine will, which she so eagerly sought to reveal to me; and every day I found in my pockets, in my hat when I dropped it on the ground, in my colour-box, in the fresh-cleaned shoes standing outside my door in the morning, those little pious tracts which she doubtless received direct from heaven.

'I treated her with frank cordiality, like an old friend. I soon began to perceive, however, that her behaviour had altered a little, though I had not noticed how it came about.

'When I was at work, either down in the valley or in some deep lane, I would see her suddenly appear, coming on at a rapid, rhythmical walk. She would sit down abruptly, breathing quickly as if she had been running, or some deep emotion were at work within her. Her face, too, would be red all over, that peculiar English red that no other nation possesses. Then, without any cause, she would turn pale, a sort of earthy colour, and seem about to faint. Gradually she would recover her ordinary looks and begin to talk.

'But suddenly she would leave off in the middle of a sentence, get up, and make off at such a pace and in such a strangely abrupt way, that I used to rack my brains to see if I had done anything to displease or wound her.

'At last I decided that this must be her usual method of behaving, which had been a little modified no doubt for my sake during the first moments of our acquaintanceship. When she came back to the farm after hours of walking along the coast, battling with the wind, her long corkscrew ringlets were often out of curl, and hung as if their springs had broken. Formerly she had never bothered about them, and used to come into dinner unceremoniously, all ruffled by that sister of hers, the breeze. But now she would go up to her room to adjust what I called her lamp-chimneys; and when, with one of those chaffing compliments that always scandalized her so, I said gallantly, "Why, you're as beautiful as a star today, Miss Harriet!" a little blush would cover her face, like the blush of a girl of fifteen.

'Presently she reverted entirely to the wild state, and ceased coming to see me paint. "It's a mood," thought I, "that will pass off." But it did not. If I spoke to her now, she either replied with affected indifference or glum exasperation. And she had fits of abruptness, impatience, and nerves. I only saw her now at meals, and we scarcely spoke at all. I thought I really must have annoyed her in some way, and one evening I asked her:

'"Miss Harriet, why aren't you the same to me as you used to be? What have I done to offend you? You're making me quite unhappy!"

'She answered angrily in the queerest tone of voice:

'"J'été toujours avec vô le mème qu'autre fois! Ce n'été pas vrai, pas vrai!"* and she ran off and shut herself up in her own room.

'Sometimes she would look at me very strangely. I have often thought since, that prisoners condemned to death must look like that when they are called on the morning of their execution. There was a sort of madness in her eye, a mystic, violent madness; and something besides, a fever, an overstrained longing, chafing at the impossibility of its fulfilment or realization. And it seemed to me as if there were a fight raging within her, and her heart were struggling with some unknown force which she was trying to subdue. Ah! yes, and something else too . . . how can I express it?

---

* 'I am just the same to you as I always was. It's not true, it's not true.'

III

'THE REVELATION WAS strange to a degree.

'For some time I had been working every day, from dawn on, at a picture which had the following for its subject:

'A deep sheltered ravine, overtopped by two slopes covered with trees and brambles, stretching away from the eye till it was lost in a bath of the milky vaporous mist that floats over valleys at sunrise. And coming towards you from far away through the heavy transparent haze, you saw, or rather divined, two human forms, youth and maiden, linked in a close embrace, her face raised to his, his bent to hers, their lips meeting.

'A first ray of sunlight, gliding through the branches, shot across this daybreak mist, and, turning it to a shaft of rose colour behind these simple lovers, made their dim shapes move as it were through silver light. It was good, I can tell you; really good!

'I was working on the slope leading to the little Étretat valley, and was lucky enough that particular morning to have just the sort of floating wrack I wanted. Suddenly something rose up in front of me like a ghost; it was Miss Harriet. Catching sight of me she was on the point of running off, but I called out to her:

'"Ah! do come here, Mademoiselle; I've got a little picture to show you."

'She came, reluctantly enough as it seemed, and I held out my sketch. She said nothing, but remained looking at it a long time motionless; then suddenly — she began to cry. She wept with the spasmodic sobbing of one who has long fought against her tears, and worn out, abandons herself, still protesting.

'I started up, myself moved by this grief that I could not understand; and with the instinct of a true Frenchman, who acts before he thinks, I gave her hands a quick affectionate grasp. She left them in mine for some seconds, and I felt them tremble as if all her nerves were writhing. Then suddenly she drew, or rather tore them away. But I had recognized that shiver. I had felt it before — there's no mistaking it. Ah! that quiver of a woman's love, whether she's fifteen or fifty, gentle or simple, goes straight to your heart, you can't mistake it. All her poor being was vibrating, responding, swooning; and I knew it. Before I could say a word, she was gone, leaving me as amazed as though I had seen a miracle, as unhappy as if I had committed a crime.

'I did not go in for lunch, but took a stroll along the cliff, feeling as much like crying as laughing; the affair was so comic, yet so lamentable; my position was so ridiculous, and hers miserable enough to drive her mad.

'I asked myself what on earth I ought to do.

'I felt there was nothing for it but to go away, and made up my mind to do so. After wandering about sad and thoughtful till dinner time, I went in as the soup appeared.

'We sat down to table as usual. Miss Harriet was there, eating solemnly, and neither speaking nor raising her eyes. In other respects she looked and behaved as usual. I waited for the end of the meal, then turned to our hostess and said :

'"Well, Mme Lecacheur, I shall have to be off in a day or two!"

'The good woman, surprised and vexed, instantly droned out:

'"What's that you say, sir? Going to leave us? Why, we we've got so used to havin' you!"

'I was looking at Miss Harriet out of the corner of my eye; her face did not change. But Céleste, the little maid, looked up at me. She was a big, ruddy, fresh-looking girl of eighteen, as strong as a horse, and, strange to say, very clean. I used to kiss her sometimes in the corner, just to keep myself in practice, nothing more. Dinner came to an end.

'I went out to smoke my pipe under the apple trees, walking backwards and forwards from one end of the yard to the other. All the reflections I had made during the day, the morning's weird discovery of that grotesque passionate love which had fixed on me, and all sorts of sweet and disturbing reminiscences that followed in the train of that discovery, perhaps even the look the servant girl had given me when I spoke of departure, all these joined in putting me into a wanton mood. My lips began tingling as if they had been kissed, and the blood ran madly in my veins.

'Night came, throwing dark shadows under the trees; I caught sight of Céleste going to shut the fowl-house at the far side of the enclosure. I ran forward on tiptoe, so that she heard nothing, and just as she was raising herself, after having lowered the little trap-door where the fowls go in and out, I seized her in my arms, and covered her moon face with a shower of kisses. She struggled with me, but, laughing all the time, pretty well used, no doubt, to that sort of thing. Something made me leave hold of her suddenly and fly round. I felt somehow there was someone behind us!

'It was Miss Harriet on her way indoors; she had seen us, and stood petrified, as if she had seen a ghost. Then she disappeared in the darkness.

'I went back to the house ashamed and disturbed, more miserable at being caught by her doing such a thing than if she had found me committing a criminal act.

'My nerves were all unstrung, and I slept badly, haunted by dismal thoughts. I seemed to hear someone crying. No doubt I was mistaken; several times I thought I heard footsteps about the house, and someone opening the outer door. Towards morning fatigue overwhelmed me, and I slept at last. I woke late, and only made my appearance at lunch time, still upset, and without having made up my mind what line to take.

'No one had seen Miss Harriet. We waited for her; she did not appear. Mme Lecacheur went into her room. The English-woman was not there. She must have gone out at daybreak, as she often did, to see the sun rise. No one expressed surprise, and we began the meal in silence.

'It was extremely hot, one of those burning, heavy days, when not a leaf is stirring. The table had been dragged out of doors, under an apple tree, and from time to time Sapeur went to the cellar to fill the cider jug, everyone was so thirsty. Céleste brought the dishes from the kitchen, a ragoût of mutton with potatoes, a fried rabbit, and a salad. Then she placed before us a dish of cherries, the first of the season.

'Thinking they would be more delicious if they were freshened up, I begged the little maid to draw me a bucket of cold water from the well.

'She came back in five minutes saying there was something wrong with it. She had let the rope out to the full, and the bucket had touched the bottom, but had come up again empty. Mme Lecacheur wished to see for herself, and went off to peer into the depths. She came back saying that she could see something in her well that oughtn't to be there. A neighbour must have thrown in some bundles of straw out of spite. I also went to have a look, hoping to be better able to make out this object, whatever it was. I leaned over the edge, and saw something that seemed white. But what? It then occurred to me to let down a lantern on the end of a rope. The yellow glare danced about on the stone sides, sinking deeper and deeper. Sapeur and Céleste had joined us, and we were all four leaning over the opening. The lantern stopped above an indistinct mass of black and white, of a strange, puzzling appearance.

'"It's an 'orse," cried out Sapeur. "I can see the 'oof. For sure 'e got out of the medder last night and fell in!"

'But suddenly a shiver went through me to the very marrow.

I had just distinguished a foot and then a leg straight upon end; the whole body and the other leg were hidden under the water.

'Trembling so violently that the lantern danced wildly above that shoe, I stammered out in an almost inaudible voice:

'"It's a woman down there . . . it's – it's – Miss Harriet!"

Sapeur was the only one who did not move a muscle. He had seen all sorts of things in Africa!

'Mme Lecacheur and Céleste, uttering piercing shrieks, fled from the spot.

'The body had to be recovered, so I tied the rope firmly round the man's waist, and let him down very slowly by means of the pulley, watching him as he sank into the shadow. He had the lantern and another rope in his hands. Presently his voice, which seemed to come from the middle of the earth, cried, "Stop!" and I saw him fishing something up from the water; it was the other leg; then he tied the heels together with the spare rope, and cried again, "Haul away!"

'I pulled him up, but I felt my arms cracking, and the muscles going slack. I was terrified I should leave go of the rope and let him fall.

'"Well?" I exclaimed, as his head appeared above the curb, as if I had expected him to give me tidings of her who was lying there at the bottom.

'We both got on to the stone ledge, and, face to face, bending over the orifice, began to hoist the body.

'Mme Lecacheur and Céleste watched us from a distance, hiding behind the house wall. When they perceived the black shoes and white stockings of the drowned woman appearing, they vanished.

'Sapeur seized the ankles, and in this attitude the poor modest old maid was dragged out. The head was in a frightful state, black with mud and wounds, her long grey hair, quite loose, and out of curl for all time, hung dripping and slimy. Sapeur said scornfully:

'"Oh! Lor! ain't she lean?"

'We carried her to her room, and as the two women did not appear, the stableman and I laid out the body. I washed the sad, distorted face. Under my touch one eye opened a little and gazed at me with the pale, cold, terrible gaze of a corpse, the gaze that seems to come from so far beyond all life. I did the best I could with the scattered hair, and, with my clumsy hands, arranged it on her forehead in a new and odd-looking fashion. Then bashfully, as though committing a sacrilege, I took off her soaked garments, exposing her shoulders, her chest, and her long arms that were as thin as sticks.

'Then I went out to look for flowers – poppies, cornflowers, marguerites, and fresh sweet-scented grasses – and with these I covered her death-bed.

'Being the only friend near her, I had to fulfil the usual formalities. A letter found in her pocket, written at the last moment, asked that she might be buried in the village where her last days had been spent. A terrible thought wrung my heart. Was it because of me that she wished to be laid to her rest here?

'Towards evening all the gossips and neighbours came to have a look at the body, but I kept them out; I intended to be alone with her, and to watch there all night. I gazed at her by the light of the candles, poor unhappy woman, dying, an utter stranger, so pitifully, so far from home. Somewhere perhaps she had friends and relatives; and I wondered what her childhood and her life had been like! From whence had she come, wandering, all by herself, like a lost dog driven from home? What secret of suffering and despair lay hidden in that poor body, the awkward body she had carried about with her throughout life, like some shameful burden; the ridiculous exterior which had driven far away from her all affection and love?

'How many unhappy creatures there are in this world! Upon this poor human being I felt the eternal injustice of implacable Nature had been laid! All was over for her, and perhaps she had never felt the one thing that sustains the greatest outcast, that hope of being loved some day! Else why did she hide herself like this, why shun people so? Why love so passionately, so tenderly, every living thing and creature that was not man? And I began to understand that here was one who really believed in God, believed that hereafter her sufferings would be made up to her. And now she was going to become one with the earth, to return to life as a plant, to blossom in the sun, yield grass for the cattle, grain for the birds, and so through the flesh of animals once more become the flesh of human beings. But that which we call her soul was quenched for ever at the bottom of that dark well. She would never suffer again. She had exchanged that life of hers for those other lives that would be born again of her.

'Hours passed in our sinister, silent communion. A pale glimmer heralded the dawn; there came a rosy beam gliding to the bed, laying a bar of light across the sheets and on the hands. It was the hour she loved so much. The awakening birds began singing in the trees.

'I threw the window wide open, flung back the curtains that the whole sky might see us, and bending over the icy body, I took her poor bruised head between my hands, and slowly, without any feeling of terror or disgust, I gave those lips a long kiss – the first they had ever known . . .'

Léon Chenal ceased speaking. The women were all in tears. The Comte d'Etrailles could be heard using his handkerchief vigorously on the box. The coachman, alone unmoved, had fallen into a doze; and his horses, no longer feeling the touch of the whip, had slackened their pace to a lazy walk. The waggonette seemed hardly to move; it had suddenly grown heavy, as though laden with grief.

The Holy Relic

To MONSIEUR THE Abbé Louis d'Ennemare Soissons:

My dear Abbé,

Here is my marriage with your cousin suddenly broken off, and in the most absurd way, because of a silly joke which I played almost involuntarily on my betrothed.

I have recourse to you, my old friend, in the embarrassing situation in which I find myself. You, if anyone, can get me out of this scrape, and I shall be grateful to you to the end of my days.

You know Gilberte, or rather you think you know her, but does anyone ever know anything of women? All their opinions, their beliefs, their ideas are in the nature of surprises for us. All their mental processes are full of turns and tricks, full of unforeseen and inconceivable reasoning, of a sort of wrong-headed logic, of obstinate resolutions which seem fixed for ever and give way suddenly for no better reason than that a little bird has come to sit on the window-sill.

I need not tell you that your cousin is pious in the extreme, brought up as she was in a convent, by the nuns in Nancy.

That you know as well as I do. What you may not know is the fact that she takes an exalted view of everything else, as well as of religious matters. Her mind is apt to be carried away like a leaf whirling in the wind; and she is a real woman, or rather truly girlish; perhaps more markedly so than the average run of them, ready to be suddenly angry or suddenly moved to tenderness; rushing impetuously into affection as into hatred, and coming back from either in the same way; and pretty, as you know; more charming than one can say – than you will ever know.

Well, we were engaged; I adored her as I still adore her. She seemed to love me.

One evening I received a telegram, summoning me to Cologne, for a consultation, to be followed, perhaps, by a serious and difficult operation. As I had to start the next day, I hastened to say good-bye to Gilberte, and to explain why I could not dine at the house till next Friday – the day on which I hoped to be back. Oh! Beware of Fridays; I assure you that they are most unlucky.

When I spoke of my departure, I saw tears in her eyes, but when I announced my speedy return, she clapped her hands directly, and cried: 'How delightful! You must bring me back something; some trifle, a simple keepsake, but a keepsake selected for me especially; you must find out what is likely to please me most – do you hear? I shall see if you have any imagination.'

She remained thoughtful for a time, then added: 'I forbid you to spend more than twenty francs. The value will consist for me in the intention, in the invention, monsieur, not in the price.'

Then, after another silence, she said, in a low voice, and with downcast eyes: 'If it doesn't cost you anything in the way of money, and the idea is very ingenious, very delicate, I will . . . I shall give you a kiss.'

I was at Cologne the next day. It was a bad case, resulting from an awful accident, which had driven an entire family to despair: Amputation was urgent. They put me up, they almost shut me in. I saw around me no one but people in tears, who deafened me with their lamentations, I had to operate upon an exhausted man, who nearly died under the knife: I remained two more nights with him; then, with the first gleam of hope for recovery, I broke away, and got myself driven to the railway station.

But I had made a mistake as to time, I had an hour to wait for my train. I wandered out into the streets, still thinking of my poor patient, when a perfect stranger accosted me.

I do not know German; he was ignorant of French; at last I understood that he was offering holy relics for sale. Gilberte's request for a keepsake flashed into my mind: I knew her fanatical piety. I followed the fellow into a shop full of saintly knick-knacks, and ended by selecting one which he described as 'a little piece of a bone from the Eleven Thousand Virgins'.

The so-called relic was in a beautifully chased old silver medallion box, which really decided my choice.

I slipped the thing into my pocket, and got into my train.

On arriving home, I wanted to examine my purchase again. I took it out . . . The lid had come off, the relic was lost! . . . I ransacked my clothes, I turned my pockets inside out; but the little bone, not as big as a small pin, had utterly disappeared.

I am, as you know, my dear Abbé, a moderate believer; your broad-minded friendship tolerates my attitude and leaves me free, trusting to the future, as you say; but I am absolutely unbelieving as to the virtues of relics obtained from dealers in such objects of piety, and I know that in this respect, at least, you share my complete scepticism. Therefore, the loss of this particle from the skeleton of some sheep did not at all distress me; and I procured a similar fragment without difficulty, which I carefully fastened with glue into the chased receptacle.

And I went off to see my fiancée. As soon as I entered the room, she ran up, anxious and smiling: 'What have you brought me?'

I pretended to have forgotten all about it; she refused to believe me; I let her beg, pray, and entreat, and when I saw that she was nearly beside herself with curiosity, I produced the holy locket.

She was overwhelmed with delight. 'A relic! Oh! A holy relic!' And she kissed the box passionately. I felt ashamed of my trick.

But a slight uneasiness appeared on her face, and passed at

once into the horror of doubt. She gazed searchingly into my eyes:

'Are you sure that the relic is genuine?'

'I am absolutely certain.'

'How so?

I was fairly caught. To confess that I had bought this bone from a dealer of sorts, who had spoken to me casually in the street, would have been fatal. What could I say? A mad notion came into my head, I replied, lowering my voice, mysteriously:

'I stole it for your sake.'

She looked at me with her big eyes, marvelling and radiant. 'Oh! you stole it. Where from, tell me?'

'In the cathedral, from the very shrine of the Eleven Thousand Virgins.' Her heart was beating fast. She seemed ready to faint with the excess of happiness.

She murmured:

'Oh! you have done that . . . for me. Tell me . . . tell me all about it.'

This was final. I could not think of going back. I invented a fantastic story, full of precise and surprising details. I had given the beadle a hundred-franc note to be left alone; the shrine was being repaired, but it happened to be the dinner hour; the workmen and the clergy were away; and so, by raising up a panel, which I fastened down again afterwards carefully, I had been able to get hold of a little bone (oh, such a little one) from amongst a heap of others (I said a heap, thinking what a lot the remains of Eleven Thousand Virgins' skeletons would amount to). Then I had gone to a jeweller's and bought a precious case worthy of the relic.

I was not sorry, either, to let her know that the medallion had cost me five hundred francs.

But she cared nothing about the cost; she listened to me, trembling with ecstasy. She murmured: 'How I love you,' and nestled into my arms.

Pray observe: I had committed a sacrilegious theft, I had robbed a church, I had violated the sanctity of a shrine, stolen and profaned the most holy remains. She adored me for that deed; she thought me tender, perfect, divine. There you have the woman, my dear Abbé, the whole woman.

For two months I remained the most admirable of future husbands. In her bedroom she decked out a sort of chapel, magnificently, wherein she deposited that bit of chop-bone, which had, as she believed, made me perpetrate a divine crime of love; and she went into ecstasies before the thing every evening and every morning.

I had begged of her inviolable secrecy, in my fear, I said, of being arrested, prosecuted, perhaps delivered over to the German authorities. She had kept her word.

Well, it happened that early in the summer she experienced a violent desire to behold, with her own eyes, the very place of that feat of mine. She worried her father so successfully (without, of course, confessing the secret reason of her insistence) that he ended by taking her over to Cologne, concealing the plan of their little excursion from me, in accordance with his daughter's wish.

I need not tell you that I have never seen the interior of the cathedral. I do not know in the least where the tomb (is there any tomb?) of the Eleven Thousand Virgins is situated. It appears that this sepulchre is quite inaccessible, alas.

At the end of the week I received ten lines of her writing, breaking off the engagement; and an explanatory epistle from the father, now taken, at last, into her confidence.

One glance at the shrine was enough to reveal to her my fraudulent pretence, all my falsehood, and, at the same time, my perfect innocence. She had asked the beadle whether no theft had ever been committed in the cathedral, and the man, laughing at the mere idea, had shown her clearly the impossibility of such a thing.

Therefore, since I had not desecrated a holy edifice, and disturbed, with a profane hand, the repose of venerated remains, I was no longer worthy of my blonde and delicate betrothed.

I was forbidden the house. All my entreaties, prayers, and supplications failed to soften the heart of the beautiful devotee.

I was positively ill with grief.

Thereupon, last week, Mme d'Arville, her cousin, and related to you also, sent word for me to call.

I have just seen her; and here are the conditions on which I may hope to receive forgiveness.

I am to procure a relic, a real, undeniable relic, certified genuine by our Holy Father, the Pope, a relic of some virgin martyr or other.

I am going almost out of mind with worry and anxiety.

I shall go to Rome if necessary. But I cannot appear suddenly before the Pope with the story of this imbecile affair. Moreover, I doubt whether true relics are ever given to private individuals.

Could you give me an introduction to a Monsignor, or, perhaps, to a French prelate, the possessor of some fragments of a saint? You yourself, have you not by chance in your collection the precious object of my desire?

Save me, my dear Abbé, and I promise you to hasten my conversion by ten years at least.

Mme d'Arville, who takes a most gloomy view of the matter, remarked to me: 'That poor Gilberte will never marry now.'

My dear fellow, will you let your cousin die the victim of a stupid imbroglio?

I beseech you, contrive something to save her from becoming the eleven-thousand-and-first.

Pardon this. I know I am unworthy; but I embrace you, and I love you with all my heart.

Your old friend,

Henri Fontal

The Wreck

Yesterday was the 31st of December.

I had been lunching with my old friend Georges Garin, when his man brought in a sealed letter, covered with postmarks, and with a foreign stamp.

Georges said:

'You'll allow me?'

'Of course.'

He began to read through eight pages of large English handwriting, with the lines crossed in every direction. He read slowly, with great attention — with that profound interest one gives to matters near one's heart.

Then he put the letter down on the mantelpiece, and said:

'Well, it's a queer story I never told you — a sentimental adventure, though, which happened to me once. Ah! it was a curious way of seeing the New Year in! And it was twenty years ago . . . I was thirty then, and now I am fifty!

'I was inspector for the Marine Insurance Company, of which I am the chairman today.

'It had been my intention to spend the first of January in Paris, as everyone makes a festival of that day, but I received a letter from the managing director, desiring me to go at once to the Île de Ré, where a ship belonging to Saint-Nazaire, and insured in our office, had been wrecked. That was at eight o'clock in the morning. I called at the Company's office at ten, to get my instructions, and the same evening I took the fast train, which put me down at La Rochelle the next day. It was the thirty-first of December.

'Having two hours to spare before the departure of the steamboat *Jean Guiton*, which served the Île de Ré, I went for a stroll in the town. It is really a curious town, and with a great deal of character, this La Rochelle. Its streets wind about like a labyrinth; its foot-pavements run under endless arcaded galleries, like those in the Rue de Rivoli, but very sombre; and these galleries, these low-arched mysterious arcades seem to have been erected and left standing like the scenery of dramatic conspiracies, the antique and striking scenery of the far-away past – the heroic and savage past of religious wars. It is quite the true old Huguenot city, grave and discreet, without the superb art, without the wonderful edifices which make Rouen so magnificent, but all the same remarkable in the severity of its aspect, which is also a little sinister: a city of obstinate struggles, where fanaticism hatched its plots, the town where the Calvinist faith found its highest expression, and where the conspiracy of the four sergeants was conceived.

'After wandering about these curious old streets for some time, I went on board a little short steamboat, black and obese, which was to take me to the Île de Ré. She started off puffing irritably, passed between the two antique towers which guard the port, crossed the roadstead, cleared the breakwater constructed by Richelieu, where one sees just awash the enormous boulders enclosing the town like a gigantic necklace; then we swung round to the right.

'It was one of those sad, depressing days, which weigh on one's mind, oppress the heart, extinguish all strength and energy; a grey, chilly day, dulled by a heavy fog, which was as wetting as a shower, as cold as frost itself, and as repulsive to breathe as the exhalation of a sewer.

'Under this ceiling of low, sinister vapour, the yellow and shallow sea of this vast sandy shore remained without a ripple, without any movement, without life; a sea of muddy water, of thick water, of stagnant water. The *Jean Guiton* rolled a little, from force of habit, cut through this opaque and smooth sheet of water, and passed on, leaving a few waves behind, a few undulations which soon calmed down in her wake.

'I began to talk to the captain, a little short-legged man, nearly as round as his ship, and always swaying like her. I wanted to obtain some details about the disaster that it was my mission to investigate. A large ship from Saint-Nazaire, the *Marie Joseph*, had gone ashore one stormy night, on the sands off the Île de Ré.

'The gale had driven this vessel so far up, her owner had written, that it had been impossible to get her off again, and there had been hardly any time to rescue her moveable fittings and salve the cargo. I had, therefore, to investigate the situation of the wreck, to estimate her value, to find out if every attempt had been duly made to get her afloat before she was abandoned. I had to act as representative of the Company, which would call me as an expert on their side, should an action in a court of law be found necessary.

'After receiving my report, the directors would take all measures advisable for the protection of our interests.

'The captain of the *Jean Guiton* knew the affair perfectly, having been called to take part with his boat in the attempts made to salve ship and cargo. He related the very simple facts of the story: the *Marie Joseph*, driven by a furious gale, lost in the night, driving blindly upon a sea of foam – "a sea as white as milk," said the captain – had struck on one of these sand banks, which at low water change the aspect of this part of the coast into that of a boundless Sahara.

'Whilst we talked, I kept on looking about me. Between the ocean and the overhanging sky there was an open space where the eye could travel afar. We were steaming along the land. I asked:

'"Is that the Île de Ré over there?"

'"Yes, monsieur."

'And suddenly the captain, pointing ahead with his right hand, showed me, far away in the offing, an almost imperceptible object, and said:

'"Look, there's your ship!"

'"The *Marie Joseph*?"

'"Yes."

'I was astounded. This black speck, almost invisible, appeared to me at least three miles distant from the coast.

'I objected:

'"But, Captain, there should be a hundred fathom of water on the spot you are pointing at?'

'He began to laugh.

'"A hundred fathom, my friend! . . . Not two fathom, I can tell you!"

'He was a native of Bordeaux. He continued:

'"Here you are, high-water now, 9.40. Go along over the sands, your hands in your pockets, after lunch at the Hotel Dauphin, and I promise that at 2.50 or three at the latest you will reach the wreck dryshod, my friend, and you will have one hour forty-five minutes to two hours, to hang about there – no more, mind, or you will be caught by the tide. The further the sea goes out the quicker it comes back. It is as flat as the back of a bed bug, this coast! Start for the land again at ten minutes to five – no later, believe me – and at half-past seven you get safe and sound aboard the Jean Guiton, which will put you alongside the Quay of La Rochelle the same evening."

'I thanked the captain, and went away forward to look at the little town of Saint Martin, which we were nearing rapidly.

'It was like any other tiny seaport, of the sort that serve for capitals to the barren strings of small islands scattered along the shores of continents. It was a big fishing village, with one foot in the water and one on land, living on fish and fowl, on vegetables and herrings, on radishes and mussels. The island is quite low, with few signs of cultivation, and nevertheless seems thickly populated; but I did not explore the interior.

'After my lunch, I strolled round a small headland; then, as the sea was ebbing rapidly, I started off across the sands and made for what resembled a black rock, which I could see above the water, very far away, out there.

'I walked quickly over this yellow plain, as elastic as living flesh, which seemed to sweat a little under my feet. The sea had been there a moment ago, and now I saw it far away, escaping out of sight, and I could not distinguish any longer the dividing line between the sands and the ocean. It was as if, by enchantment, I had been allowed to look at a gigantic and supernatural event. The Atlantic was before me just now, and it had disappeared into the vast and arid expanse, as stage scenery sinks through trap-doors, and had left me walking in the midst of a desert. Only a flavour, a scent of salt water lingered around me. I sniffed the odour of seaweed, the odour of the surge, the coarse and wholesome odour of the sea-shore. I walked quickly; I did not feel cold any more. I watched the motionless wreck, which grew bigger as I advanced, and now resembled the carcass of a stranded whale.

'She seemed to grow out of the earth, and, on this immense,

flat, and yellow expanse, took on an aspect of surprising size. I reached her at last, after an hour's walking.

'She lay over with a heavy list; she was already beginning to break up, and her sides, like the flanks of a dead animal, showed her bared ribs, huge ribs of tarred timber, studded with the heads of enormous nails. The sand had already invaded her interior, had entered through the torn sides, had got a hold on her, had taken possession of her, and would never let her go again. She seemed to have taken root in the sandbanks; her bows had sunk deeply into the soft and perfidious surface, whilst the raised stern seemed to throw up to heaven, like a desperate appeal, the two words painted in white on the black planking: *Marie Joseph*.

'I climbed up this corpse of a ship from the lowest side, then, having reached the deck, I descended into the hold. The daylight came through the broken hatchways, and through the rents in the sides; it lighted up, sadly, a sort of long and gloomy chamber, full of demolished woodwork. There was nothing in there but sand, which made a floor to this cavern of planks.

'In order to jot down a few notes as to the state of the vessel, I sat down on the head of an empty cask, and began to write by the light of a large hole, through which I could see the boundless extent of the sands. A queer shuddering sense of cold and solitude ran through me from time to time; and, ceasing to write, I began to listen to the faint, mysterious noises pervading the wreck, to the noise of the crabs scuttling along the planks on their fang-like claws, to the noises of a thousand tiny creatures, already making a home of this lifeless thing, and also to the soft and rhythmical sound of the teredo, that gnaws and bores unceasingly, with its whisper, as of a gimlet at work in the old ship's frame, which it excavates and devours.

'Suddenly I heard human voices, at my elbow as it were. I started up as though faced by an apparition. It really seemed, for a moment, as if I were about to see, arising in the depths of this sinister hold, two drowned bodies, ready to tell me all about their deaths. I assure you that it did not take me long to scramble out on deck, hand over hand, and I saw then, standing under the bows of this wreck, a tall man, with three young girls, or rather, a tall Englishman, with three young "misses". Certainly they were a good deal more frightened than I, myself, at this swift apparition of a man upon the deserted ship. The youngest of the girls ran off; the two others clung to their father desperately; as for him, he had opened his mouth, and this was the only sign of emotion he allowed himself.

'Then, after a few seconds, he spoke up:

'"Oh, monsieur, you are the owner of this vessel?"

'"Yes, monsieur."

'"May I visit it?"

'"Yes, monsieur."

'He uttered a long English phrase, of which I caught only the word "gracious", repeated several times.

'As he was looking for the best place to climb up, I directed him, and, with the help of my extended hand, he got up first;

then we assisted the three girls, who had recovered from their alarm. They were charming, all three, especially the eldest, with fair hair, eighteen years old perhaps, as fresh as a flower, and so delicate! So pretty! Really, pretty English girls are just like the tender products of the sea. You would have said that this one had come out of the sand, and that her hair had retained its hue. With their exquisite freshness, and delicate colouring, they make one think of pink shells, of nacreous pearls, rare and mysterious, opening out in the unknown depths of the ocean.

'She spoke French a little better than her father; and she served as an interpreter in the conversation. I had to relate the story of the wreck, with precise details (which I had to invent), as though I had been present at the catastrophe. Then the whole family party went down into the hold of that hulk. As soon as they had got into this sombre, dimly lighted gallery, they uttered cries of astonishment and admiration; and instantly the father and the girls produced their sketch books, which had been hidden, doubtless, in their ample waterproof cloaks, and commenced, simultaneously, four pencil sketches of this weird and mournful place.

'They were sitting down, side by side, on one of the beams, and the four books on the eight knees were being covered with little black pencil strokes, which were to represent the devastated interior of the *Marie Joseph*.

'I went on with my inspection of the wreck, whilst the eldest of the girls talked to me as she worked.

'I learned from her they were staying for the winter at Biarritz, and that they had come from there to the Île de Ré on purpose to see this stranded ship. They had none of the English stiffness, these good people; they belonged to that harmless eccentric class of everlasting wanderers, which England sends out all over the world. The father, tall, spare, with a red face framed in white whiskers, a real living sandwich, a slice of ham cut out in the likeness of a human head, and laid between two pads of hair; the girls, long in the leg, like young storks, thin too, except the eldest, who was also the prettiest of the three.

'She had such a funny way of speaking French, of talking, of laughing, of understanding you, and of not understanding you, of raising her eyes inquiringly, her blue eyes, blue like the deep sea, of leaving off her sketching to ponder over what you said, of going to work at it again, of saying "yes" or "no", that I would have remained there an indefinite time only to listen to her voice and to watch her movements.

'Suddenly she murmured:

'"I hear a little stir on this boat."

'I listened, and I became aware too of a slight noise, of a whispering continuous sound. What was it? I got up to look through an opening, and could not help crying out. The sea had returned, the tide was flowing all around the hulk. I ran up on deck in a hurry. It was too late. The sea hemmed us in, running towards the coast with prodigious speed. No, it was not running, it was gliding, creeping, spreading out like a huge wet blot. No more than a few inches of water covered the sands, but already the head of the stealthy flood was out of sight between us and the coast.

'The Englishman wanted to hurry off at once, but I held him back. Flight was impossible, on account of the deep pools, which we had avoided easily when coming out, but in one of which, now that they were invisible, we would infallibly be drowned if we tried to get back.

'For a moment our hearts were filled with horrible anxiety. Then the eldest of the young girls murmured, with a smile:

'"It is we who are the castaways."

'I tried to smile too, but I was seized with fear, a cowardly fear, that had come upon me stealthily, like this treacherous flood tide. All the dangers of our position appeared to me at once. I felt inclined to shout for help. But who was there to hear?

'The two younger girls had sidled up close to their father, who stood looking with dismay at the sea that had surrounded us.

'The night came upon us as rapidly as the rising tide of the ocean; a heavy, damp, and icy darkness.

'I said:

'"There is nothing else for us to do but to stay on board here and wait."

'The Englishman replied:

'"Oh, yes."

'We remained quite still for a quarter-of-an-hour, for half-an-hour – I don't really know how long, watching around us that yellow water which rose and eddied, which seemed to bubble and swirl as if at play upon the immensity of the reconquered sands.

'One of the girls complained of the cold, and the idea of going below occurred to us, to find some shelter from the light nipping breeze, which stung our faces with its chilly breath.

'I looked down the hatchway. The water had flowed into the ship's hold too. There was nothing for it then but to crouch aft in a body, where the bulwarks protected us a little from the wind.

'Darkness now enveloped us, and we remained huddled together, surrounded by water and the shades of night. I felt the shoulder of the English girl pressing against me; she trembled; her teeth chattered now and then; but I felt also the gentle warmth of her body penetrating me; and the communicated warmth was as delicious to me as a kiss.

'We did not talk; we crouched low, very still and silent, like animals sheltering under a hedge during a storm. And all the same, in spite of everything, in spite of the night, in spite of the terribly dangerous situation, I felt distinctly happy at being there. I was happy during these long hours of darkness and anxiety spent on these shaky planks, so near to this pretty, tender, and charming young girl.

'I asked myself, whence came this delightful absorption; why this sensation of pleasure and joy?

'Why? Who can tell? Because she was there? Who was she? An unknown little English girl! I did not love her, I did not know her at all, and I felt myself softened, conquered! I desired to save her, to devote myself to her service, to commit innumerable follies for her sake. Strange! How is it that the mere presence of a woman can affect us so profoundly? Is it the emanation of her grace that envelops us with a potent spell, the seduction of prettiness and youth which intoxicates us like a draught of wine?

'Or is it not rather the touch of love, of mysterious love, which for ever seeks to unite human beings, which tries its power as soon as it has placed a man and a woman face to face, and which sends over them awakening emotion, a confused, deep, and sweet emotion, as a falling shower moistens the earth to make the flowers grow out of the ground?

'But the silence of the darkness above was becoming awful, the silence of the heavens – for we could hear around us a vague and continuous swirling of water, the low, deadened murmur of the rising sea, and the monotonous lapping of the current against the side of the ship.

'Suddenly I heard a great sobbing. The youngest of the girls had begun to cry. Her father tried to comfort her, and they went on talking in their own language, which I did not understand. I guessed only that he was telling her that there was no danger, but that she was still afraid.

'I said to my neighbour:

'"You must be very cold, mademoiselle?"

'"Oh, yes – I am very cold."

'I wanted to give her my cloak; she refused to have it; but I had taken it off already, and I covered her with it, disregarding her resistance. In the short struggle her hand touched mine, and this contact caused a shiver of delight to run through my whole body.

'For some time before this the breeze had seemed fresher, the wash of the water sounded louder against the side of the vessel. I stood up; a blustering gale blew in my face. The wind was getting up.

'The Englishman noticed this, as well, and remarked, simply:

'"It is bad for us, this . . ."

'Without doubt, it was bad enough, it was certain death for us if the sea rose ever so little and began to batter this hulk, so shaken and disjointed already, that the first touch of rough weather would be certain to send her to pieces.

'Every moment our anxiety increased, with the greater strength of the squalls. Now the sea was beginning to break a little; and I saw white lines appearing and disappearing in the darkness, the lines of foam; whilst each wave that struck against the *Marie Joseph* sent a shock through her that went straight to our hearts.

'The young girl was trembling; I felt her shivering against me, and I felt a mad impulse to seize her in my arms.

'Far off, before us, to the left, to the right, behind us, the white, yellow, and red lights of the lighthouses shone along the coast: they turned and blinked like enormous eyes, like the eyes of giants, glaring at us, watching us, waiting eagerly for our disappearance. One of them, especially, irritated me greatly. It went out every thirty seconds, to flash up again immediately, and this one, really, was like an eye, with its eyelid lowered, time after time, over its brilliant glance.

'Now and then the Englishman would strike a match to see the time, then he would silently put his watch back into his pocket. Suddenly he said to me, over the heads of his daughters, with supreme gravity:

'"Monsieur, I wish you a happy New Year."

'It was midnight. I extended my hand, which he grasped; then he said something in English, and suddenly he and his three daughters began to sing, all together, "Rule Britannia". The grave tune rose up into the black, silent air, and seemed to ascend and vanish into space.

'I felt inclined to laugh at first, then I was seized by an overwhelming and bizarre emotion.

'It was something sinister and superb, this song of the castaways, of the condemned: something like a prayer, and also something greater still, something that one might compare to the old and sublime "*Ave Cæsar, morituri te salutant*".

'When they had ceased, I asked my neighbour to sing something for us – a ballad, a romance, what she liked – in order to make us forget our distress. She consented, and immediately her clear young voice rose lightly into the night. She sang something sad, no doubt, for the long-drawn notes came slowly out of her lips, and went away fluttering, like wounded birds, over the waves.

'The sea got up and rolled upon the dismantled hulk.

'As for me, I thought only of this voice. I thought also of the sirens. If a boat had been passing near us, what would the sailors have thought? My tormented mind strayed away into a dream! A siren! Was she, indeed, not a siren, this girl of the sea, who had made me stay on this wrecked ship, and who would be soon sinking with me into the waves!

'But all at once the five of us went rolling headlong to the other side of the deck, for the *Marie Joseph* had heeled over heavily to the right. The English girl had fallen upon me; I clasped her in my arms, and wildly, without knowing, without understanding what I was doing, but thinking that our last hour had come, I showered kisses on her cheeks, on her forehead, on her hair. The ship did not move after this, and we lay without stirring at all for a time.

'The father's voice said: "Kate!" She whom I held in my arms answered: "Yes," and tried to free herself. Certainly, at that moment, I wished the hulk would fall to pieces, and let me sink with her into the sea.

'The Englishman was heard again:

'"A little capsize – it is nothing. I still have my three daughters."

'Not being able to see the eldest, he had thought, at first, that she was lost overboard. I got to my feet slowly, and suddenly I saw a light on the sea, quite close to us, too. I shouted; a hail came back. It was a boat which was out looking for us; the hotel-keeper had foreseen our imprudence.

'We were saved! I was extremely sorry. They took us off the wreck, and sailed back to Saint Martin.

'The Englishman kept on rubbing his hands and murmuring:
'"A good supper! A good supper!"

'We did indeed sup. I was not happy, I regretted the *Marie Joseph.*

'We had to part the next day, after many embraces and promises to write to each other.

'They started for Biarritz. I was very near following them there.

'I was hard hit. I had been on the point of asking this girl to marry me. Certainly, if we had spent a week together, it would have ended in marriage. How weak and incomprehensible a man shows himself sometimes.

'Two years passed away without my hearing from them; then I received a letter from New York. She was married, and wrote to tell me so. And since then we have written to each other every year on the first of January. She tells me her life, speaks of her children, of her sisters, but never of her husband! Why? Ah, why? And I, I speak only of the *Marie Joseph* . . . She is, perhaps, the only woman I have truly loved . . . No . . . that I should have truly loved . . . Ah! there it is . . . who knows? . . . Events carry you away . . . And then . . . all is over . . . She must be old now . . . I should not know her . . . Ah! that one of former times . . . the one of the wreck . . . what a creature! . . . Divine! She writes that her hair has turned white now, it has upset me horribly . . . Ah! her hair that was so golden! . . . No, my young girl does not exist any longer . . . How sad it is, all this.'

At Sea

THE FOLLOWING paragraph appeared recently in the newspapers:

FROM OUR BOULOGNE CORRESPONDENT,

January 22nd.

A terrible disaster has just spread consternation among our fisher-folk, so severely tried during the last two years. The fishing-boat belonging to Captain Javel, on its way into port, was driven to the west of the harbour mouth, and dashed to pieces on the rocks forming the breakwater of the jetty.

In spite of the efforts of the life-boat and the rocket-apparatus, four men and the boy were lost. The bad weather still continues, and further accidents are to be feared.

I wonder who this skipper Javel is? Is it the brother of the man who had lost an arm?

If this poor fellow, carried off by the seas, and dying, entangled perhaps in the wreckage of his own boat, is the man I am thinking of, he took part eighteen years ago in another drama, terrible and simple as are all these formidable dramas of the sea.

This Javel, the elder of two brothers, was then skipper of a trawler. Of all fishing-boats the trawler is the most staunch. Strong enough to stand any kind of weather, round-flanked, tumbling about perpetually like a cork on the waves, lashed by the harsh, salt winds of the Channel, it toils upon the sea, with a bellying sail, untiring, dragging on its beam a great net that, scraping in the bed of the ocean, sweeps up and gathers in all the creatures that sleep among the rocks, flat fish sticking to the sand, heavy crabs with crooked claws, and lobsters with pointed whiskers.

When the breeze is fresh, with a short sea running, the boat starts work. The net of the trawl is fixed the whole length of a great wooden beam, banded with iron, which is let down by means of two ropes running over rollers at either end of the vessel.

And the boat, drifting broadside to wind and tide, drags with it this contrivance for the spoiling and devastation of the ocean plains.

Javel had with him on board his younger brother, four men, and a boy. He had left Boulogne in fine weather to start trawling.

But the wind soon rose, and a gale coming on, the trawler was forced to run before it.

They made for the English coast, but a heavy sea was beating against the cliffs, and hurling itself on shore with such baffled fury that it was impossible to attempt the entrance to any port. The little boat stood out again and made for the French coast. But the heavy weather still made it dangerous to go near the jetties, enveloping all approaches to the sheltering harbours with foam, uproar, and peril.

The trawler had to stand off again, riding over the waves, tossed and shaken and streaming, struck by great lumps of water, but behaving well in spite of all, quite used to rough weather that often kept her out five or six days at a time, stretching back and forth between the two neighbouring coasts, unable to land on either.

At last, while they were far from land, the storm abated, and though the seas still ran high, the skipper ordered the trawl to be got overboard.

The huge fishing machine was accordingly put over the side, and two men at bow and two at stern began to pay out the ropes of it. Suddenly it touched bottom, but a big sea making the boat roll, Javel the younger, who was in the bow tending the fore-warp of the trawl, stumbled, and got his arm caught between the momentarily eased rope and the roller over which it was passing. He made a desperate effort to lift the rope with his other hand, but the trawl was dragging already, and the taut warp could not be moved.

Writing with pain, the man called for help. Everyone came running to him. His brother left the tiller. They threw themselves all together on the rope, trying to free the limb that was being crushed by it. It was no use.

'Must be cut!' said one of the 'hands', pulling out of his pocket a huge knife, which was capable in a stroke or two of saving young Javel's arm.

But to cut the warp meant losing the net, and the net meant money, a great deal of money, fifteen hundred francs, and it was the property of the elder Javel, who could not bear to lose it. With anguish in his heart, he called out, 'No, don't cut – wait! I'll luff up!' and rushing to the tiller he put it hard down. But the boat would not answer, her way deadened by the net which hampered her steering, and she swept on with the wind and the drift she already had on her.

Javel the younger had dropped on to his knees, with clenched teeth and haggard eyes. He did not utter a word. In continual dread of the knife being used, his brother came back again, 'Hold on, hold on, don't cut; we'll let go the anchor.'

The anchor was let go, the whole long chain running out; then they began heaving in at the capstan, to ease the trawl ropes, which slackened at last, and the inert limb was disengaged, in its blood-stained woollen sleeve.

Javel the younger seemed to have become imbecile. His peajacket was removed, revealing a horrible sight, a shapeless pulp of flesh which spurted blood in jets as if forced from a pump. Then the man gazed at his arm, and muttered, 'It's done for!' And, as the blood was making a pool on the deck one of the men exclaimed, 'He'll bleed to death; we must tie the veins.' Then they took a line, a coarse, brown, tarry yarn, and, twisting it round the limb above the wound, drew it taut with all their strength. The jets of blood grew gradually less, and at last ceased entirely.

Javel the younger got up, his arm dangling at his side. He took hold of it with the other hand, lifted it, turned it about, shook it. Everything was broken, the bones smashed; this fragment of his body hung by the muscles alone. He contemplated it with gloomy, thoughtful eyes. Then he sat down on a spare sail, and his mates advised him to keep the wound continually wet, to keep mortification from setting in.

They put a bucket near him, and every few minutes he dipped a glass into it and bathed the horrible place, letting a thin stream of clear water trickle over it.

'You'd be better down below,' said his brother. He went below, but came up again in about an hour's time, not liking to be alone; he had need of the fresh air too. So he sat down again on his sail and recommenced bathing his arm.

They had a good catch. Great white-bellied fish lay alongside of him, tossing about in their death-throes; he gazed at them without ever stopping the bathing of his mutilated flesh.

Just as they were nearing Boulogne a fresh gale sprang up; the little boat started off again on her senseless cruise, plunging and dipping, knocking the poor sad-faced wretch about.

Night came on. The bad weather continued till dawn. At daybreak they were again in sight of the English coast, but as the sea was going down, they started once more for France, tacking.

Towards evening Javel the younger called his mates to look at some black marks, an ugly appearance of decay in that part of the limb which could hardly be said to be his any longer. The 'hands' gazed at it, and gave their opinions.

'It's the black rot, sure enough,' thought one.

'Better pour salt water over it,' declared another.

Some seawater was brought and poured on to the wound. The sick man turned livid, ground his teeth, writhed a little, but did not cry out.

Then, when the burning pain had abated, he said to his brother, 'Give me your knife.'

The brother held out his knife.

'Hold up my arm, straight out; hang on to it tight.'

What he asked was done.

Then he himself began to cut. He cut quietly and thoughtfully, severing the last sinews with that blade, which had an edge as keen as a razor's; and at last there was only the stump left. He heaved a deep sigh, and declared: 'It had to be done! 'Twould ha' been all up with me!'

He seemed relieved, and kept taking deep breaths. He began again to pour water over the stump.

It was another rough night, and they were unable to get in.

When day dawned, Javel the younger picked up his severed

arm and examined it minutely. Decomposition had set in. His messmates also came and examined it, passing it from hand to hand, tapping it, turning it over, sniffing at it.

His brother said: 'It's about time to throw that into the sea.'

But Javel the younger was annoyed. 'Not if I know it! Not if I know it!' said he. 'It belongs to me, I suppose, seeing it's my own arm.'

He took hold of it again, and placed it between his knees.

'T'll go bad all the same,' said the elder. Then an idea seemed to strike the maimed man. When the boats are kept out a long time, the catch of fish is packed in barrels of salt to keep it fresh.

He asked: 'Couldn't I put it in the brine?'

'Yes, you could do that,' declared the others.

Whereupon they emptied one of the barrels already full of fish from the catch of the last few days, and right at the bottom they laid down the arm. A layer of salt was put over it, then, one by one, the fish were replaced.

One of the 'hands' made the following joke: 'Let's hope it won't get sold in the auction!'

At which everyone laughed except the two Javels.

The wind had not abated. They tacked about in sight of Boulogne till ten o'clock on the following morning. And the injured man continued without ceasing to pour water over his stump. Now and then he would get up and pace the deck from end to end. His brother, at the tiller, gazed after him, shaking his head.

At last they entered the harbour.

The doctor examined the wound, and pronounced it to be going on as well as possible. He dressed it thoroughly, and prescribed rest for the patient. But Javel would not go to bed without having regained possession of his arm, and returned at once to the harbour to find the barrel, which he had chalked with a cross.

It was emptied in his presence, and he snatched up his arm, which, thoroughly pickled by the brine, was shrivelled, but quite fresh. He wrapped it in a cloth he had brought for the purpose, and went back home.

For a long time his wife and children examined this fragment of the father, touching the fingers, brushing away the grains of salt that had got under the nails. Then the carpenter was sent for, to take measurements for a little coffin.

Next day the whole of the trawler's crew followed the funeral of the severed arm. The two brothers, side by side, were chief mourners.

The sexton of the parish carried the corpse under his arm.

Javel the younger gave up the sea. He obtained some light employment at the harbour, and later on, when talking about his accident, he would whisper confidentially in his listener's ear: 'If my brother would only have cut the rope, I should have had my arm now, right enough. But he was thinking of his pocket.'

Minuet

GREAT MISFORTUNES seldom affect me, said Jean Bridelle, an old bachelor, who passed for a sceptic: 'I have seen war at close quarters, I strode over corpses without a feeling of pity. Violent outrages of nature or of human beings can make one utter cries of horror or indignation, but do not give one that gnawing sensation at the heart, that shiver that runs up one's back at the sight of certain little distressing things.

Certainly, the most terrible affliction that one can experience is, for the mother the loss of a child, and the loss of a mother for the man. That is awful, fearful; it unhinges and lacerates; but one recovers from these catastrophes as from deep and dangerous wounds. But certain chance meetings, certain things half perceived, divined, certain secret griefs, certain treacheries of fate which stir up in us a whole world of sorrowful thoughts, and afford us, as through a half-opened mysterious door, a swift glimpse of moral sufferings, complicated and incurable, all the deeper for their seeming placid, all the more piercing for their seeming inaccessible, all the more tenacious for their seeming artificial; these things leave in the soul a trail of sadness, a taste of bitterness, a feeling of disenchantment, which cling to one for a very long time.

I have always before my eyes two or three things which others very likely might never have noticed, and which have penetrated into my heart like long, sharp, and incurable stings.

Perhaps you will not understand the emotion that has remained in me after these fleeting impressions. I will only tell you of one. It is very old now, but as vivid to me as if it had occurred yesterday. It may be that my imagination only is responsible for these feelings.

I am fifty. I was young then, and I was studying the law. Rather gloomy, rather a dreamer, steeped in a philosophic melancholy, I hardly ever cared for glaring cafés, brawling companions, or stupid girls. I got up early, and one of my greatest pleasures was to walk about alone, towards eight o'clock in the morning, in the Pépinière of the Luxembourg.

You people of today cannot remember that Pépinière. It was like a forgotten garden of another generation, a garden as beautiful as the gentle smile of an old lady. Clustering hedges bordered the straight narrow paths, peaceful little avenues between two walls of formally trimmed foliage. The gardener's large shears kept these bushy partitions incessantly in line, and in certain places there were beds of flowers, or borders of young trees, arranged like school children out for a walk, or groups of magnificent rose bushes, and regiments of fruit trees.

A whole corner of this enticing grove was given up to bees. The straw skeps, carefully spaced about on the beds, opened to the sun their little doors no larger than the hole of a thimble, and all along the pathways one met the bees humming and gleaming like gold, real mistresses of this peaceful spot, real haunters of these tranquil corridor-like walks.

I went there almost every morning. I sat down on a seat and read. Sometimes I let the book fall on my knees to dream, to listen to bustling Paris all around me, and to enjoy the infinite repose of those old-fashioned hedges of hornbeam.

But I noticed presently that I was not the only one who frequented this place, as soon as the gates were opened; for I met now and then, at the corner of a thicket, face to face, a strange little old man.

He wore shoes with silver buckles, knee-breeches, a snuff-coloured frock coat, a lace ruffle instead of a tie, and an extraordinary grey hat, with a wide brim and a long nap, which made one think of an antediluvian epoch.

He was very slight, thin, angular, full of smiles and grimaces. His alert eyes danced and quivered with a continual movement of the lids, and he always carried a superb walking-stick with a gold head, which must have been some splendid keepsake.

This old fellow astonished me at first, then interested me beyond measure. I watched him through the walls of leaves, I followed him at a distance, and I waited behind thickets so as not to be seen.

And it happened one morning, when he thought he was alone, that he began to make some curious movements; first, some little gambols and then a bow; then he struck up with his slender feet a sprightly *entrechat*, then he began to turn round courteously, frisked about in a droll way, smiled as though he were before an audience; he saluted gallantly, he waved his arms, his poor little body writhed like a marionette, he directed his lithe, tender, and ridiculous bows to no one. He was dancing!

I remained petrified with astonishment, asking myself which of us two were mad, he or I.

Suddenly he stopped, came forward, as actors do on the stage, then bowed again, retreating with the gracious smiles and kisses of a comedian, which he threw with a trembling hand to the two rows of pruned bushes.

Then he resumed his walk gravely.

From this day I did not lose sight of him, and each morning he recommenced this incredible performance.

I had an irresistible desire to speak to him. I ventured, and, having greeted him, I said:

'It is a nice day, monsieur.' He bowed.

'Yes, monsieur, it is quite like the olden days.'

A week after we were friends and I learned his history. He had been a dancing master at the Opéra, in the reign of Louis

XV. His beautiful stick was a gift from the Comte de Clermont. When one spoke to him of dancing, there was no stopping his chatter.

One day he confided to me:

'I married "La Castris", monsieur. I will introduce you if you wish it, but she does not come here so early. You see, this garden is our joy and our life. It is all that we have of past times. It seems as though we should not be able to exist without it. It is ancient and distinguished, don't you think so? I believe that there is an atmosphere here that has not changed in the least since my youth. My wife and I spend every afternoon here. But I come in the mornings, because I rise early.'

When I had finished my lunch, I returned to the Luxembourg, and I soon perceived my friend, who was giving his arm ceremoniously to a little old woman, dressed in black, to whom I was presented. She was 'La Castris', the celebrated dancer; beloved by princes, beloved by the king, beloved by the gallant circle who seem to have bequeathed to the world an atmosphere of love.

We sat down on a stone seat. It was in May. A perfume of flowers pervaded the neat walks; the bright sun-rays glided through the leaves and scattered yellow patches of light over us.

La Castris's black dress seemed mellowed in the splendour of the afternoon.

The garden was empty. One could hear the fiacres rumbling in the distance.

'Tell me, please,' I said to the old dancer, 'what is the minuet?'

He started.

'The minuet, monsieur, is the queen of dances, and the dance of Queens, do you understand? Since we have had no king, we have not had the minuet any more.'

He commenced in a pompous style a long dithyrambic eulogy, of which I understood nothing. I wanted him to describe the steps, all the movements, and the attitudes. He became confused, exasperated with his inability, nervous and discomposed.

But suddenly turning to his old companion, who remained silent and serious, he said:

'Élise, tell me . . . shall we . . . it would be so nice of you . . . shall we . . . show this gentleman what it is?'

She looked all round her uneasily, she rose without saying a word, and placed herself opposite him.

Then I saw something unforgettable.

They went to and fro with childish affectation, smiled, wavered, bowed, and skipped, like two old-fashioned puppets, set dancing by an ancient mechanism a little worn, constructed long before by a skilful workman, after the fashion of his day.

I watched them, with extraordinary sensations disturbing me, with my soul moved by an indefinable melancholy. I seemed to be looking at a mournful and comic apparition; the old-fashioned spirit of a long-past age. I wanted to smile and cry at the same time.

Suddenly they stopped, they had come to the end of the figures of the dance.

They stood for some moments looking at one another, making surprising grimaces; then they embraced; they were both sobbing.

I went away into the country three days after; I have never seen them again. When I returned to Paris, two years later, the Pépinière had been cleared away. What has become of them without their dear garden of olden times, with its labyrinth of walks, its fragrance of the past, and its beautiful winding avenues of hornbeam?

Are they dead? Do they wander along the modern streets like exiles without hope? Do they dance, quaint phantoms, a fantastic minuet, between the cypress trees in the cemetery, along the paths bordered with tombstones, in the moonlight?

Their memory clings to me, it haunts me, tortures me, and remains in me like a wound. Why? I cannot tell.

Doubtless, you will think this ridiculous!

Night

A Nightmare

I LOVE THE NIGHT passionately. I love it as a man loves a woman or his own country, with an instinctive, deep, and invincible love. I love it with all the senses of my being, with my eyes that see it, with my ears that listen to its silence, and with my whole body, which the darkness caresses. The larks sing in the early sunlight, high up in the blue sky, in the warm atmosphere, in the clear air of light mornings. In the night the owl passes, a black spot that flits across a black space, and rejoicing, intoxicated by the black infinity, utters his cry, vibrating and sinister.

The daylight is fatiguing and wearisome to me. It is brutal and noisy. I get up with difficulty, I dress myself overcome by lassitude, I go out reluctantly, and each step, each movement, each gesture, each word, each thought, demands an effort, as if I had to lift up an overwhelming burden.

But when the sun is sinking, a confused joy invades me, a joy that enters into all my limbs. I am aroused, I become animated. With the deepening of the twilight I begin to feel myself another man, younger, stronger, more alert, much happier. I watch the gradual increase of the vast shadow falling softly down from heaven; it rolls over the town like an impalpable and impenetrable sea wave; it hides, blots out, destroys all colour and form, enveloping houses, beings, and monuments in the clasp of its imperceptible embrace.

Then it seems to me that I must cry out with pleasure like the owls, run along the roofs like the cats; and an impetuous, an overpowering desire for love flames up in my veins.

I walk about, I tramp on for hours, sometimes in the shadowy outskirts of the town, or else in the woods, near Paris, where the wild creatures of my kin, and my brothers the poachers, are astir.

Death lurks continually in the passion of a violent love. But how can I relate clearly what is happening to me? How can I explain even that I am able to tell you my tale at all? I do not know; I know nothing; I only know that it is so. Listen!

Yesterday – was it yesterday? – yes, without doubt, it must have been, unless it happened before, on some day, in another month, in another year – I do not know. It should be yesterday, however, because daylight has not returned, because the sun has not risen again. But how long has this night lasted? Since when? . . . Who can tell? Who will ever know?

Yesterday, I went out, as I go out every evening, after

my dinner. The weather was very fine, very still, very warm. Strolling towards the boulevards, I watched above me the stream of black sky, glittering with stars, between the roofs of the street, which, winding away, made this rivulet of stars curve and undulate like a real river.

Everything, from the planets to the gas jets, appeared brilliant in the clear air. So many lights sparkled overhead and in the town below, that they made the darkness luminous. The sheen of brilliant nights is infinitely more joyous than the garish light of day.

On the boulevard, the cafés blazed, people laughed, strolled by, people sat drinking. I entered a theatre for a few moments. What theatre was it? I don't remember now. The amount of light in there depressed me so much, that I went out again, with my heart a little cast down by the shock of the crude glitter on the gilded balconies, by the artificial scintillation of the lustrous crystal, by the fiery barrier of the footlights, by the melancholy of all this brutal and false brilliancy. I reached the Champs Élysées, where the café concerts appeared like centres of conflagrations in the midst of the foliage. The chestnuts, touched with the yellow light, looked as if they had been painted, as if they had a phosphorescent glow. And the electric globes, shining like pale moons, like egg-shaped moons fallen from the sky, like enormous pearls, made the lines of gaslight, the odious, filthy gaslight, and the festoons of coloured lamps, look warm in the flood of their nacreous, mysterious, and regal splendour.

I stopped under the Arc de Triomphe, to look at the avenue, the long and beautiful starlit avenue, going towards Paris, between two long rows of lights and the stars! The stars up there, the unknown stars, cast by haphazard into the infinite space, and tracing those curious figures which cause so much wonder, and give rise to so many dreams.

I went into the Bois de Boulogne, and I stayed there a long time, a long time. A strange shudder passed through me, an unexpected and powerful emotion, an exaltation of mind which verged on madness.

I walked on for a long time, for a long time. Then I retraced my steps. What time was it when I went under the Arc de Triomphe again? I don't know. The town had gone to sleep, and a few clouds – thick, black clouds – had spread themselves slowly over the sky.

For the first time I felt that something extraordinary was going to happen, something unheard of. It seemed to me that the night was turning cold, that the air was thickening, that the night, that my beloved night, was gathering around my heart. The avenue was deserted now. Two policemen, only, walked about the fiacre-stand, on the highway, lit up faintly by the gas-lights, which seemed on the point of dying, a line of waggons, loaded with vegetables, were going to the Halles. They went slowly, laden with carrots, with turnips, and with cabbages. The drivers were lying back asleep, out of sight, and the horses went along, stepping deliberately, each one at the tail of the waggon in front, without any noise on the wooden pavement. In the light of each street lamp, the carrots glowed red, the turnips white, the cabbages green; and they continued, one after the other, those red carts, as red as fire, the white as white as silver, the green as green as emeralds. I followed them for a time, then, turning into the Rue Royale, I came back to the boulevards. No more people anywhere, no more lit-up cafés, only some belated figures hastening along. I had never seen Paris so dead, so deserted. I pulled out my watch: it was two o'clock.

I was impelled by a force, a necessity to go on. I went as far as the Bastille. There, I observed that I had never before seen so dark a night, for I could not even distinguish the commemorative column, whose golden genius above was lost in the impenetrable obscurity. A canopy of clouds, as massive as immensity itself, had obliterated the stars, and seemed to crouch down over the earth, as if to swallow it up for ever.

I turned back. There was no one near me now. In the Place du Château d'Eau, however, a tipsy man lurched against me, and vanished directly. For some time I could hear his uneven and sonorous footsteps. I went on. At the top of the Faubourg Montmartre a fiacre passed me, going down towards the Seine. I shouted after it. The driver did not answer. A woman was roaming about in the neighbourhood of the Rue Drouot; 'Monsieur, just listen to me.' I quickened my pace in order to escape the outstretched hand. Then nothing more. Before the Vaudeville, a ragpicker was turning over the rubbish in the gutter. His little lantern wavered about on a level with the ground. I asked him: 'What time is it, my good fellow?'

He growled: 'How am I to know? – I haven't got a watch.'

Then I noticed, suddenly, that the gas lights had been put out. I was aware that, at this season, they are turned off early, before the break of day, through economy; but daylight was yet very far away, so very far from appearing.

'I had better go to the Halles,' I thought: 'there, at least, I shall find some life.'

I started off, but I could not even see enough to find my way. I advanced slowly, as one moves through a dense wood, identifying the streets only by keeping count of those I passed.

Before the Crédit Lyonnais, a dog growled. I turned into the Rue de Grammont. I had lost myself. I wandered about; then I recognized the Bourse by the iron railings outside. All Paris was sleeping, with a profound and terrifying slumber. In the distance, however, a fiacre was rumbling, a solitary fiacre, perhaps the one that had passed me some time before. Trying to overtake it, I made for the sound of the wheels, crossing the deserted, black streets, quite black, as black as death.

I lost my way again. Where was I? What stupidity to turn the gas off so early! Not a passer, no one out late, not a single prowler, not even a howl of an amorous cat. Nothing.

Where were the policemen? I said to myself: 'I will shout, they will come.' I shouted. No one answered.

I cried out louder. My voice went forth without an echo,

feebly, smothered up, overwhelmed by the night, by the impenetrable night.

I began to yell: 'Help! Help! Help!' My desperate appeal remained without response. What time was it then? I pulled out my watch, but I had no matches. I listened to the faint ticking of the little piece of mechanism with a strange and extravagant delight. It seemed to be alive! I felt less solitary. What a mystery! I started off again, like a blind man, tapping the walls with my stick, and every moment I would raise my eyes towards the sky, hoping that the day was coming at last; but all space was black, completely black, more profoundly black than the town below.

What hour could it be? I walked on, it seemed to me, for an infinite time; my legs were giving under me, my chest heaved, and I suffered horribly from hunger.

I made up my mind to ring at the first door I came to. I pulled at the brass knob, and the bell rang within the enormous house; it rang out strangely, as though there had been nothing in the house but that vibrating sound.

I waited; there was no answer, no one opened the door. I rang once more, and waited again. Nothing came of it.

I became scared. I ran to the next house and, twenty times in succession, I made the bell ring in the dark lobby where the concierge should have been sleeping. But I could not wake anyone, and I went on further, pulling at the rings, or at the knobs, with all my might, kicking, beating with my stick, with my hands, these doors so obstinately closed.

And suddenly I perceived that I had arrived at the Halles. The great market was deserted, without a sound, without a stir, without a single cart, without a man anywhere, without a heap of vegetables or a bunch of flowers. It was empty, lifeless, abandoned, dead!

I was seized with terror – a horrible terror. What is happening? Oh, my God! what does this mean?

I went away again. But the time? What was the time? Who would tell me the time? No clock up in the towers or on the monuments would strike. I thought, 'I will open my watch glass and feel the hands with my fingers.' I pulled it out . . . it ticked no more . . . it had stopped. There was nothing left. Nothing. No more; no movement in the town, not a glimmer of light, not a rustling in the air. Nothing! Nothing more; not even a distant rumble of a fiacre – nothing whatever!

I was on the quays and an icy freshness rose up from the river. Was the Seine still flowing?

'I wanted to know; I found the steps, and went down . . . I could not hear the swirling of the current under the arches of the bridge . . . A few more steps . . . then sand . . . and . . . then water . . . I plunged my arm into it . . . it was flowing . . . it was flowing . . . cold . . . cold . . . cold . . . almost frozen . . . almost dried up . . . almost dead.

And I felt, indeed, that I should never have strength enough to climb up again . . . and that I should die there . . . I also . . . die of hunger . . . of fatigue . . . and of cold.

Yvette

I

COMING OUT OF the Café Riche, Jean de Servigny said to Léon Saval: 'Shall we walk? It's too fine to drive.'

'All right!' replied his friend.

Jean continued: 'It's barely eleven; let's take it easy, or we shall get there long before twelve.'

A busy crowd was eddying on the boulevard – such a crowd as on summer nights is always to be seen in the streets, stirring, halting, murmuring, flowing along like a river, full of placid gaiety. Here and there a café threw a brilliant shaft of light over groups on the pavement sitting round little tables covered with bottles and glasses, and so closely packed as to completely block the pathway. And in the road, cabs with red, and blue, and green eyes, shooting swiftly across the glare of the lighted front, showed for a second the lean and ambling silhouette of the horse, the profile of the driver up above, the sombre bulk of the vehicle, while the *Urbaine* cabs made pale and fleeting flashes as their yellow panels caught the light.

The two friends strolled slowly along, smoking, in evening dress, with greatcoats over their arms, flowers in their button-holes, and their hats a trifle on one side, as hats are sometimes worn, after a good dinner, when the breeze is warm.

They were old school friends, sincerely, firmly devoted to each other. Jean de Servigny, short, slight, rather bald, frail-looking, but exceedingly elegant, with curled moustache, clear eyes, and sensitive lips, was one of those night-birds who seem born and bred on the boulevards; indefatigable in spite of his look of exhaustion, vigorous in spite of his pallor, one of those wiry Parisians whom gymnastics, fencing, and Turkish baths endow with a nervous, carefully disciplined strength. He was known everywhere for his wild ways, his wit, his wealth, his amours, and for the genial amiability and worldly charm innate in certain men.

A true Parisian, light, sceptical, capricious, impulsive, energetic, irresolute; capable of everything, and yet of nothing; selfish on principle, but generous by fits and starts, getting comfortably through his income, and carefully through his constitution. Cool, yet passionate, he was continually letting himself go and continually pulling himself up, a prey to the most contrary instincts, and yielding to them all, by way of living up to his ideal of the shrewd man of the world, with weathercock logic swinging to all the winds, and profiting by every turn, while he never stirs a finger to set it in motion.

His companion, Léon Saval, equally well off, was one of those superb giants who make women turn round and stare after them in the streets. He gave the impression of a statue come to life, a model of the human race, after the fashion of those works of Art that get sent to exhibitions. Too fine, too tall, too broad, and too strong, he sinned by the very extravagance of his good points. He had inspired innumerable passions.

'Have you informed this lady that you're bringing me?' he asked, as they passed the Vaudeville.

Servigny burst out laughing. 'What! inform the Marquise Obardi? Do you inform the driver of an omnibus that you're going to get up at the next corner?'

'Why! who is she, exactly, then?' asked Saval, rather puzzled.

'A parvenue, a charming rascally adventuress,' replied his friend, 'from the devil knows where, who turned up one day in Bohemia, the devil knows how, and has managed to cut a dash there. What does it matter? They say her real name, I mean her maiden name — she's remained a maiden lady except in reality of course — is Octavie Bardin; keep the first letter of the Christian, and clip the last of the surname, and you get Obardi. An attractive person; and with your physique you're bound to be her lover. Hercules isn't introduced to Messalina without something coming of it. I must say one thing, though: the entrance to the place is as free as the entrance to a shop, and you're not in the least obliged to buy what's exhibited. The stock consists of love and cards; they don't bother you to take either the one or the other. And the exit's just as free.

'It's three years since she pitched her shady tent in the Quartier de l'Étoile, and opened its doors to the cosmopolitan scum who come to exploit Paris, to exercise their dangerous talents there.

'I can't for the life of me remember how I came to know her. Suppose I must have gone, like everyone else, because there's gambling, because the women are easy-going, and the men scamps. I can't help being fond of that crowd of decorated rascals – all foreign, all noble, all titled, and all unknown at their Embassies, except, of course, the spies. There they are, trotting out their honour on every imaginable occasion, quoting their ancestors for no reason at all, telling you all about their lives – braggarts, liars and thieves, as dangerous as the cards they play; brave simply because they have to be, like robbers, who can't strip their victims without risking their own lives. In a word, the aristocracy of the hulks – yes, I'm fond of them. They're interesting to study, amusing to listen to, often witty; never commonplace, like our own blessed officials. Their womenkind, too, are always pretty, with a little flavour of foreign rascality in them, and a sense of mystery about their past lives, spent probably half the time in reformatories. They've almost always got splendid eyes and hair, the true professional physique, a sort of grace that intoxicates and seduces you into making a fool of yourself, and a charm that's altogether unholy and irresistible. They rob you in the real old highway fashion, take everything you have. Ah, yes; they're regular female birds of prey. Well, I'm fond of them too.

'The Marquise Obardi is the very type of these charming villains – full-blown, of course, but still beautiful – the sort of feline sorceress that you feel to be vicious to the very marrow. Oh! it's an amusing house. Gambling, dancing, supper – in fact, all the pleasures of this wicked world.'

'Have you ever been, or are you, her lover?' asked Saval.

Servigny replied: 'I haven't been, am not, and never shall be. I go there for the sake of the daughter.'

'Ah! there's a daughter?'

'There is indeed! A miracle, my dear fellow. She's just at present the principal attraction of the den. A glorious creature, perfection itself, eighteen years old, as fair as her mother is dark; always in high spirits and ready for fun, always laughing and dancing like a mad thing. Who's to be the lucky man? Who *is* the lucky man? No one knows. There are ten of us waiting and hoping. A girl like that in the hands of a woman like the Marquise is a fortune. And they play such a dark game, the rogues! Can't make out what they're at – waiting for a better chance than me, I suppose. Well, I can only tell you – if the chance comes my way, I shall seize her. This girl Yvette nonplusses me completely. She's a mystery. If she isn't the most perfect monster of subtle perversity you ever saw, she's the most marvellous piece of innocence. She lives amongst all these disreputable surroundings with a quiet, triumphant unconcern that's quite amazing in its artfulness or its artlessness. There she is, an exotic offshoot of this adventuress, grown on the dunghill of Bohemia, like a magnificent plant that's nourished on manure – the child, I shouldn't wonder, of some man of rank, some great artist or great lord – a casual prince or king, perhaps – who turned in there one night. Impossible to understand what she is or what her thoughts are. But you'll see for yourself.'

Saval began to laugh, and said: 'You're in love with her.'

'No – I'm in the running; not at all the same thing. I'm going to introduce you to my most serious rivals. But I've got a fair chance – I'm ahead even: she smiles on me.'

'You're in love!' repeated Saval.

'No-o! She disturbs and allures me; she makes me uneasy, attracts, and scares me, all at the same time! I distrust her as if she were a trap, and I long for her as I long for a drink when I'm thirsty. I feel the charm of her, but I never go near her without the sort of fear one has of a pickpocket. While I'm with her I've an irrational belief in her innocence – which, mind you, is possible – and a most rational distrust of her villainy, which is just as probable. I feel I'm in contact with an abnormal being, outside the pale of natural law. Which is she, exquisite or abominable? I really can't tell you.'

For the third time Saval said: 'I tell you you're in love. You're talking of her with the fervour of a poet, and the sing-song of a troubadour. Come, look into yourself, sound your heart, and confess!'

Servigny took several paces without speaking, and then replied: 'Well, you may be right after all. Anyway, I'm very much interested in her. Yes – perhaps I *am* in love. I think of her too much. I think of her when I'm going to sleep, and when I wake up . . . Yes, it's pretty serious. Her image follows me, actually pursues me, it's always with me, before me, around me, in me. Can you call such a physical obsession love? Her face has gone so deep into my brain that I see her the moment I shut my eyes. My heart leaps each time I catch sight of her. I don't deny it. So be it! I love her; but in a queer sort of way. I want her frightfully, but the idea of making her my wife would seem to me mad, idiotic, monstrous. I'm a little afraid of her too, like a bird with a hawk above it. And I'm jealous, jealous of everything I don't know in that incomprehensible heart. I'm always asking myself: "Is she simply a charming tomboy, or an abominable jade?" She says things that would make a trooper blush; but – so do parrots. She's sometimes so imprudent, or – impudent, as to make me believe in her spotless innocence, and sometimes so simple, with a kind of impossible simplicity, that it makes me doubt whether she ever was innocent. She provokes and excites me like a courtesan, and defends herself all the time like a vestal. She seems to be fond of me, yet she's always making fun of me; in public she labels herself my mistress, in private she treats me like her brother or her valet. Sometimes I fancy she has as many lovers as her mother; sometimes I think she hasn't a suspicion of what life really is like – not the smallest suspicion. Then again, she's a tremendous novel-reader – while I'm waiting like this for better days, I keep her supplied with books – she calls me her librarian. By my orders, the New Library sends her weekly every mortal thing that comes out; I believe she reads the lot pell-mell. It must make a strange salad in her head. Perhaps indeed this literary stew counts for something in her extraordinary behaviour. Anyone who looks at life through the medium of fifteen thousand novels must see it in a funny sort of light – get quaint ideas about things, eh?

'Well, I'm waiting. On the one hand, I've never had for any woman the fancy I have for this one, that's certain – as certain as that I shall never marry her. So, if she's had lovers, I shall swell the number; if not, I shall take number 1, like a tram ticket. It's a simple case. Obviously, she'll never marry. Who'd marry the daughter of the Marquise Obardi, of Octavie Bardin? No one, for a thousand reasons. Where could they find her a husband? In our class? Never. The mother's house is a place of public resort, where the daughter acts as bait. We don't marry into that sort of thing. In the middle class? Still less. Besides, the marquise is a woman of business; she'll never give Yvette for good and all to anyone but a man of high position – and him she'll never catch. That leaves the lower classes – still less chance there. No, there's no way out of it. This young lady is not of our class, not of the middle class, not of the people; she can't marry into any of them. She belongs, by reason of her mother, her birth, education, heredity, manners, habits, to – gilded prostitution.

'She can't escape without turning nun, which is not at all likely, considering her ways and tastes. There's only one profession possible to her: Love. She'll come to it, if she hasn't already. She can't avoid her fate. From a "young woman" she'll simply become a "woman", and I should much like to be the pivot of the transformation.

'So I'm waiting – the gentlemen-in-waiting are numerous. You'll see a Frenchman, M. de Belvigne; a Russian, called Prince Kravalow; and an Italian, Chevalier Valréali; these are definite candidates, busy canvassing already. But there are a lot of unconsidered hangers-on. The marquise is watching. I think she's got views about me. She knows I'm very well off, and she's less sure of the others. Her house is really the most astonishing place that I've ever met with of its kind. You even come across very decent fellows there – we're going ourselves, you see, and we shan't be the only ones. As to the women, she's found, or rather, skimmed off the cream of all those ladies who pillage our purses. Goodness knows where she discovered them. It's apart from the regular professionals, it's not Bohemia, it's not exactly anything. She's had an inspiration of genius, too, in pitching on adventuresses with children, particularly girls. So much so that a greenhorn might fancy he was among good women!'

They had reached the Avenue of the Champs Élysées. A gentle breeze stirred softly among the leaves, touching their faces

233

like soft sighs from a giant fan wafted to and fro somewhere in the sky. Dumb shadows wandered among the trees, or made dusky blurs on the benches. And these shadows spoke very low, as if confiding to each other weighty or shameful secrets.

Servigny resumed: 'You've no idea what a collection of fancy titles we shall meet in this menagerie. Talking of that, I shall introduce you as Count Saval. An unadorned Saval would be unpopular – oh! very unpopular!'

'No! no! by Jove!' cried his friend; 'I won't for a moment, even in a place like that, have them suppose me ass enough to deck myself out with a title – no, no!'

Servigny laughed. 'Don't be such a duffer,' said he; 'they've baptized me the Duke of Servigny – I haven't the least notion how or why. And I remain the Duke of Servigny without a murmur. It really doesn't hurt, and without it I should be awfully looked down on.'

But Saval was by no means open to conviction: 'Ah! you've a title of your own, that's quite another thing. But as for me, for better or worse, I'll be the only commoner in the place. It'll be my distinguishing mark – my superiority.'

Servigny persisted: 'It can't be done, absolutely can't be done. It would seem quite monstrous. You'd be like a ragpicker in an assembly of emperors. Leave it to me; I'll present you as the Viceroy of the Upper Mississippi, nobody'll be astonished. When one's going in for titles, they can't be too big.'

'No; once for all, I won't.'

'Very well. I was an ass to try and persuade you, for I defy you to get in there without being decorated with a title; there are some shops, you know, where ladies can't get past the door without having a bunch of violets given them.'

They turned to the right in the Rue de Berri, ascended to the first floor of a fine modern house, and gave their overcoats and sticks into the hands of four lackeys in breeches. A warm odour of festivity, suggestive of flowers, perfumes, and fair women, and a loud, sustained, confused murmur, issued from the crowded rooms.

A sort of master of the ceremonies, a tall, upright, stout, and solemn person, whose face was framed in white whiskers, came up to the newcomer, and, with a slight but haughty bow, asked:

'What name may I announce?'

'Monsieur Saval,' replied Servigny.

At which, opening the door, the man shouted into the crowd of guests:

'M. le Duc de Servigny.'

'M. le Baron Saval.'

The first room was full of women, and the eye alighted at once on an array of bare necks, emerging from billows of brilliant drapery. The lady of the house, who was standing talking to three friends, turned round and majestically came forward with graceful movements, and smiling lips.

Her forehead, narrow and very low, was covered with a mass of shining black hair, thick as fleece, encroaching a little on the temples. She was tall and rather too plump and full-blown, but very beautiful, with a heavy, warm, compelling beauty. Her helmet of black hair had the power of conjuring up delightful visions, of making her mysteriously desirable; beneath it were great black eyes. The nose was rather small, the mouth large, yet infinitely seductive, eloquent of love and conquest.

But her most living charm was in her voice. It came from that mouth like water from a spring, so natural, so soft, so true in tone, so clear, that it was a physical joy to listen to it, a delight for the ear to hear the subtle words flowing out like a stream from its source, a delight for the eye to see those beautiful lips part to give them passage.

She stretched out a hand to Servigny, who kissed it, and, letting her fan drop to the full length of its thin gold chain, she gave the other to Saval, and said:

'Welcome, Baron; any friend of the Duke is welcome here.'

And she fixed her glowing eyes on the giant presented to her. There was a tiny black down on her upper lip, the suspicion of a moustache, more visible when she spoke; a delicious scent clung about her, strong and intoxicating – some American or Indian perfume. But fresh people kept arriving, marquises, counts, or princes; and saying to Servigny with motherly graciousness: 'You'll find my daughter in the other room – make yourselves at home, gentlemen, the house is yours,' she left them, to meet her new guests, casting at Saval that smiling, fleeting glance by which a woman shows a man that he has pleased her.

Servigny seized his friend's arm: 'Come on,' said he, 'I'll pilot you. This room belongs to the ladies – temple of the Flesh, fresh or otherwise. Bargains as good as new, and better still, high-priced articles to be had cheap. To the left is the gambling room – temple of Gold. You know all about that . . . In the room at the far end, they dance – temple of Innocence, the sanctuary, the maidens' market. It's there that these ladies show off their produce. Why, even real marriages would be tolerated. Yes, over there is the Future, the hope of our days and nights. And really, the most curious feature in this museum of moral maladies is the sight of these young girls, with souls as out of joint as the bodies of little clowns born of acrobats. Let's go and have a look at them.'

He kept bowing courteously to right and left, distributing his compliments, and glancing rapidly with the eye of a connoisseur at every bare-necked woman that he knew.

A band at the far end of the second room was playing a waltz; and they stopped in the doorway to watch. Some fifteen couples were dancing; the men solemn, the girls with a smile fixed on their lips. Like their mothers they showed a good deal of skin, and the bodices of one or two were merely secured by a narrow ribbon over the shoulders.

Suddenly from the very end of the room darted a tall girl, rushing along past everyone, pushing the dancers aside, and holding up the outrageously long train of her dress in her left hand. She ran with quick little steps, as women do in a crowd, and cried:

'Ah! here's Muscade! How *are* you, Muscade?'

Her face was like the Spring, alight with happiness. Her warm white skin, the skin that goes with auburn hair, seemed to sparkle. And that mass of hair, twisted round her head, flame-bright, hung heavy on her forehead, and looked too weighty for her supple and still slender neck. She seemed made for motion, as her mother was made for speech, so natural, noble and simple were her gestures. To see her walk, turn, bend her head, lift her arm, was to feel a moral joy, a physical delight. She repeated:

'Ah, Muscade, how are you, Muscade?'

Servigny shook her hand violently, as he would have shaken a man's, and said:

'Mam'zelle Yvette, this is my friend, Baron Saval.'

She bowed, and staring at the stranger, said: 'How do you do, Monsieur; are you always as big as that?'

In the chaffing tone that he adopted with her to hide his distrust and uncertainty, Servigny replied: 'No, Mam'zelle. He's brought his largest dimensions tonight to please your mother; she's fond of the gigantic.'

The young girl answered in a serio-comic voice: 'All right! But when you come for me, make yourself a little smaller, please; I like moderation. Muscade, now, is just my size.'

She gave the newcomer her little, wide-open hand, and said: 'Are you going to dance, Muscade? Come along, do let's have a turn!'

Without answering, Servigny, with a quick, eager movement,

clasped her round the waist, and they disappeared at once with the fury of a whirlwind.

They danced faster than all the others, turning and turning, flying along, whirling round and round; clasped so close that they looked like one, with bodies upright and legs almost still, as if an invisible machine hidden under their feet had made them so to twirl. They seemed tireless. The other couples stopped one by one. They alone remained, waltzing unendingly. They had a look of being far away from the dance, in ecstasy. And the band played on, their eyes fixed on this treadmill couple; every eye was fixed on them, and when they stopped at last, everyone applauded.

She was a little flushed now, with strange-looking eyes, ardent, yet timid, less frank than before; troubled, and so blue, with such black pupils, that they seemed quite unnatural.

Servigny was like a drunken man. He leaned against a door to recover himself.

'No head, my poor Muscade!' she said; 'I'm tougher than you!'

He laughed nervously, devouring her with greedy longing in his eyes and in the curve of his lip; he continued to gaze at her standing before him with her bare throat heaving tumultuously.

'Sometimes,' she went on, 'you look just like a cat that's going to fly at someone. Come along; give me your arm, and let's go and find your friend.'

Without a word he offered his arm, and they crossed the

room. Saval was no longer alone. The Marquise Obardi had rejoined him. She was murmuring trivial commonplaces in that entrancing voice of hers. And looking deep into his eyes, she seemed to be meaning quite other words than those her lips pronounced. The moment she saw Servigny her face became smiling, and, turning towards him, she said: 'My dear Duke, did you know that I've just taken a villa at Bougival for two months? You must come and see me, and bring your friend. Let's see, I'm going in on Monday – will you both come and dine next Saturday, and stay all Sunday?'

Servigny abruptly turned his head towards Yvette. She was smiling, tranquil and serene, and said with an assurance that left no loop-hole for hesitation: 'Of course Muscade will come to dinner on Saturday! You needn't take the trouble to ask him. We'll have tremendous fun in the country.'

He fancied he could detect the birth of a promise in her smile, some hidden intention in her voice.

The Marquise lifted her great dark eyes to Saval: 'And you, Baron?' she said; and her smile, at any rate, was not ambiguous.

He bowed: 'I shall be only too happy, Madame!'

'Ah!' said Yvette slyly, 'we'll scandalize everyone down there, won't we, Muscade? We'll make my regiment mad with rage?'

There was again that artless or artful meaning in her voice, and with a glance she pointed to a group of men, watching them from a distance.

'As much as ever you like, Mam'zelle,' replied Servigny. In

talking to her he never said Mademoiselle, by virtue of a sort of comradeship established between them.

'Why does Mademoiselle Yvette always call my friend Servigny "Muscade"?' asked Saval.

The young girl put on an innocent expression: 'Because he's always slipping through one's fingers, Monsieur. You think you've got hold of him, but you never have.'

The Marquise, who was visibly occupied with other thoughts and had not taken her eyes off Saval, said absently: 'Aren't these children funny?'

'I'm not funny,' answered Yvette crossly, 'I'm simply frank! I like Muscade, and he's always deserting me; it's so annoying!'

Servigny made a deep bow: 'I'll never leave you again, Mam'zelle, day or night!'

She made a movement of alarm: 'Ah, no! The day's all very well, but at night you'd be a mistake.'

'Why, how?' he asked wickedly.

She answered with calm audacity: 'Because I'm sure you can't look so nice in *déshabille*.'

The Marquise, without appearing in the least disturbed, cried out: 'Why! they're saying the most awful things! One can't be as innocent as all that.'

Servigny replied chaffingly: 'That's just what I think, Marquise!'

Yvette fixed her eyes on him: 'You –' she said haughtily in a wounded voice; 'you've made a hole in your manners: you've been doing that too often lately.'

And, turning her back on him, she called out: 'Chevalier, come and defend me, I'm being insulted.'

There came up a lean, dark man, slow of movement, who said with a forced smile: 'Which is the culprit?'

She nodded her head towards Servigny. 'He!' she said; 'but all the same, I like him better than the rest of you put together; he's less tiresome.'

Chevalier Valréali bowed: 'We do what we can,' said he; 'we've fewer attractions perhaps, but not less devotion.'

At this moment a tall, corpulent man, with grey whiskers, approached, and said in a big voice: 'Mademoiselle Yvette — your servant.'

'Ah! Monsieur de Belvigne.' she cried, and turning to Saval, remarked: 'This is my best young man; tall, fat, rich, and stupid. That's how I like them. A real knight — of the trencher. Why! you're even taller than he! I *must* give you a nickname. Good! I shall call you "young Mr Rhodes", after the Colossus — he must have been your father. But I'm certain you two have any amount of interesting things to tell each other up there over our heads — so good-night!' And off she went towards the band, to ask the musicians to play a quadrille.

Mme Obardi, who seemed lost in reverie, turned slowly to Servigny: 'You're always teasing her. You'll spoil her temper, and give her all sorts of bad habits'; but it was clearly said for the sake of talking.

'Ah! then you've not finished her education?' he retorted.

She looked as if she did not understand, and went on benignly smiling.

Just then she saw approaching a solemn personage, starred with crosses, and hastening towards him, cried: 'Ah! Prince, how delightful!'

Servigny again took Saval's arm, and drew him away. 'That's the latest suitor, Prince Kravalow,' he said. 'Well now, isn't she superb?'

Saval replied: 'I call them both superb. The mother's good enough for me.'

Servigny bowed: 'She's quite at your service, my dear chap,' he said. The dancers elbowed them, taking their places for the quadrille, couple by couple, in two opposing lines.

'Let's go and see the Greeks,' said Servigny, and they made their way into the gambling room.

Round each table stood a circle of men watching, who spoke but seldom, while the chink from the gold thrown on the cloth, or sharply raked in, mingled its light, metallic murmur with the murmur of the players, as though the voice of money were making itself heard among the voices of human beings.

These men were all decorated with strange orders, and curious sorts of ribbons; and though their faces were so different, they all had the same severe expression, and were most readily distinguished one from the other by the cut of their beards. The stark American with a horseshoe round his jaw, the haughty Englishman with a hairy fan divided on his chest, the Spaniard with a fleece of black up to the eyes, the Roman with the huge moustache presented to Italy by Victor Emanuel, the Austrian with his whiskers and clean-shaven chin, a Russian general with an upper lip armed, as it were, with two lances of waxed hair, and the Frenchman with his gay moustache – revealed the fantasies of all the barbers in the world.

'Aren't you going to play?' asked Servigny.

'No, are you?'

'Never here! If you're ready, we'll be off, and come again some quieter evening. It's too crowded tonight, one can't stir.'

'All right.'

They disappeared through a curtained doorway which led to the vestibule.

As soon as they were in the street, Servigny said: 'Well, what do you think of it?'

'Oh! interesting enough! But I prefer the women's quarters to the men's.'

'Rather! Those women are our very finest specimens. One scents love in them as one scents perfumes at a hairdresser's. This is really the only kind of house where you get your money's worth. Ah! and what craftswomen, my dear chap! What artists! . . . Have you ever eaten tarts at a baker's? They look good, but they're good-for-nothing. The man who made them is a fellow who only knows how to make bread. Well, the love of an ordinary woman of the world always seems to me like baker's pastry. Whereas, the love that one gets at these Marquise

Obardis, well — it's the real thing. Ah! they know how to make cakes, those little confectioners! One pays 2½d. for what costs a penny anywhere else, that's all!'

'Who's the lord of the manor just now?' asked Saval.

Servigny shrugged his shoulders. 'I know nothing about it,' said he; 'the last I heard of was an English peer, who departed three months ago. Just now she must be living on the community, perhaps on the gambling, for she's capricious. But we've settled to dine with her at Bougival next Saturday, haven't we? In the country one has more opportunity; I shall find out at last what Yvette has in that head of hers!'

'There's nothing I should like better. I've no engagements that day,' replied Saval.

Returning through the Champs Élysées, under the fiery field of the stars, they disturbed a couple on a bench, and Servigny muttered: 'Love! How idiotic, and yet how tremendous it is! How commonplace, and yet how amusing! It's always the same, and always different. And the ragamuffin who pays that girl a franc asks of her the very same thing for which I should pay ten thousand to some Obardi, no younger or less stupid perhaps than that drab. What folly!'

He said nothing for some minutes, then began again: 'It would be rare luck all the same to be Yvette's first lover. Ah! for that I'd give — I'd give —'

He did not discover what he would give. And Saval wished him good-night at the corner of the Rue Royale.

II

THE DINNER TABLE had been laid on the verandah over-looking the river. The Villa Printemps, taken by the Marquise Obardi, was placed half-way up the slope, just where, below the garden wall, the Seine made a curve in the direction of Marly.

Opposite the house loomed the island of Croissy, a mass of great trees and foliage, and a long reach of the broad river was visible, stretching as far as the floating café of *La Grenouillière*, hidden amongst the green.

The evening was falling, a calm, river-side evening, full of sweetness and colour, one of those quiet evenings that bring with them a sense of happiness. Not a breath stirred the leaves, no puff of wind ruffled the smooth, pale surface of the Seine. It was not too hot; just pleasantly warm – good to be alive. The benign sweetness of the riverbanks mounted towards the quiet sky.

The sun was going down behind the trees, on its way to other lands, and one seemed to inhale the peace of the sleeping earth, inhale the unheeding breath of life itself, in that calm, broad space.

When the party came out from the drawing-room to sit down to dinner, they were all in ecstasies. A tender gaiety invaded their hearts; it seemed so delicious to be dining out there in the open, breathing the clear sweet-scented air, with the great river and the sunset for background.

The Marquise had taken Saval's arm, and Yvette Servigny's.

There were only the four of them. The two women seemed quite unlike what they had been in Paris, particularly Yvette; she hardly spoke, and appeared languid and grave.

Saval had difficulty in recognizing her: 'What's the matter, Mademoiselle?' he asked; 'you're utterly changed since the other day. You've become quite a reasonable being!'

'It's the country,' she replied; 'I *am* changed. I feel quite strange. But then, you know, I never do feel the same for two days running. One day I'm full of mischief and the next I'm like a funeral. I change like the weather, I can't think why. You see, I have all sorts of moods. Some days I could really kill people – not animals, I could never kill an animal – but people I could, and at other times I could cry for nothing at all. I get so many different ideas into my head. It depends a good deal on how you get up in the morning. When I wake, I could tell you what I'm going to be like all day. Perhaps it's one's dreams that make one like that; or perhaps the book one's just been reading has something to do with it.'

She had on a dress of white flannel, falling about her in soft, delicate folds. The loose bodice, with big pleats, set off, without too much defining, her firm, free, well-formed figure. Her slender throat rose out of a foam of heavy lace, and, whiter than her dress, curved softly, a miracle of beauty, beneath the heavy burden of her red-gold hair.

Servigny looked at her fixedly. 'Yes,' he said, 'you're adorable this evening, Mam'zelle. I should like to see you always like this.'

With a touch of her usual mischief she answered: 'Don't

247

offer me your heart, Muscade; I might take it seriously today, and that would cost you dear!'

The Marquise looked supremely happy. She was dressed in a dignified and simple robe of black, which showed the statuesque lines of her fine figure; there was a touch of red in the bodice, a garland of red carnations falling from the waist like a chain, looped up on the hip, and a red rose in her dark hair. In that simple toilette with the sanguine flowers, in those eyes with their compelling gaze, in that slow speech and infrequent gesture, her whole personality gave the idea of hidden flame.

Saval, too, seemed serious and absorbed. He now and then caressed his brown beard – pointed *à la Henri III* – with a gesture habitual to him, and appeared to be lost in thought. For several minutes no one spoke.

Then, while some trout were being served, Servigny remarked: 'Silence is a fine thing sometimes. It can often make a closer link between two people than speech – don't you think so, Marquise?'

Turning a little towards him, she replied: 'You are right. It's so beautiful to be thinking at the same moment about the same delightful things.'

She rested her ardent glance on Saval; and for some seconds they remained so, gazing into each other's eyes. A tiny movement, almost imperceptible, occurred beneath the table.

Servigny began again: 'Mam'zelle Yvette, you'll make me think you're in love if you keep on being as good as this. Now, with whom could you be in love? Let's see; shall we run through them together? I'll leave out the rank and file, and only take the chiefs. Is it Prince Kravalow?'

At this name Yvette roused herself. 'My poor Muscade, what are you thinking of? Why, the prince looks like a waxwork Russian who's taken a prize in a hairdresser's competition.'

'Good! Off with the prince! Then you must have favoured the Vicomte Pierre de Belvigne?'

This time she burst out laughing: 'Ha, ha, ha! Can't you see me hanging round Raisiné's neck' (she called him indifferently Raisiné, Malvoisie, Argenteuil, for she nicknamed everyone), 'murmuring in his ear: "Dear little Pierre, my divine Pedro, my adored Pietri, my darling little Pierrot, put down your dear, fat, ducky head for your own little wife to kiss"?'

Servigny proclaimed: 'Off with those two! That leaves the marquise's favourite – Chevalier Valréali!'

Yvette recovered all her gaiety: 'Watery Eyes? I'm sure he's a professional weeper at the Madeleine, hired out for first-class funeral processions. I always fancy I'm dead every time he looks at me.'

'Three gone! Well, then, you're smitten with the Baron Saval, here present?'

'With young Mr Rhodes? No, there's too much of him. I should feel as if I were in love with the Arc de Triomphe!'

'Then, Mam'zelle, you must be in love with me – I'm the only one of your adorers we haven't mentioned. I kept myself in the background in my modesty and prudence. It only remains for me to thank you.'

In an ecstasy of mirth she replied: 'You, Muscade? No-o. I like you very much – but I don't love you. Wait a moment, though – I don't want to discourage you. I don't love you – yet. You've got a chance – perhaps. Persevere, Muscade; be devoted, eager, humble, full of attentions and forethought, submissive to my smallest caprice, ready to do everything to please me – and, we'll see – later on.'

'But, Mam'zelle, I'd rather exhibit all those qualities after, than before, if you don't mind.'

She asked with a soubrette-like air of innocence: 'After what, Muscade?'

'Why! after you've shown that you love me!'

'Well, *pretend* that I love you; believe it if you like – !'

'But—'

'Be quiet, Muscade, that's enough.'

He gave her a military salute and held his tongue.

The sun had hidden itself behind the island, but the whole sky remained flaming like a brazier, and the still water of the river seemed turned to blood. Houses, things, people, all were reddened by the glow of the sunset. The crimson rose in the marquise's hair looked like a drop of carmine fallen from the clouds on to her head.

Choosing a moment when Yvette's eyes were far away, her mother, as though by accident, laid her hand upon Saval's. The young girl stirred, and the marquise's hand flew lightly back to adjust something in the folds of her bodice.

Servigny, who was watching them, said: 'Shall we take a turn on the island after dinner, Mam'zelle?'

She was charmed with this idea: 'Yes, yes! That will be lovely; we'll go all alone, won't we, Muscade?'

'Yes, all alone, Mam'zelle.'

And silence fell on them again.

The broad stillness of the horizon, the sleepy quiet of the evening stole over their hearts, and bodies, and voices. There are tranquil, precious hours, when it is well-nigh impossible to speak. Noiselessly the lackeys served the dinner. The blaze in the sky died down, and the slow-falling night marshalled its shadows over the earth.

'Are you going to make a long stay?' asked Saval.

'Yes,' replied the marquise, dwelling on each word; 'just so long as I am happy here.'

When the light failed, lamps were brought, and cast on the table a weird, pale light amid the vast, indefinite darkness; and instantly a rain of flies began falling on the cloth – tiny flies, which burned themselves passing over the lamp chimneys, and with scorched legs and wings powdered the damask, the plates, the glasses, with a sort of grey, dancing dust. The diners swallowed them in their wine, ate them in the sauces, saw them struggling about the bread, and all the time their faces and hands were tickled by this countless flying swarm of tiny beasts.

The wine had constantly to be thrown away, the plates covered, the courses eaten furtively, with infinite precautions. This game amused Yvette, Servigny taking care to shelter all she put to her lips, to guard her wine-glass, and hold over her head, like a roof, his outspread napkin. But the marquise, a little nauseated, began to show signs of upset nerves, and the dinner came quickly to an end.

Yvette had by no means forgotten Servigny's proposition: 'Now we're going to the island, aren't we?' she said to him.

'Be sure not to stay long,' advised her mother languidly. 'We are coming with you as far as the ferry.'

They started along the towing-path, two by two, the young girl and her friend in front. Behind, they could hear the marquise and Saval talking very low and very quick. All was black, velvet black, as black as ink; but the sky, swarming with grains of fire, seemed to be sowing them in the river, for the dark water was powdered with stars. The frogs were croaking now, raising all along the banks their rolling, monotonous chant; and innumerable nightingales flung their soft song into the calm air.

All of a sudden Yvette said: 'Why! they're not following! Where are they?' And she called out: 'Mother!'

No voice replied. The young girl continued: 'They can't be far off, at any rate; I heard them just now.'

'They may have turned back,' murmured Servigny. 'Perhaps your mother was cold.' He drew her along.

In front of them glowed a light. It came from the inn of

Martinet, fisherman and vendor of refreshments. At the call of the strollers a man came out of the house; they embarked in a broad punt moored in the middle of the reeds at the water's edge. The ferryman took his oars, and the advance of the heavy boat awoke the stars sleeping on the water, making them dance a frenzied dance, which little by little came to rest again behind them.

They touched the other bank, and stepped out under the great trees. The freshness of damp earth floated there, below those high, clustering branches, which seemed to harbour as many nightingales as leaves. A distant piano began playing a popular waltz.

Servigny had taken Yvette's arm, and very quietly he slipped his hand round her waist and pressed it gently. 'What are you thinking of?' he said.

'Nothing! I'm just happy.'

'So you don't care for me at all, then?'

'Of course I care for you, Muscade; I care a great deal; but do drop all that now! It's too beautiful here to listen to your nonsense!'

He pressed her against him, for all she tried with little jerks to get free, and through the soft texture of her flannel dress he could feel the warmth of her body.

'Yvette!' he stammered.

'Well, what?'

'*I* care for *you*.'

'You're not in earnest, Muscade?'

'I am; I've cared for you a long time.'

She was trying all the time to get away from him, trying to pull away her arm, crushed between them. And they walked with difficulty, hindered by this link and by their struggles, zigzagging like a couple of drunkards.

He knew not what to say to her next, feeling it was impossible to speak to a young girl as he would have spoken to a woman; in his perplexity he kept seeking for the right thing to do, wondering whether she consented or simply did not understand – ransacking his brain for just the right, tender, irrevocable words.

He kept on saying: 'Yvette! No – but – Yvette!'

Then, suddenly, he hazarded a flying kiss upon her cheek.

She swerved a little, and said in a vexed voice: 'Oh! how silly you are! Why can't you leave me alone?'

The tone of her voice told nothing of what she was feeling or wishing; but, judging that she was not so very angry, he put his lips to the nape of her neck, close to the lowest-growing golden down of her hair, that fascinating spot he had coveted so long.

Then she struggled hard to escape, with jerks and starts. But he held her tight, and throwing his other hand upon her shoulder, forced her face round to his own, and stole from her lips a maddening, long kiss.

She slipped down through his arms with a quick undulation of her whole body, dived, and freeing herself swiftly from his embrace, disappeared in the darkness with a great rustling of skirts, like the noise of a bird taking flight.

He stood for a moment quite still, astounded by her suppleness and her disappearance, but, hearing no further sound, he called softly: 'Yvette!' There was no answer. He started walking, probing the darkness with his gaze, searching the bushes for the white blur that her dress must surely make. It was all dark. Again he cried, and louder: 'Mam'zelle Yvette!'

The nightingales stopped singing.

He hastened on, vaguely alarmed, calling louder and louder: 'Mam'zelle Yvette! Mam'zelle Yvette!'

Nothing! He stopped and listened. The whole island was still – scarcely a shiver among the leaves above his head. Alone, the frogs continued their sonorous croaking on the banks.

Then he proceeded to range from copse to copse, descending to the steep, bushy bank of the main stream, and returning to the bare, flat bank of the backwater. He went on till he found himself opposite Bougival, came back to *La Grenouillière*, searched in all the thickets, crying continually: 'Mam'zelle Yvette! Where are you? Do answer! It was only a joke! I say, do answer! Don't keep me hunting for you like this!'

A distant clock began to strike. He counted the strokes: Midnight! He had been patrolling the island for two hours. Then he thought that perhaps she had gone home, and he returned also, very uneasy, making the round by the bridge.

A servant, asleep in an armchair, was waiting up in the hall.

Servigny woke him and asked: 'Has Mlle Yvette been in long? I was obliged to leave her over there, to pay a call.'

The man replied: 'Oh yes, M. le Duc, Mlle came in before ten o'clock.'

He reached his room and went to bed, but his eyes remained wide open, he was unable to sleep. That stolen kiss had disturbed him, and he mused: What was she meaning? What was she thinking? What did she know? How pretty she was, how maddening!

His senses, jaded by the life he led, by all the women he had known, all the loves he had exploited, awoke before this strange child, so fresh, so exciting, so inexplicable.

He heard the clock strike one, then two. Assuredly he would never get to sleep! He was hot, perspiring, the blood pulsing hard in his temples; he got up and opened the window.

A puff of fresh air came in, and he drew in a long, deep breath of it. The night was silent, densely dark, unmoving. But suddenly he perceived before him, in the depths of the garden, a glowing speck, like a little live coal. 'Hallo!' he thought; 'a cigar! That must be Saval'; and he called out softly: 'Léon!'

A voice replied: 'Is that you, Jean?'

'Yes; wait for me, I'm coming down.'

He dressed, went out, and joined his friend, who was smoking, astride of an iron garden-chair.

'What are you up to at this time of night?'

'I? Resting!' replied Saval, with a laugh.

Servigny pressed his hand: 'My compliments, my dear fellow. And I – am not.'

'That's to say?'

'That's to say that Yvette and her mother are not alike.'

'What's happened? Tell me!'

Servigny recounted his efforts, and their failure. 'This child beats me altogether,' he went on; 'just think – I haven't been able to get to sleep. What an odd thing a young girl is! She looks simplicity itself, but one really knows nothing about her. A woman who has lived, and loved, and knows what life is, one sees into at once. When it's a question of a young girl, on the contrary, one can't deduce anything at all. At the bottom of my heart, I begin to think she's making a fool of me.'

Saval tilted his chair, and said very slowly: 'Take care, my dear fellow, she's leading you towards marriage. Remember all the illustrious examples. By that same process Mlle de Montijo, who was at any rate well-born, became an empress. Don't play at being Napoleon!'

'Don't be afraid of that!' murmured Servigny; 'I'm neither a fool nor an emperor, and you must be one or the other to do anything so mad. But, I say, are you sleepy?'

'No, not a bit!'

'Then let's go for a stroll along the river!'

'All right!'

They opened the gate, and started along the river-side towards Marly. It was the chill hour that precedes the dawn, the hour of deepest sleep, of deepest rest, of profound quiet. Even the vague noises of the night were hushed. Nightingales no longer sang; frogs had ceased their uproar; alone, some unknown creature, a bird, perhaps, was making somewhere a sound as of a grating saw, feeble, monotonous, and regular, like something mechanical at work.

Servigny, who had his moments of poetry as well as of philosophy, said all of a sudden: 'Look here! This girl is too much for me. In arithmetic, one and one make two. In love, one and one ought to make one, but they make two for all that. Have you ever felt this longing to absorb a woman into yourself, or to be absorbed in her? I'm not speaking of the animal instinct, but of that moral, mental torment to be at one with her, to open all one's heart and soul to her, to penetrate to the very depths of her thought. And yet one never really knows her, never fathoms all the ups and downs of her will, her wishes, her opinions; never unravels even a little the mystery of that soul so near you, the soul behind those eyes that look at you, as clear as water, as transparent as if there were nothing hidden behind; the soul speaking to you through lips you love so that they seem to be your very own; the soul which utter its thoughts to you, one by one in words, and yet remains further from you than those stars are from each other, and more inscrutable. Odd, isn't it?'

Saval replied: 'I don't ask so much from them. I don't look past their eyes. I don't bother myself much about the inside, but a good deal about the out.'

'The fact is,' murmured Servigny, 'that Yvette is abnormal. I wonder how she'll greet me this morning!'

Just as they reached Marly they noticed that the sky was growing lighter; cocks were beginning to crow in the poultry-houses, and the sound came to them deadened by the thickness of the walls. A bird chirped in an enclosure on the left, repeating ceaselessly a simple, comic little flourish.

'It's about time we went home,' remarked Saval.

They returned. And Servigny, entering his room, noticed the horizon all rosy through the still open window. He closed the shutter, drew and pulled together the thick curtains, went to bed, and at last fell asleep. He dreamed of Yvette all through his slumbers. A singular noise awoke him. He sat up in bed, listened, and heard nothing. Then suddenly, against his shutters came a curious crackling like falling hail.

He jumped out of bed, ran to the window, threw it open and saw Yvette standing in the garden path, flinging great handfuls of gravel up into his face.

She was dressed in pink, with a large, broad-brimmed straw hat trimmed with one cavalier plume, and laughing a sly, malicious laugh, she cried: 'Well, Muscade! are you still asleep? What *can* you have been doing last night to wake up so late? Did you meet with an adventure, my poor Muscade?'

He was dazzled by the brilliant daylight suddenly striking on eyes still heavy with fatigue, and surprised at the young girl's mocking serenity.

'Coming, coming, Mam'zelle!' he called back; 'just a second to dip my head in water, and I'll be down.'

'Well, be quick,' she cried; 'it's ten o'clock. And I've a splendid plan to tell you about; a conspiracy we're going to carry out. Breakfast's at eleven, you know.'

He found her sitting on a bench, with a book on her knees. She took his arm with a friendly familiarity, as frank and gay as if nothing had happened the night before, and drawing him away to the end of the garden, said: 'Now, this is my plan. We're just going to disobey mother, and you're going to take me to *La Grenouillière*. I want to see it. Mother says that decent women can't go there. But I don't care whether they can or can't. You will take me, won't you, Muscade? We'll have such fun with all those boating people!'

There was a sweet scent about her, and he could not determine what that vague and delicate aroma was. It was not one of her mother's heavy perfumes, but a subtle fragrance in which he seemed to catch a suspicion of iris powder, and possibly a touch of verbena.

Whence came that undefinable scent? From her dress, her hair, her skin? He wondered, and as she spoke quite close to him, her fresh breath came full in his face, and that too seemed delicious to inhale. Then he fancied that this fleeting perfume, so impossible to put a name to, was perhaps conjured up by his fascinated senses – nothing but a sort of delusive emanation of her young, seductive grace.

'That's settled, then, Muscade?' she said. 'It will be very hot after breakfast, and mother's sure not to wish to go out. She's always so limp when it's hot. We'll leave her with your friend, and you shall take me. We shall be supposed to be going into the wood. Oh, if you only knew how much I want to see *La Grenouillière*!'

They came to the gate opposite the river. A ray of sunlight fell on the slumberous, glistening stream. A light heat mist was rising, the fume of evaporated water, which lay on the surface of the river in a thin, shining vapour. Now and then a boat would pass, a rapid yawl, or clumsy wherry, and they heard in the distance short or prolonged whistles, of trains pouring the Sunday crowd from Paris into the surrounding country, and of steam-boats giving warning of their approach to the lock at Marly.

But a little bell rang, announcing breakfast, and they went in. The meal was a silent one, almost. A heavy July noon crushed the Earth, weighed down all her creatures. The heat seemed nearly solid, paralysing to body and spirit. Torpid words refused to leave the lips, and movement was laborious, as if the air had acquired the power of resistance, and become a difficult medium. Yvette alone, though silent, seemed brisk and nervously impatient. When dessert was over she said: 'Now, shall we go for a walk in the wood? It would be so jolly under the trees!'

The marquise, who seemed quite done up, murmured: 'Are you mad? As if one could go out in such a heat!'

Delighted, the young girl went on: 'All right, then! We'll leave the baron to keep you company. Muscade and I are going to climb the hill and sit on the grass and read!'

She turned towards Servigny: 'Well, is that settled?' she said.

'At your service, Mam'zelle,' he replied.

She flew off to get her hat.

The marquise shrugged her shoulders:

'She's mad, really,' she sighed. Then, with languid fatigue in the slow, amorous gesture, she stretched her fine, white hand to the baron, who kissed it solemnly.

Yvette and Servigny started. Following the river at first, they crossed the bridge, went on to the island, and sat themselves down on the bank of the main stream under the willows, for it was still too early to go to *La Grenouillière*.

The young girl at once drew a book from her pocket and said with a laugh: 'Now, Muscade, you're going to read to me!'

She held the book out to him.

He made a gesture towards flight. 'I, Mam'zelle? But I don't know how to read!'

She went on gravely: 'Come, now, no excuses, no explanations! There you are again, you see – a fine sort of suitor! "Everything for nothing", that's your motto, isn't it?'

He took the book, opened it, and was amazed. It was a treatise on entomology – a history of the ant, by an English writer. And he remained silent under the impression that she was chaffing, till at last she grew impatient, and said: 'Come, begin!'

'Is this for a bet, or is it simply a whim?'

'No my dear sir, I saw that book at a book-shop. They told me it was the best thing written on ants; I thought it would be amusing to learn about the life of the little beasts, and watch them running about in the grass at the same time; so now, begin!'

She stretched herself out on her face, her eyes fixed on the grass, and he began reading: 'Without doubt the anthropoid apes are, of all animals, those which most nearly approach to man in their anatomical structure; but if we consider the habits of ants, their organization into societies, their immense communities, their dwellings, the roads they construct, their custom of keeping domestic animals, and sometimes even of having slaves, we are forced to admit that they have the right to claim a place near to man on the ladder of intelligence . . .' And he went on in a monotonous voice, stopping now and then to ask: 'Isn't that enough?'

She shook her head, and having caught a wandering ant on the point of a blade of grass she had plucked, was amusing herself by making it run from end to end of the stalk, which she turned the moment the creature had reached one extremity. She listened with a quiet, concentrated attention to all the surprising details in the life of these frail creatures, their subterranean works, their habit of rearing, stabling, and feeding greenfly, so as to obtain the sugary liquor secreted by them, just as we ourselves keep cows in stables; their customs of domesticating little blind insects to keep their establishments clean, and of going to war and bringing back slaves to take such care of the conquerors that the latter even lose the habit of feeding themselves.

And gradually, as though a motherly tenderness had awakened in her heart for this beastie, so minute and so intelligent, Yvette made the ant climb up her finger, and looked at it with soft eyes, quite longing to kiss it. And as Servigny read of how they live in a commonwealth, how they have sports and friendly trials of strength and skill, the young girl in her enthusiasm actually attempted to kiss the insect, which escaped from her finger and ran about her face. Whereupon she gave as piercing a scream as if she had been threatened by some terrible danger, and, with the wildest gestures, brushed at her cheek to get rid of the creature. Servigny, in fits of laughter, caught it on her forehead, and planted a long kiss on the spot he had taken it from, without her turning away her face.

Then, rising, she declared: 'I like that better than a novel. Now let's go to *La Grenouillière*.'

They came to a part of the island planted like a park with huge, shady trees. Along the river, where boats kept gliding by, some couples were strolling under the branches; work-girls and their lovers, who slouched along in their shirt-sleeves, with a dissipated, jaded air, tall hats on the back of their heads, and coats over their arms; citizens, too, and their families, the women in their Sunday clothes, the children trotting around their parents like broods of chickens.

A distant, continuous hubbub of human voices, a dull and

muttering clamour, proclaimed the favourite spot of the river crowd. They came in sight of it all of a sudden – a huge barge crowned with a roof, moored to the bank, and crowded with males and females, some seated drinking at little tables, others on their feet, shouting, singing, howling, dancing, capering, to the sound of a wheezy piano all out of tune and as vibrant as an old kettle.

Great red-haired girls, displaying all the curves of their opulent figures, were promenading round, three parts drunk, with provocation in their eyes and obscenities on their crimson lips. Others danced wildly in front of young men dressed in rowing shorts, cotton vests, and jockey caps. And the whole place exhaled an odour of heat and violet powder, of perfumery and perspiration.

Those seated at the tables were gulping down white, and red, and yellow, and green drinks; shouting and yelling all the time, yielding apparently to a violent longing to make a noise, an animal desire to fill their ears and brains with uproar.

Every minute or so, a swimmer, standing erect on the roof, would spring into the water, showering splashes on those at the nearest tables, who yelled at him like savages.

On the river a fleet of boats kept passing. Long, slender, gliding skiffs, lifted along by the strokes of oarsmen with bare arms, whose muscles rolled under the burnt skin. Their dames, in red or blue flannel, with blue or red sunshades open, dazzling in the brilliant sunlight, lolled on the rudder seats, and seemed to float along the water in their slumberous immobility. A tipsy student, bent on showing off, was rowing a kind of windmill stroke, and knocking up against all the boats, whose occupants greeted him with howls. He just missed drowning two swimmers, then disappeared aghast – followed by the jeers of the crowd packed on the floating café.

In the midst of this raffish medley Yvette strolled, all radiant, on Servigny's arm; she seemed quite content to be jostled by these dubious people, and stared undisturbed with her friendly eyes at the women.

'Look at that one, Muscade!' she said; 'what pretty hair! They *do* look as if they were enjoying themselves!'

The pianist, an oarsman in red, hatted with a sort of enormous parasol of straw, dashed into a waltz; Yvette, seizing her companion round the waist, carried him off with the fury she always threw into her dancing. They went on so long and so frenziedly that everyone looked at them. Some mounted the tables and beat a kind of measure with their feet; others clinked their glasses. The musician seemed suddenly to go mad, and, throwing his hands about, banged the keys with wild contortions of his whole body, nodding his head passionately under its vast cover. All at once he stopped, and, sliding to the floor, flattened himself out at full length, enshrouded under his headgear, as if he had perished of fatigue.

A roar of laughter burst out all over the café, and everyone applauded. Four friends hastened forward as if there had been an accident, and picking up their comrade, carried him off by his four limbs, after carefully depositing on his stomach the sort of roof he had worn on his head.

A joker, following them, intoned the *De Profundis*; and a procession was formed behind the counterfeit corpse, winding along the paths of the island, and gathering in its wake topers, and strollers, and everyone it met.

Yvette flew along delighted, laughing heartily, chatting with any and everyone, half wild with the noise and excitement. Young men looked right into her eyes and pushed against her; their glances were full of meaning, and Servigny began to fear the adventure might turn out ill.

The procession, however, continued its course, faster and faster, for the four bearers had begun to race, followed by the yelling crowd.

But suddenly they made for the bank, stopped dead at the edge, swung their comrade for a second, and, letting go all together, shot him into the river.

An immense shout of delight burst from every mouth, while the bewildered pianist shivered, swore, coughed, spat out the water, and, sticking in the mud, strove to remount the bank. His hat, floating down stream, was brought back by a boat.

Yvette, hopping with joy and clapping her hands, kept crying, 'Oh! Muscade! oh! Muscade! What fun!'

But Servigny, who had recovered his seriousness, was watching her uneasily, annoyed to see her so thoroughly at home in these dubious surroundings. He instinctively revolted; for there was in him the natural aversion to vulgarity of every well-bred man, who, even in letting himself go, avoids familiarities too vile, contacts too soiling.

'Great Scot!' he thought, marvelling: 'you must have some nice blood in you, my dear!' He felt inclined to use out loud the familiarity that already he applied to her in thought; the familiarity men use to women who are common property, the first time they set eyes on them.

In his thoughts he hardly distinguished her now from the auburn-haired creatures who brushed against them, bawling coarse words in their raucous voices. The air was full of those words – gross, short, and sounding – that seemed to hover over their heads, born of the crowd as flies are of a dunghill. They appeared to surprise and shock no one, and to pass unnoticed by Yvette.

'Muscade, I want to bathe,' she said; 'we'll go right out into mid-stream.'

'Very well,' he replied; and they went off to the office for bathing-dresses. She was ready first, and waited for him, standing on the bank, and smiling, under the eyes of all. They started side by side into the sun-warmed water.

Her swimming was full of a sort of ecstatic delight; and lapped by the ripples, shivering with a sensuous joy, she rose with every stroke as if she would spring out of the river. He followed with difficulty, panting, and by no means pleased to find himself so second-rate a performer. Then, slackening speed, she turned over abruptly and floated, with her arms crossed and her eyes lost in the blue of the sky. He gazed at her stretched thus on the surface of the water, at the curving lines of her body, her bosom firm and round under the stuff of the clinging gown, her half-submerged limbs, her bare calves gleaming through the water, her little feet peeping out.

There she was from head to foot, as if thus displayed on purpose to tempt, and once more to fool him. His nerves were all on edge with the intensity of his exasperated longing. Suddenly she turned over again, and said laughingly:

'Oh, you do look funny!'

Piqued by her raillery, and possessed by the spiteful rage of a baffled lover, he gave way suddenly to a subtle desire for reprisals, a longing to avenge himself and wound her.

'So that sort of life would suit you?' he said.

'What life?' she asked, with her most innocent air.

'Don't play the fool with me! You know very well what I mean!'

'No, honour bright.'

'Now, let's have done with this nonsense. Will you, or won't you?'

'I don't in the least understand.'

'You're not so stupid as that. Besides, I told you last night.'

'What? I forget.'

'That I love you.'

'You?'

'I.'

'Rubbish!'

'I swear it.'

'Very well, then; prove it.'

'That's just what I want.'

'How do you mean, what you want——?'

'To prove.'

'Very well, do.'

'You didn't say that last night.'

'You didn't propose anything.'

'This is absurd!'

'Besides, it's not to me you ought to speak.'

'You're very kind. To whom then?'

'Why, to mother, of course!'

He gave a shout of laughter.

'To your mother? Oh no! That's a little too much.'

She had suddenly become very serious, and looking straight into his eyes, said: 'Listen, Muscade, if you really love me enough to marry me, speak to mother first; I'll give you my answer afterwards.'

He still thought she was chaffing him, and losing his temper completely, cried, 'Mam'zelle, what do you take me for?'

She still gazed at him with her soft, clear eyes; and hesitating, said, 'I still don't understand you, really!'

Then, with something harsh and stinging in his voice, he

exclaimed, 'Now then, Yvette, once for all let's have done with this absurd farce; it's been going on too long. You're playing the little simpleton; believe me, it's a rôle that doesn't suit you. You know well enough it can't be a question of marriage between us – but of love. I told you I loved you – it's the truth, and I say it again, I love you. Don't pretend not to understand me any longer, and don't treat me as if I were an idiot.'

They were face to face in the water, keeping themselves up simply by little movements of their hands. She remained quite still for some seconds, as if she could not decide to take in the sense of his words, then suddenly blushed to the roots of her hair. The whole of her face was flooded with crimson from her throat to her ears, which grew almost purple, and, without answering a word, she fled towards the bank, swimming with all her strength. He could not catch her up, and gasped with the effort of following. He saw her leave the water, snatch up her cloak and gain her cabin, without once turning her head. He was a long time dressing, completely puzzled as to what to do next, racking his brains for what to say to her, and asking himself whether he ought to apologize or to persevere. When he was ready, she was gone, alone. He walked home slowly, anxious and perturbed.

The Marquise, on Saval's arm, was strolling round the path encircling the lawn.

On seeing Servigny she said with the air of serene indolence she had worn since the night before: 'What did I tell you about going out in such a heat? There's Yvette with a sort of sunstroke.

She's gone to lie down. The poor child was as red as a poppy, and has got a frightful headache. You must have been walking in the hot sun; you know you've been up to some nonsense – you're just as crazy as she!'

The young girl did not come down to dinner. When asked what she would have, she replied, without opening the door, that she was not hungry – she had locked herself in – and begged only to be left alone. The two young men departed by the ten o'clock train, promising to come again on the following Thursday; and the Marquise sat down to dream happily at her open window, while in the distance the orchestra at *La Grenouillière* flung its flighty music into the solemn silence of the night.

There were times when a passion for love would sweep over her, as a passion for riding or rowing will seize on a man; a mood of sudden tenderness would take possession of her like an illness. These passions pounced on her, invaded her body and soul, maddened, enervated, or overwhelmed her, according as they were of an inspiring, violent, dramatic, or sentimental nature.

She was one of those women born to love and to be loved. From a very low beginning she had climbed by means of that love, of which she had made a profession almost without knowing. Behaving intuitively with innate ability, she accepted money and kisses without distinction, employing her wonderful instinct in the natural, unreasoning way that animals, made sagacious by their daily needs, have. She had had many lovers for whom she had felt no tenderness, yet at whose embraces she had known no disgust. She endured all their caresses with a quiet indifference, just as, when travelling, a man eats all sorts of foods to keep himself alive. But, now and then, her heart or her flesh took fire, and she gave way to a real passion, which lasted weeks or even months, according to the physical or moral qualities of her lover. These were the perfect moments of her life. She loved with all her soul, with all her body, with enthusiasm, with ecstasy. She cast herself into that love as one flings oneself into a river to drown; and she let herself be swept away, ready to die, if so she must, intoxicated, maddened, yet infinitely happy. Each time she imagined that never before had she felt anything so wonderful; and she would have been vastly astonished if you had recalled to her all the different men over whom she had dreamed passionately, the whole night long, gazing at the stars.

Saval had captured her, body and soul. Under the spell of his image she mused over precious memories, deep in the supreme calm of fulfilled happiness, of present and certain joy.

A sound from behind made her turn. Yvette had just come in, dressed as she had been all day, but pale now, with the brilliant eyes that great fatigue will cause.

She leaned against the side of the window, opposite her mother.

'I've something to tell you,' she said.

The Marquise looked at her in surprise. She was fond of her daughter in a selfish sort of fashion, proud of her beauty as one might be of great wealth; she was herself still too handsome to be jealous, and too lazy to make the plans that others credited her with; at the same time she was too subtle not to be aware of the girl's value.

'I'm listening, child,' she said; 'what is it?'

Yvette gazed at her as if she would read the depths of her soul, as if she meant to grasp all the shades of expression that her coming words might awaken.

'It's — Something extraordinary happened today!'

'What?'

'M. de Servigny told me he loved me.'

The Marquise waited uneasily, but as Yvette said nothing, she asked: 'How did he tell you that? Let me hear!'

Yvette nestled down in her favourite attitude at her mother's feet, and squeezing her hands, said: 'He asked me to marry him.'

Mme Obardi made an abrupt movement of stupefaction, and cried out: 'Servigny! You must be mad.'

Yvette had not taken her eyes off her mother's face, searching for the true meaning of her astonishment.

In a grave voice she asked: 'Why mad? Why shouldn't M. de Servigny want to marry me?'

The Marquise stammered in embarrassment: 'You've made a mistake — it's out of the question. You couldn't have heard — you misunderstood. M. de Servigny is too rich for you, and too — too — Parisian ever to marry.'

Yvette got up slowly. 'But if he loves me, mother, as he says he does?' she asked.

Her mother went on with a certain impatience: 'I thought

you were big enough and knew enough about things not to have any such ideas as that. Servigny is a selfish man of the world. He'll only marry a woman of his own rank and fortune. If he did ask you to marry him, he simply meant—'

The Marquise, unable to speak out her suspicions, was silent for a moment, then went on: 'There, don't bother me; go to bed.'

And the young girl, as if she now knew all she wanted, replied obediently: 'Yes, mother.'

Just as she was going out of the door, however, the Marquise called: 'And what about your sunstroke?'

'I never had one. It was all this other affair.'

'We'll talk about that again,' added the Marquise; 'but take care not to be alone with him after this; you may be quite sure he doesn't mean to marry you, only to – to – compromise you.'

She could find no better words to express her thought. Yvette went back to her room.

Mme Obardi set to work to reflect.

Living for years in the serene atmosphere of gilded love, she had carefully guarded her mind from every thought that could preoccupy, trouble or sadden it. Never once had she allowed herself to face the question of what would become of Yvette; it would be time enough to think about that when the difficulty arose. Her courtesan's instinct told her that her daughter could never marry a rich and well-born man save by some quite improbable chance, one of those surprises of love that have placed adventuresses upon thrones.

She was not counting on any such thing, moreover, being too self-centred to make any plans not directly concerned with her own affairs.

Yvette would live for love, as her mother had done, no doubt. But the Marquise had never dared to ask herself when or how it would come about. And now here was her daughter, suddenly, without preparation, demanding of her an answer to one of those questions to which no answer could be given, forcing her to take up a definite attitude in an affair so difficult, so delicate, so dangerous in every way, so disturbing to her conscience, the conscience a mother is bound to have towards her child, in matters such as these. She had too much natural acumen, slumbering, it is true, but never quite asleep, to be deceived for a moment as to Servigny's intentions, for she had acquired a wide knowledge of men, and particularly of men of his kind. So, at the first words Yvette had spoken, she had been unable to help that exclamation: 'Servigny marry you! you must be mad!'

Why had he made use of such a stale trick? He, that shrewd man of the world, that pleasure-loving rake? What would he do now? And how should she warn the child more plainly, how defend her? Obviously she was capable of making a complete fool of herself. Who would have believed that that great girl had remained so simple, so ignorant, so artless?

And the Marquise, puzzled, and already fatigued with too much thinking, racked her brains for what to do now, without finding any way out of so truly embarrassing a situation.

Tired of this bother she suddenly decided: 'Ah, well! I'll watch them carefully, and act according to circumstances; if necessary, I'll speak to Servigny; he's sharp enough to understand a hint.'

She did not ask herself what she would say to him, nor what he might reply, nor what sort of arrangement could be arrived at between them, but happy at having smoothed out this troublesome matter without having had to make any decision, she went back to dreams of her Saval. With eyes lost in the night, turned towards the glowing haze that hung over Paris, she wafted kisses towards the great city, flinging them with both hands into the darkness, one after another, kisses without number; and in a low voice, as though still speaking to him, she murmured: 'I love you! I love you!'

III

YVETTE, TOO, DID not sleep. Like her mother, she leaned on her elbows at the open window, and tears, the first tears of real sadness, filled her eyes.

Till now she had grown up in the heedless, confident serenity of a joyous youth. What was there indeed to make her brood, reflect, or wonder? What to make her different from other young girls? Why should doubt, or fear, or painful suspicions visit her? She had seemed knowing because she had seemed to talk knowingly, having, naturally, caught up the tone, the manner, the risky sayings of the people round about her. But in reality she knew little more of life than a child brought up in a convent; her audacious speeches were like a parrot's, and came rather from her feminine faculty for assimilation and mimicry, than from any daring depth of knowledge.

She talked of love as the son of a painter or musician will talk of painting or music at the age of ten or twelve. She knew – or rather suspected – what sort of mystery lay behind that word; too many jokes had been whispered in her hearing for her inno-cence to have remained entirely unenlightened. But was that a reason for concluding that other families were not like her own?

Everyone kissed her mother's hand with ostentatious respect; their friends were all titled, and all were, or appeared to be, rich; all talked familiarly of royal personages. Two princes of the blood had actually come to some of her mother's evenings. How was she to know? Then, too, she was by nature simple, and far from inquisitive; she had none of her mother's intuitive perception. Her mind was undisturbed, she was too much in love with life to worry over things which might have seemed suspicious to a quieter, more thoughtful, more reserved nature – to one less open-hearted, less exultant.

And now, in a moment, Servigny, with a few words, whose brutality she had felt rather than comprehended, had roused in her a sudden and at first unreasoning disquiet, which had grad-ually become a galling dread. She had fled home like a wounded creature, pierced to the heart by those words which she kept repeating over and over again, in the effort to sound all their meaning, and grasp their true import: 'You know well enough it can't be a question of marriage between us – only of love!'

What had he meant by that? And why had he insulted her? There was clearly something that she did not know, something secret or shameful! No doubt she was the only one in ignorance. But what was it? She felt scared, overwhelmed, as if she had discovered some hidden infamy, treachery in some beloved friend – one of those disasters that wring the heart.

And she went on brooding, reflecting, searching, weeping, consumed by her doubts and fears.

But at last her young, buoyant nature reasserted itself. She began constructing a story, an abnormal and dramatic situation woven out of many memories of the many romantic novels she had read. She recalled startling turns of fortune, sombre, heart-breaking plots, and out of the jumble made up a life-story of herself, to adorn this half-hidden mystery surrounding her life.

She was already a little less miserable, and, wrapped in reverie, began lifting mysterious veils, imagining impossible complications, a thousand curious and terrible events, whose very strangeness had a fascination.

Could she, by any chance, be the natural child of some prince? Her poor mother, seduced and abandoned, created Marquise by the King, Victor Emanuel himself perhaps, and obliged to fly from the wrath of the family? Or was she not more likely the offshoot of a guilty passion, abandoned by very illustrious parents, and rescued by the Marquise, who had adopted her and brought her up?

And fresh ideas kept coming into her head, which she accepted or rejected according to her fancy. She began to have a sort of tender pity for herself, happy and sad, too, in the depths of her heart, yet on the whole content to find herself a heroine of romance, who would have to show herself capable of playing a dignified and noble part.

And she thought over the rôle she would assume, according to these various sets of circumstances. She pictured it vaguely, this rôle, like a character of M. Scribe's or Mme Sand's. It should be made up of devotion, nobility, self-sacrifice, greatness of soul, tenderness, and beautiful speeches. Her flexible nature almost rejoiced in this new prospect.

So she stayed until the evening, thinking what she was going to do, and how best she should set to work to drag the truth out of the Marquise. And when night was come, the hour of tragic situations, she had at last devised this simple but subtle trick to obtain what she wanted:

To tell her mother suddenly that Servigny had asked her to marry him.

At the news Mme Obardi, in her surprise, would certainly let fall some word, some ejaculation that would throw light into her daughter's soul.

And Yvette had forthwith carried out her plan.

She had expected an outburst of astonishment, an outpouring of love, some disclosure full of caresses and tears.

And behold! Her mother, neither astounded nor distressed, had only seemed annoyed; and from the embarrassed, displeased, troubled tone of her reply, the young girl, in whom had suddenly awakened all a woman's shrewd subtlety and dissimulation, understood that she must not insist, that the mystery was of some other kind, more painful to learn, probably, and that she would have to guess it for herself. She had gone back to her room with a heavy heart, in dire distress, crushed now by the sense of a real misfortune, without knowing exactly whence or wherefore came this new feeling. Leaning on her elbows at the window, she wept.

She sobbed a long time, without thinking at all now, or trying to make any more discoveries; then little by little fatigue overcame her, and her eyes closed. She fell for a few minutes into that unrefreshing slumber of people too exhausted to make the effort of undressing and getting to bed – a heavy sleep, broken by sudden starts, as her head kept slipping between her hands. She did not go to bed till the first gleam of dawn, when the penetrating chill of the early morning forced her to leave the window.

The next day, and the day after, she maintained a reserved and melancholy demeanour.

A ceaseless ferment of thought was going on within her; she was learning to watch, and deduce, and reflect. A new and lurid light seemed cast on everyone and everything around; she was beginning to look with suspicion on all she had once believed in, even on her mother. During those two days all kinds of surmises flitted through her brain, and, facing each possible contingency, she flung herself, with all the abruptness of her headlong, unbalanced nature, from one extreme decision to another.

On the Wednesday she fixed on a plan which embodied a complete scheme of conduct, and a system of espionage. She got up on Thursday morning with the resolve to outvie the subtlety of a detective, to be armed for battle against all the world. She even resolved to take for her motto the two words, 'Myself alone!' and considered for over an hour how they would make the best effect engraved round the monogram on her writing paper.

Saval and Servigny arrived at ten o'clock. The young girl held out her hand to them quite simply, but coolly, saying in a friendly, rather grave voice: 'How do you do, Muscade?'

'Thank you, Mam'zelle, pretty well – and you?'

He watched her. 'What game is she up to now?' he asked himself.

The Marquise had taken Saval's arm, and he gave his own to Yvette; they all sauntered round the lawn, winding in and out of the clumps of bushes and trees. Yvette moved along reflectively, her eyes fixed on the gravel path; she hardly seemed to listen to her companion, hardly answered him. All at once she asked: 'Are you really my friend, Muscade?'

'I am, Mam'zelle.'

'Really, really and truly?'

'Absolutely your friend, Mam'zelle, body and soul.'

'Friend enough not to tell me a fib for once, just for this once?'

'Even for twice, if necessary.'

'Friend enough to tell me the whole truth, the whole horrid truth?'

'Yes, Mam'zelle.'

'All right then: what do you really, *really* think of Prince Kravalow?'

'Phe-e-ew!'

'There, you see, you're getting ready to tell me a fib directly.'

'Not at all, I'm merely choosing the exact words. Well, then, Prince Kravalow is a Russian – a Russian of the Russians, speaks Russian, was born in Russia, who quite possibly had a passport for France, and has nothing false about him but his name and his title.'

She looked straight into his eyes: 'You mean that he's . . .'

After a moment's hesitation he replied: 'An adventurer, Mam'zelle.'

'Thank you. And the Chevalier Valréali is no better, I suppose?'

'Just so.'

'And M. de Belvigne?'

'Ah! he's different. He's a gentleman – provincial, of course; honourable – up to a certain point – but a little burnt about the wings, from having flown too fast—'

'And you?'

He answered without hesitation: 'I? Oh, I'm what you call a

"gay bird" – of good enough family, who once had brains, and has hashed them up making jokes; who once had a constitution, and has run through it playing the fool; who once had a certain value perhaps, and has squandered it doing nothing. To sum up, I've got money, and experience of life, a complete absence of prejudice, a pretty fair contempt for men, including women, profound consciousness of my own futility, and vast toleration of riff-raff in general. However, I've still got my moments of frankness, you see, and I'm even capable of affection, as you *might* see – if you liked. With these defects and qualities, I put myself, morally and physically, at your service, to dispose of as you please. There!'

She did not laugh; but seemed, as she listened, to be weighing the meaning of his words.

She began again: 'What do you think of the Comtesse de Lammy?'

He said very quickly: 'Ah! Allow me to give no opinion on women.'

'On none?'

'None.'

'Then, it's because you think very badly of them all. Come, now, can't you think of a single exception?'

His insolent smile that was half a sneer reappeared, and with the cynical audacity he used like a weapon, both for attack and defence, said: 'Present company always excepted.'

She flushed a little, but asked quite calmly: 'Well, what do you think of *me*?'

'You *will* have it? Very well. I think that you're a person of excellent practical sense, or, if you like it better, of excellent common sense, understanding perfectly how to mask your game, amuse yourself at other people's expense, hide your plans, throw out your nets, and wait calmly – for the result.'

'Is that all?'

'That's all.'

'I shall make you change that opinion, Muscade,' she said very gravely; and joined her mother, who was strolling languidly along with her head bent, like a woman talking of tender, intimate things, and tracing as she went patterns, or perhaps letters, on the gravel path with the point of her sunshade. She was not looking at Saval, but speaking on and on in a slow voice, leaning on his arm, and pressing against him. Yvette suddenly fixed her eyes upon her; a suspicion, so vague that she could not seize it, a sensation rather than a doubt, flitted through her brain, like the shadow of a wind-chased cloud passing over the earth.

The bell sounded for breakfast.

It was a silent, almost mournful meal.

There was the feeling of storm in the air. Great motionless clouds seemed ambushed on the far horizon, dumb, weighty, loaded with tempest. They had just taken coffee on the terrace, when the Marquise said: 'Well, darling, are you going for a walk today with M. de Servigny? It's just the weather for strolling under the trees!'

Yvette gave her a rapid glance, quickly averted: 'No, mother, I'm not going out today.'

The Marquise seemed annoyed: 'Oh! go and take a turn, my child,' she persisted; 'it's so good for you.'

'No, mother,' repeated Yvette brusquely, 'I mean to stay at home today, and you know quite well why, I told you the other evening.'

Mme Obardi, absorbed in the desire to be alone with Saval, had forgotten. She reddened, grew confused; and, uneasy on her own account, wondering how on earth she would get an hour or so free, she stammered: 'Of course, that never occurred to me; you're quite right. I don't know what I was thinking about.'

Taking up a piece of embroidery which she had nicknamed the 'public welfare', and on which she employed her fingers when in the doldrums — perhaps five or six times in the year — Yvette sat down in a low chair near her mother, while the two young men, astride of their seats, smoked their cigars.

So the hours passed, in languid talk that was continually dying away. The Marquise, her nerves on edge, and casting despairing glances at Saval, was seeking some pretext for getting rid of her daughter. She realized at last that she would never succeed, and at her wits' end said to Servigny: 'You know, my dear Duke, I mean to keep you both here tonight. Tomorrow we'll go and breakfast at the Restaurant Fournaise, at Chatou.'

He understood at once, smiled, and replied with a bow: 'We are entirely at your disposal, Marquise.'

The day slipped slowly and sadly away, under the menace of

the storm. At last the dinner-hour came. The lowering sky kept filling with slow, heavy clouds. There was not a breath of air.

The evening meal was silent too. A feeling of discomfort and constraint, a sort of vague fear, seemed to hold the two men and the two women dumb.

When the table was cleared they stayed on the terrace, speaking only now and then. The night fell, a stifling night. All at once, the horizon was torn by a great hook of fire, which, with a blinding, wan flame, illumined the four faces shrouded in the gloom. And a distant sound, a dull, faint noise, like the rolling of a carriage over a bridge, travelled along the earth, and the heat of the atmosphere seemed to increase, to become suddenly more overwhelming, the silence of the evening more profound.

Yvette got up. 'I'm going to bed,' she said; 'the storm makes me feel so queer.'

She bent her forehead to the Marquise, gave her hand to the two young men, and disappeared.

Her room was just over the terrace, and the leaves of a great chestnut tree planted opposite the front door were presently lit up with a greenish light; Servigny kept his eyes fixed on that pale glow among the foliage, across which he fancied he could now and then see a shadow pass. But suddenly the light went out. Mme Obardi drew a long, deep breath. 'My daughter's in bed,' she said.

Servigny got up: 'I think I'll follow her example, Marquise, if you'll excuse me.'

He kissed the hand she gave him, and disappeared.

She remained alone with Saval in the darkness, and the next moment she was in his arms, clasping him to her. Then, though he tried to prevent it, she knelt before him, murmuring: 'I must look at you by the blaze of the lightning.'

But Yvette, having blown out her candle, had come back to her balcony, stealing barefoot like a shadow; she listened, consumed by painful and confused suspicions.

She could not see, being exactly above them, on the roof of the verandah itself.

She heard nothing but a murmur of voices, and her heart beat so fast that it filled her ears with its noise. A window was suddenly shut above her head. So Servigny had gone up to his room! Her mother was alone with the other. A second flash cleft the sky in two, and for a second made the whole well-known landscape start forth with a violent, sinister clearness; and she saw the great river, the colour of molten lead, like a river in the fantastic land of dreams. And at that moment a voice beneath her said: 'I love you!'

She heard no more. A strange shiver passed through her whole body, and her brain wandered in the whirl of a frightful emotion. A heavy, unending silence, that seemed the very silence eternal, brooded over the world. She could no longer breathe, her heart weighed down by something unknown and horrible. Once more a flash kindled the sky, and illumined the horizon, another followed, and yet others.

And the voice that she had already heard repeated in a louder tone: 'Ah! how I love you! how I love you!'

Yvette knew that voice too well – the voice of her mother.

A large drop of lukewarm water fell on her forehead, and a tiny tremor, barely perceptible, ran through the leaves, the shiver of the rain just beginning.

Then a clamour came hurrying from afar, a confused clamour, like wind among branches; the heavy shower beating in a sheet upon the earth, the river, the trees. Quickly the water streamed all round her, splashing, covering, soaking her like a bath. She did not stir, thinking only of what they were doing on the terrace. She heard them get up, and mount the stairs to their rooms; the noise of doors shutting in the house. And, obeying an irresistible longing to know, that tortured and maddened her, the young girl flew down the stairs, gently opened the outer door, and crossing the lawn under the furious beat of the rain, ran and hid herself in the bushes, to watch the windows.

Her mother's alone was lighted. And suddenly two shadows appeared, framed in the bright square, side by side. Then, drawing closer, they made but one; and by the lightning which again flung a vivid blinding jet of fire on the face of the house, she saw them embracing, their arms clasped around each other's necks.

Wildly, without thinking or knowing what she did, she cried with all her strength, in a piercing voice: 'Mother!' as one cries out to warn another of some deadly danger.

Her despairing appeal was smothered in the splashing of the rain, but the embracing couple started uneasily apart, and one of the shadows vanished, while the other sought to distinguish something among the dark shadows of the garden.

Then, fearing to be discovered, to meet her mother at such a moment, Yvette fled towards the house, flew up the stairs, leaving behind her a trail of water that dripped from step to step, and shut herself in her room, resolved to open her door to no one.

Without taking off the streaming dress that clung to her skin, she fell on her knees, and clasping her hands, implored in her distress, divine protection, that mysterious help from heaven, that unknown aid we pray for in hours of agony and despair.

Every minute great flashes kept throwing their livid light into the room, and suddenly she saw her reflection in the glass of her wardrobe, with hair unbound and dripping, so strange that she failed to recognize herself.

She remained there a long time, so long that the storm had passed over without her being conscious of it. The rain ceased falling, light came into the sky, though it was still dark with clouds, and a warm, sweet, fragrant freshness, the freshness of wet grass and leaves, drifted in at the open window.

Yvette rose, mechanically took off her limp, cold clothes, and went to bed. There she remained, with eyes fixed on the dawn.

She wept again, then again she began thinking.

Her mother with a lover! The shame of it! But she had read so many books where women, mothers even, abandoned themselves like that, to rise again to honour at the end of the story, that she was not beyond measure amazed to find herself thus entangled in a drama so like all the dramas she had read of.

Her grief, the cruel bewilderment of the shock, were already losing a little of their violence in the confused memory of similar situations. Her thoughts had roved among such tragic adventures, so romantically introduced by novelists, that the horrible discovery began little by little to seem like the natural continuation of a story commenced yesterday.

'I will save my mother,' she said to herself. And, almost tranquillized by this heroic resolve, she felt strong, great, ready all at once for her devoted struggle. She thought over the means she would employ. One only commended itself to her romantic nature. And as an actor prepares the scene he is about to play, so she began to prepare the interview she would have with the Marquise.

The sun had risen. The servants were busy about the house, and the maid came with her chocolate. Yvette told her to put the tray down on the table, and said: 'Go and tell my mother that I'm not well today, that I'm going to stay in bed till those gentlemen are gone. I haven't been able to sleep all night, and I don't wish to be disturbed; I'm going to try and rest now.'

The maid looked in surprise at the wet dress, lying like a rag on the carpet: 'Why, Mademoiselle, you've been out!' she said.

'Yes, I went for a walk in the rain to freshen myself up.'

The girl picked up the petticoats, stockings, and muddy

shoes, and went off, carrying them over one arm, with disdainful precautions; they were soaked for all the world like the clothes of a drowned woman. Yvette waited, knowing that her mother would come. The Marquise entered, having jumped out of bed at the first words of the maid, for a doubt had remained in her mind ever since that cry of 'Mother!' heard out of the darkness.

'What's the matter with you?' she asked.

Yvette looked at her, and faltered: 'I – I've –' Then, overcome by a sudden and terrible emotion, she began to choke with sobs.

The Marquise, in astonishment, asked again: 'What *is* the matter with you?'

Forgetting all her plans and prepared phrases, the young girl hid her face in her two hands and sobbed out: 'Oh! mother, oh! mother!'

Mme Obardi remained standing by the bedside, too disturbed to altogether understand, but guessing nearly all, with that subtle instinct wherein lay her strength.

And since Yvette, choked by her sobs, could not speak, her mother, at last quite unstrung, and feeling the approach of some formidable explanation, abruptly asked: 'Come, will you tell me what's taken possession of you?'

Yvette could scarcely articulate the words: 'Last night – I saw – your window!'

Very pale, the Marquise exclaimed: 'Well, what then?'

Her daughter continued to sob: 'Oh! mother, oh! mother!'

Mme Obardi, whose dread and embarrassment were quickly

changing into anger, shrugged her shoulders, and turned to go away: 'I really think you're mad,' she said; 'when this is over, perhaps you'll let me know.'

But the young girl suddenly took her hands from her face, which was streaming with tears. 'No! listen! I *must* speak – listen! Promise me ! – we'll go away together, ever so far, into the country, and live like peasants; and no one will know what has become of us! Oh! mother, will you? I beg, I implore – will you?'

The Marquise, dumbfounded, remained in the middle of the room. She had the irascible blood of the 'people' in her veins. Then, a feeling of shame, the shame of a mother, began to mingle with the vague alarm and exasperation of a passionate woman whose love is menaced; she was shivering, ready either to ask pardon or fling herself into a fury. 'I don't understand you,' she said.

Yvette went on: 'I saw you! Oh! mother – last night. It must never – if you only knew! Let's go away together – I'll love you so, that you'll forget . . .'

In a trembling voice Mme Obardi began: 'Listen, my child; there are things that you don't yet understand. Well – don't forget – never forget, that I forbid you – ever to speak to me – of – of those things.'

But Yvette, suddenly assuming the rôle of saviour she had marked out for herself, declared: 'No, mother, I'm no longer a child; I've a right to know. Well, I *do* know that we receive all sorts of people, adventurers – and that we're not respected,

293

because of that; and I know something else too. It mustn't be, can't you understand? I can't bear it; we'll work if we must, and live like honest women, somewhere, far away. And if I should happen to marry, so much the better.'

Her mother looked at her with her black, angry eyes, and answered: 'You're mad. You'll do me the favour of getting up, and coming down to lunch with us all.'

'No, mother. There's someone I won't see again; you know what I mean. He must leave this house, or I will. You must choose between us.'

She was sitting up in bed, and she raised her voice, speaking as people speak on the stage, entering fully at last into the drama of which she had dreamed, and almost forgetting her grief in the absorption of her mission.

The Marquise, finding nothing else to say, repeated the words: 'You must be mad . . .'

Yvette continued with theatrical energy 'No, mother, that man must leave the house or I will myself – I shan't flinch.'

'And where will you go? What will you do?'

'I don't know; I don't care. Only let us be honest women!'

The recurrence of this expression, 'honest women', aroused the fury of a street girl in the Marquise, and she shouted: 'Hold your tongue! I won't allow you to speak to me like that! I'm as good as anyone else, d'you hear? I'm a courtesan! and I'm proud of it! I'm worth a dozen of your "honest women"!'

Yvette gazed at her aghast, stammering: 'Oh, mother!'

But the Marquise, more and more excited, cried: 'Well, I *am* a courtesan; what then? If I were not a courtesan, you'd be a kitchen-maid, as I was once; and you'd earn thirty sous a day, and wash up plates and dishes, and your mistress would send you on errands to the butcher's – do you hear? and she'd turn you out of doors if you idled; whereas you idle and amuse yourself all day long, just because I *am* a courtesan. So there! When you're only a servant, a poor girl with fifty francs of savings, you've got to find a way out of it, if you don't mean to die in the workhouse; yes, and there are no two ways for us women, d'you hear, no two ways, when you're a servant! Women can't make their fortunes by jobbery and swindling. We've nothing but our bodies – nothing but our bodies!'

She beat her breast like a penitent confessing, and all flushed and excited, came towards the bed, crying: 'So much the worse for a girl that's handsome, she must live on her looks, or grind along in poverty all her life – all her life! There's no choice!'

Then, reverting to her original idea: 'And do *they* starve themselves, your good women? Not they! It's *they* who are the drabs, d'you hear? – because they're not obliged to. They have money, plenty to live on, plenty to amuse them – and yet they have their lovers! That's vice! It's *they* who are the drabs!'

She stood close to the bed, where Yvette, distraught, ready to shout for help, ready to rush away, was crying loudly like a child that is being beaten.

The Marquise stopped, and seeing her daughter in such a

desperate state, was herself seized with grief, remorse, tenderness, pity; falling on the bed with outstretched arms, she too began to sob, murmuring: 'My child, my poor child; if you only knew how you hurt me!'

And so they wept together, for a long time.

Then the Marquise, with whom grief never lasted, gently raised herself, and said very gently: 'Come, darling, things *are* like that, you know! We can't alter them now. We must take life as it comes!'

But Yvette continued to weep. The blow had been too heavy and unexpected for her to collect and control herself.

Her mother went on: 'Come, get up, and come to lunch, so that nobody will notice anything.'

The young girl shook her head, unable to speak; at last she said in a halting voice, strangled with sobs: 'No, mother, you know what I told you; I can't change. I will not come out of my room until they're gone. I don't want to see any more of men of that kind – never – never. If they come back I – I – you'll never see me again.'

The Marquise had dried her eyes, and, tired by her emotion, murmured: 'Come, think; be reasonable!' Then, after a minute of silence, she added: 'Well, perhaps it is better for you to rest this morning. I'll come and see you in the afternoon.'

And, already quite calm again, she kissed her daughter on the forehead, and left the room to finish dressing.

As soon as her mother had disappeared, Yvette sprang up

to bolt the door, so that she might be quite alone, and set to work to think.

Towards eleven o'clock the maid knocked, and asked through the door: 'Mme la Marquise wishes to know if Mademoiselle wants anything, and what she would like for breakfast?'

'I'm not hungry,' replied Yvette; 'I only want to be left alone.'

And she remained in bed, as though she had been seriously ill.

Towards three o'clock there came another knock. 'Who's there?' she asked.

Her mother's voice replied: 'It's I, darling; I've come to see how you are . . .'

She hesitated what to do, then unfastened the door, and went back to bed.

The Marquise came up to her, and speaking in a hushed voice, as though to a convalescent, asked: 'Well, do you feel better? Couldn't you eat an egg?'

'No, thank you, nothing.'

Mme Obardi sat down beside the bed, and they stayed without speaking; then, at last, as her daughter remained motionless, with hands resting inertly on the sheets, she asked: 'Aren't you going to get up?'

'Presently,' replied Yvette.

Then in a grave and slow voice, she added: 'Mother, I've been thinking a great deal; and this is what I've decided. The past is the past; we won't talk about it again. But the future must be different – or else – or else, I know what's left for me to do. Now, we won't talk about it any more.'

The Marquise, who had believed the explanation over, felt her impatience rising again. It was really too much. This great goose of a girl ought to have understood long ago! But she made no answer, and only repeated: 'Are you going to get up?'

'Yes, I'm ready now.'

Her mother acted as lady's-maid, fetching her stockings, corset, and petticoats; then, kissing her, said: 'Shall we go for a stroll before dinner?'

'Yes, mother.'

They went for a walk along the river-side, talking chiefly of the most trivial things.

IV

NEXT MORNING Yvette went off alone, and seated herself at the spot where Servigny had read to her the history of the ant. 'I won't stir from here until I've made up my mind,' she said to herself.

The swift current of the main stream flowed by just at her feet; it was full of eddies and great bubbles that passed in a silent flight of little swirling pools. Already she had stared at every side of the problem, at every possible way of solution.

What should she do if her mother failed to scrupulously

preserve the condition she had imposed, failed to renounce her life, her friends, everything, to go and hide with her in some far distant place?

She might run away – go alone. But where – and how? And what was she to live on?

By working! But at what? To whom would she go to find work? And then the mournful, humble existence of a poor work-girl seemed to her a little ignominious, not quite worthy of her. She thought of becoming a governess, like the young persons in novels, and of being loved and wedded by the son of the house. But for *that*, high birth was a *sine qua non*, so that when the angry father reproached her for stealing his son's love, she might be able to reply proudly: 'My name is Yvette Obardi!'

And this she could not do. Besides, it was a commonplace, stale idea.

The convent was hardly better. She felt no vocation for the religious life, having but fitful, intermittent moments of piety. No one would step in and marry a girl with her antecedents. No help from any man was to be thought of for an instant. There was no possible way out, nothing definite that she could have recourse to. And then, it must be some forceful issue, something really great and strong, that would serve as an example; and she resolved on death. She decided on it all at once, quietly, as if it were a question of taking a journey; without reflecting or realizing the nature of death, without seeing that it is the end without possibility of recommencement, the departure without return, the eternal farewell to this earth, to life.

She felt at once well-disposed towards this great resolution, with all the irresponsibility of a young, romantic spirit.

She mused over the means she might employ; but all seemed so painful and hazardous in the doing, and demanded, too, an act of violence, which was repugnant to her.

She very quickly abandoned the idea of dagger or pistol, which may merely wound, cripple, or disfigure, and require, too, a steady, practised hand; rejected hanging as too common, a ridiculous and ugly method only fit for paupers; and drowning, because she could swim. So there only remained poison; but which? Nearly all caused suffering and provoked violent sickness. She wished neither to suffer, nor to be sick. At last she thought of chloroform, having read in some paper how a young woman had set to work to suffocate herself by this method.

And she felt at once a kind of joy in her resolve, a certain private pride, a sense of self-esteem. They should see what she was made of, what she was worth!

Returning to Bougival, she went into a chemist's, and asked him for a little chloroform for an aching tooth. The man, who knew her, gave her a very small phial of the narcotic.

Then she started off on foot to Croissy, where she procured another little bottle of the poison. She obtained a third at Chatou, and a fourth at Reuil, and got home late for lunch. Being very hungry after this round, she ate a hearty meal, thoroughly famished after so much exercise.

Her mother, delighted to see her with such an appetite, and feeling herself safe at last, said, as they rose from table: 'All our friends are coming to spend Sunday with us. I've invited the prince, the chevalier, and M. de Belvigne.'

Yvette turned rather white, but made no reply.

She went out almost at once, and making for the station took a ticket for Paris.

During the whole afternoon, she went from chemist to chemist, buying from each a few drops of chloroform.

She returned in the evening with her pockets full of little bottles. This campaign she renewed on the morrow, and going by chance into a druggist's, succeeded at one stroke in buying about half a pint. On Saturday she did not go out; it was a close, overcast day, and she spent the whole of it on the terrace, lounging in a long cane chair. She hardly thought about anything at all, but felt very resolute and calm.

The next day, wishing to look her best, she put on a blue dress that suited her extremely well, and, gazing at herself in the glass, thought suddenly: 'Tomorrow I shall be dead!' A strange shiver passed through her from head to foot.

'Dead! Never to speak, never to think; no one to see me any more. And I – I shall never see all this again.'

She scrutinized her face as if she had never seen it before, and especially her eyes – discovering a thousand new traits, a hidden character in that face that she had been quite unaware of; and she was astonished at the look of herself, as if she had in front of her some strange person, some new friend. She thought: 'It's I, yes! it's I, in that glass. How weird it is to look at oneself! And yet, without mirrors we should never know our faces. Everyone else would know what we were like, but *we* should never know.' She took her thick, plaited tresses of hair, and brought them over on to her bosom, following each gesture and attitude with attentive eyes. 'How pretty I am!' she thought. 'Tomorrow I shall be dead; dead, over there, on my bed.'

She looked at her bed, and seemed to see herself stretched upon it, white, like the sheets.

Dead! in a week that face, those eyes and cheeks would be nothing but a black horror, in a box, deep down in the earth! And a terrible anguish wrung her heart.

The clear sunlight fell in flecks on all the country round, and in at the window came the sweet morning air. She sat down, still thinking: 'Dead!' It seemed as if the world must be coming to an end before her eyes; and yet, it was not that! For nothing in the world would be changed, not even her room. No, her room would be there just the same, with the same bed and chairs and mirror, but *she* would be gone for ever and ever, and no one would be grieved, except perhaps her mother.

People would say: 'Little Yvette! How pretty she was!' and that would be all. And as she looked at her hand resting on the arm of the chair, she mused again over that decay, that black nauseous mass that would be her body. And once more a great shiver of horror ran over her whole frame. She could not comprehend how it was that she could disappear without the whole world coming to naught, so deeply did she feel that she was a part of everything, of the earth, the air, the sun, and of life.

There was a burst of laughter from the garden, a hubbub of voices and cries, the noisy merriment of a country-house party just assembled; she recognized the sonorous organ of M. de Belvigne, singing:

> 'Je suis sous ta fenêtre,
> Ah! daigne enfin paraître!'

She got up without thinking, and looked out. They all applauded. The whole five of them were there, as well as two other men whom she did not know.

She started back, torn by the thought that these men had come to amuse themselves at the house of her mother, the courtesan.

The lunch-bell rang.

'I will show them how to die,' she said to herself.

And she walked firmly downstairs, with something of the resolution of the Christian martyrs entering the arena where the lions awaited them.

She shook hands with the guests, smiling rather superciliously.

'Are you less grumpy today, Mam'zelle?' asked Servigny.

In a grave and curious tone of voice she answered: 'Today I'm going to run wild. I'm in my Paris mood; take care!'

Then, turning towards M. de Belvigne, she added: 'You shall be my pet today, my little Malvoisie. I'm going to take you all to Marly fair, after lunch.' Marly fair was, in fact, going on.

The two newcomers were presented to her as Count Tamine and the Marquis de Briquetot. During the meal she hardly spoke, setting her mind hard on being gay all the afternoon, so that no one might guess anything, but be all the more astonished, and say: 'Who could have thought it? She seemed so happy and contented! What enigmas they are – people like that!'

She forced herself not to think at all about the evening, for that was the time she had chosen, when they would all be on the terrace.

She drank as much wine as she could, to raise her spirits, and two liqueur glasses of brandy; she rose from the table flushed and a little giddy, hot all over her body, hot, as it seemed to her, to the very soul; but reckless and ready for anything.

'Come along!' she cried.

Taking M. de Belvigne's arm, she issued her marching orders to the others: 'Now, battalion, form up! Servigny, you're to be sergeant; take the outside, on the right, and make the two Exotics, the foreign legion, march in front – the prince and the chevalier, of course; in the rear, the two recruits, who are under arms for the first time. March!'

They started. Servigny began to imitate the bugle, while the two newcomers made believe to play the drum. M. de Belvigne, a little embarrassed, said in a whisper: 'Do be reasonable, Mlle Yvette; you'll compromise yourself, you know!'

'It's you I'm compromising, Raisiné,' she replied; 'as to myself, I don't care a rap. It'll be all the same tomorrow! So much the worse for you; you shouldn't go about with a girl like me!'

They passed through Bougival, to the amazement of the folk in the streets, who all turned to stare at them. People came out on their doorsteps; travellers by the little railway from Reuil to Marly hooted at them, and men standing on the platform of the cars, shouted: 'Give 'em a ducking!'

Yvette marched with a military step, holding M. de Belvigne by the arm as if he were a prisoner. She was far from laughing, but had a frozen, sinister expression on her pale, grave face.

Every now and then Servigny would stop bugling and shout commands. The prince and the chevalier were vastly amused, finding it all extremely droll and *chic*; the two young men continued to play the drum without ceasing.

On arriving at the fair they made quite a sensation. Girls clapped their hands; young men sniggered; a fat gentleman with his wife on his arm said in an envious tone: 'Well, *they're* not bored!' She caught sight of a merry-go-round, and made Belvigne get up alongside her, while her squadron scrambled up behind them on to the wooden horses. And when that turn was over, she refused to dismount, compelling her escort to take five journeys running on their ridiculous nags, to the immense joy of the public, who kept up a fire of jokes. M. de Belvigne returned to earth livid and giddy.

Then she began wandering through the booths, and caused all her companions to be weighed in the midst of a ring of spectators. She insisted on their buying absurd toys and carrying them in their arms. The prince and the chevalier began to find the joke a little overdone; Servigny and the two drummers alone maintained their spirits.

At last they arrived at the far end, and she gazed at her followers with eyes full of subtle malevolence, full of a weird fancy that had come into her head. Ranging them on the right bank overlooking the river, she called out: 'Let him who cares for me most throw himself into the water!'

No one stirred. A regular mob had formed behind them. Some women in white aprons watched them open-mouthed, and two troopers, in red trousers, laughed a stupid laugh.

'So,' she began again, 'not one of you will throw himself into the water when I ask you!'

Servigny muttered: 'H'm! Needs must when the – !' and leaped upright into the river.

His plunge flung drops to Yvette's very feet. A murmur of astonishment and glee arose from the crowd.

The young girl picked up a little piece of wood from the ground and threw it out into the stream. 'Fetch it, then!' she cried.

The young man started swimming, and seizing the floating

stick in his mouth like a dog, brought it back, and climbing the bank, dropped on one knee to present it to her.

'Good dog!' she said, taking it and giving him a friendly pat on the head.

A stout lady exclaimed in great indignation: 'Is it possible!'

'Pretty way of amusing yourself!' said another.

'Wouldn't catch me taking a bath for the sake of a wench!' remarked a man.

She took Belvigne's arm once more with the cutting remark: '*You're* a slacker, my friend; you don't know what you've missed!'

And now they started for home. She flung angry looks to right and left at the passers-by. 'How silly all these people look!' she said; and, raising her eyes to her companion's face, added: 'And you too!'

M. de Belvigne bowed. Turning round, she perceived that the prince and the chevalier had disappeared. Servigny, mournful and dripping, no longer played the bugle, but walked with a melancholy air alongside the two weary young men who no longer played the drum. She laughed drily. 'You seem to have had enough of it! And yet you call this amusing yourselves, don't you? That's what you came for; well, I've given you your money's worth!'

She walked on without another word; and all of a sudden Belvigne saw that she was crying: 'What's the matter?' he asked in amazement.

'Let me alone,' she murmured, 'it's nothing to do with you.'

But like an idiot he insisted: 'Come, Mademoiselle; what *is* the matter? Has anyone annoyed you?'

'Do be quiet!' she repeated impatiently.

And suddenly, no longer able to withstand the despairing sadness that flooded her heart, she began to sob so violently that she could not go on.

Covering her face with her two hands, she stood gasping for breath, strangled, stifled by the violence of her grief.

Belvigne remained standing by her side, quite distracted, saying over and over again: 'I can't understand it!'

But Servigny came hastily forward: 'Let's get home, Mam'zelle; don't let people see you crying in the streets! Why do you do these mad things; they only upset you!' And, taking her by the elbow, he hurried her along. But as soon as they had reached the villa gate, she broke away, darted across the garden, rushed upstairs, and shut herself in her room. She did not reappear till dinner time, and then was very pale and grave. All the rest, however, were in excellent spirits. Servigny had bought a suit of workman's clothes at a neighbouring shop, corduroy trousers, flowered shirt, vest, and overall, and had assumed the accent of the working man.

Yvette longed for the end of dinner. She felt her courage failing, and as soon as coffee had been served, she again went up to her room.

Under her window she could hear their festive voices. The chevalier was indulging in risky jokes – clumsy, foreign witticisms.

She listened despairingly. Servigny, a little tipsy, began imitating a drunken workman, calling the Marquise 'Missis!' Suddenly he turned to Saval, and said, 'Hallo, Master!'

There was a general laugh.

At this Yvette hesitated no longer. She first took a sheet of her writing-paper, and wrote:

BOUGIVAL,

Sunday, 9 p.m.

I am dying, to keep myself an honest girl.

YVETTE.

Then a postscript:

Good-bye, dear mother; forgive me!

She addressed the envelope 'Mme la Marquise Obardi', and sealed it; then wheeled her sofa up to the window, drew a little table within reach of her hand, and placed on it the large bottle of chloroform beside a handful of cotton-wool.

An immense rose tree covered with flowers, which grew from the terrace close to her window, gave out into the night air a faint, sweet perfume, drifting up in soft breaths, and for some minutes she sat drinking it in. The moon in its first quarter floated in the dark sky, nibbled, as it were, on the left-hand edge, and veiled at times by little clouds.

'I am going to die!' thought Yvette; 'to die!' And sobs welled up in her heart, that seemed to be breaking, to be suffocating her. She felt a longing to ask for mercy, to be rescued, to be loved.

Then she heard Servigny's voice telling an improper story, interrupted every moment by peals of laughter. The Marquise was more amused than all the rest, and kept repeating: 'Nobody can tell a story like him! Ha! ha! ha!'

Yvette took up the bottle, uncorked it, and poured a little of the liquid on the cotton-wool. A powerful, sweet, strange odour was diffused, and putting the lump of wadding to her lips she inhaled the strong, irritating essence till it made her cough. Then, shutting her mouth, she began to breathe it steadily in. She took long draughts of the deadly vapour, closing her eyes, and striving to quench all thought within her, to deaden all reflection and consciousness.

Her first feeling was of a certain expansion and broadening of the chest, and it seemed to her that her soul, a moment before so heavy, so weighed down with grief, was growing light, as if the burden which had crushed her had been lifted, and eased, that it had finally taken wing.

A sensation both keen and pleasant penetrated her in every limb, to the very tips of her toes and fingers, permeated her whole body with a sort of vague intoxication and gentle fever.

She perceived that the cotton-wool was dry, and was surprised to find that she was not yet dead. She felt instead that her senses were sharpened, more subtle and alert.

She could now hear every single word spoken on the terrace. Prince Kravalow was relating how he had killed an Austrian general in a duel. And, far away in the country, she heard the noises of the night, the casual barking of a dog, the short croak of a toad, the lightest fluttering of the leaves.

She took up the bottle, again soaked the lump of cotton-wool, and again began to breathe it in. For some instants she felt nothing at all; then that slow, delightful sense of well-being which had already invaded her began again.

Twice she poured chloroform on the cotton-wool, greedy now for this strange mental and physical sensation, this dreamy torpor in which her soul was wandering. She felt as if she had no longer bones and flesh, legs and arms; all seemed to have gently vanished without her noticing. The chloroform had spirited away her body, leaving her brain more alert, alive, spacious, and free than it had ever felt before. She remembered a thousand things she had forgotten, details of her childhood, trifles that had pleased her. Her spirit, gifted suddenly with incredible activity, leaped far and wide from one strange notion to another, rambled through a thousand adventures, roamed in the past, strayed among happy plans for the future. And her busy, careless thoughts gave her a sensuous delight; she felt a divine joy in dreaming like that.

All the time she could hear those voices, but no longer distinguished words, which seemed indeed to have taken new meanings. She had wandered deep into a sort of weird and ever-changing fairy land. She was on a great boat, passing through beautiful country all covered with flowers. She saw people on the bank who were talking loudly, and she found herself on shore without knowing or caring how she had come there. Servigny, dressed as a prince, had come to take her to a bull-fight.

The streets were full of passers-by, all talking, and she listened to their conversation without surprise – they seemed all to be acquaintances, for throughout her dreamy intoxication she could hear her mother's friends laughing and talking on the terrace. Then everything became vague.

She awoke, deliciously numb, and had some difficulty in recalling herself to consciousness. So she was not dead yet; but she felt so rested, so full of physical well-being and mental peace, that she was in no hurry to bring it to an end. She longed for that state of exquisite assuagement to last for ever. Softly breathing, she gazed at the moon in front of her above the trees. Something in her soul was changed. She no longer thought as she had thought just now. The chloroform had enervated her, body and soul, smoothed away her grief, lulled to sleep her resolve to die.

Why should she not live, and be loved? Why not be happy? All things seemed possible now, and easy, and certain. Everything in life was sweet and good and lovely. But as it was needful to keep on dreaming for evermore, she poured more of this dream-water on to the wadding, and began again to breathe it in, removing the poison now and then from her nostrils, so as not to absorb too much, and die.

She gazed at the moon, and saw a face in it, a woman's face, and began again her flight among the dizzy pictures of her opium-dream. That face was wavering in the middle of the sky, and started singing, in a voice she knew well, the 'Alleluia of Love'. It was the Marquise who had just gone indoors, and seated herself at the piano.

Yvette had wings now. She flew through the night, the sweet, clear night, over the woods and streams. She flew with delight, opening her wings, fluttering her wings, wafted on the wind as though by caresses. She whirled through the air, it kissed her skin, and she glided along so quick, so quick, that she had no time to see what was below, and she found herself down on the bank of a pond – a line in her hand; she was fishing.

Something dragged at the line, and she pulled it out of the water, bringing up a splendid pearl necklace which she had set her heart on having, some time ago. She was not in the least surprised at this haul, and looked at Servigny, who was seated by her side, without her knowing how he had come there; he, too, was fishing, and had just caught a wooden horse. Then, again, she had the sensation that she was waking, and heard them calling her from below.

Her mother had said, 'Blow out your candle!'

Then the voice of Servigny, clear and whimsical, 'Blow out your candle, Mam'zelle Yvette!'

And they all took up the chorus, 'Blow out your candle, Mam'zelle Yvette!'

She poured more chloroform over the wadding, but now, wishing not to die, held it just far enough from her face to breathe the fresh air, yet to fill the room with the suffocating scent of the narcotic, for she realized that someone would come up. Lying back, as though dead, she waited.

'I'm a little uneasy!' said the Marquise; 'that thoughtless child has gone to sleep and left her candle alight on the table. I'll send Clémence to put it out, and shut her balcony window – it's wide open.'

Presently the maid knocked at the door and called, 'Mademoiselle, Mademoiselle!'

She paused, and began again – 'Mademoiselle! Mme la Marquise wishes you to put out your candle and shut your window.'

Again Clémence waited a little, then knocked louder, and cried, 'Mademoiselle! Mademoiselle!'

But as Yvette did not reply she went downstairs, and said to the Marquise, 'Mademoiselle must have gone to sleep; she's bolted her door, and I can't wake her.'

'But she mustn't stay like that,' murmured Mme Obardi.

At Servigny's suggestion they all stood together close under the young girl's window, and shouted in chorus, 'Hip-hip-hurrah! Mam'zelle Yvette!'

Their loud cry rose in the quiet night, took its flight under the moon, through the clear air, away over the sleeping country, and they heard it dying in the distance, like the echo of a receding train. But there was no reply from Yvette, and the Marquise said, 'I hope there is nothing wrong with her, I'm beginning to be frightened.'

Thereupon Servigny, plucking crimson flowers and buds from the great rose tree growing on the wall, began throwing them up through the window into the room.

At the first that struck her, Yvette started and nearly cried out. Some dropped on her dress, some in her hair, others, flying over her head, fell right on the bed, and covered it with a rain of flowers.

Once more the Marquise called out, in a choking voice, 'Come, Yvette – do answer!'

Servigny remarked: 'Really, it's not natural; I'm going to climb the balcony.'

But the chevalier demurred. 'Allow me,' he said; 'that's much too great a favour – I protest; both time and place are quite too perfect, for obtaining a rendezvous.'

The others, too, feeling sure the young girl was playing some joke on them, cried out: 'We protest. It's a trick! He shan't go!' But the Marquise repeated uneasily: 'Someone *must* go and see!' With a dramatic gesture the prince declared: 'She favours the Duke; we are betrayed!'

'Let's toss who shall go!' cried the chevalier. And he drew a gold five-louis piece from his pocket.

He began with the prince.

'Tails!' said he.

It came down heads.

The prince spun the coin in turn, saying to Saval: 'Your cry, sir!'

'Heads!' said Saval.

It came down tails.

Thereupon, the prince put the same question to all the others. They all lost.

'By Jove! He's cheating!' declared Servigny, with his insolent smile. He was the only one left.

The Russian placed his hand on his heart, and handed the gold piece to his rival, saying: 'Do the tossing yourself, then, my dear Duke!'

Servigny took the coin and spun it, crying: 'Heads!'

It came down tails.

He bowed, and waving his hand towards the pillar of the balcony, said: 'Climb away, prince!'

But the prince looked round about him uneasily.

'What are you looking for?' asked the chevalier.

'Well – er – I should like – a – a ladder!'

There was a general laugh, and Saval, coming forward, said: 'We will help you!'

'Catch hold of the balcony!' he said, and raised the prince in his Herculean arms.

The prince at once caught hold, but Saval, letting go, left him suspended, waving his legs in space. Whereupon Servigny, seizing the limbs that were so frenziedly hunting for a resting-place, pulled at them with all his strength; the hands gave way, and the prince fell in a lump on to the stomach of M. de Belvigne, who was advancing to his assistance.

'Whose turn now?' asked Servigny.

But no one came forward.

'Come, Belvigne, a little pluck!'

'No, thank you, my dear fellow; I prefer my bones whole!'

'Now, chevalier, *you* ought to know how to scale a fortress!'

'I resign the post to you, my dear Duke.'

'Hey – hey – I don't know that I'm so keen about it as all that!' And with a calculating eye Servigny sidled round the pillar. Then, springing, he caught hold of the balcony, raised himself by his wrists, and with a gymnastic manœuvre, surmounted the balustrade.

With noses in the air, the spectators all applauded.

He reappeared at once, crying: 'Quick! quick! Yvette's unconscious!'

The Marquise screamed loudly, and flew towards the staircase. The young girl, with closed eyes, lay like one dead. In a frenzy of terror her mother came rushing in, and threw herself down close to her. 'What is it? What is it?' she kept saying.

Servigny picked up the bottle of chloroform which had fallen on the floor. 'She's suffocated herself,' he said. Putting his ear down to her heart, he added: 'But she is not dead yet; we shall pull her round. Have you any ammonia?'

The maid repeated distractedly: 'Any what, sir? What?'

'Sal volatile.'

'Yes, sir.'

Fetch it at once, and leave the door open, to make a draught.'

The Marquise, now on her knees, sobbed: 'Yvette! Yvette, my child, my little one, my child! Listen, answer me! Yvette, my child! Oh! my God! my God! What is the matter with her?'

The frightened men moved to and fro, some bringing water, towels, glasses and vinegar, some doing nothing.

Someone said: 'She ought to be undressed!'

Half out of her senses, the Marquise tried to unfasten her daughter's clothes, but she no longer knew what she was doing – her hands trembled, all muddled and useless, and she groaned: 'I – I can't, I can't!'

The maid had returned with a medicine bottle, which Servigny uncorked and half emptied over a handkerchief. He put it close under Yvette's nose, who began to choke.

'Good! She's breathing!' he said. 'It'll soon be all right!' He bathed her temples, cheeks, and throat with the sharp-scented liquid; then signed to the maid to unlace her, and when there was nothing but a petticoat left over the chemise, took her up in his arms and carried her to the bed. He quivered all over, disturbed by the contact of the half-clothed body in his embrace. When he had placed her on the bed he raised himself, very pale.

'She'll come round,' he said; 'it's all right!' for he had heard her steady, even breathing. But, perceiving all those men with their eyes fixed on Yvette lying on her bed, he felt a sudden spasm of jealous anger shaking him. Going up to them, he said:

'Gentlemen, we're far too many in this room; kindly leave M. Saval and myself alone here, with the Marquise!'

He spoke in a dry, authoritative tone, and the others at once withdrew.

Mme Obardi had thrown her arms around her lover, and with her face raised to his, was crying: 'Save her – oh! save her!'

Meanwhile Servigny, turning round, caught sight of a letter on the table. With a quick movement he picked it up, and read the address. He understood at once, and reflected: 'Perhaps the Marquise had better not know about this!' And tearing open the envelope, he ran his eyes over the two lines which it contained:

I am dying, to keep myself an honest girl.

YVETTE.

Good-bye, dear mother; forgive me!

'The devil!' he thought. 'This needs thinking over,' and he slipped the letter into his pocket. Coming back to the bedside, he at once realized that the young girl had regained consciousness, but from embarrassment and fear of being questioned, was ashamed to show it.

The Marquise had fallen on her knees, and was weeping, her head bowed at the foot of the bed. Suddenly, she cried: 'A doctor! we must send for a doctor!'

But Servigny, who had been whispering to Saval, said:

'No! it's all right. Now, just go away for a minute, only one minute, and I promise you she shall give you a kiss when you come back!'

The baron, supporting Mme Obardi by the arm, hurried her away.

Then Servigny, sitting down by the bedside, took Yvette's hand, and said: 'Mam'zelle, listen to me!'

She did not answer. She felt so happy, so sweetly, warmly nested, that she wished never to stir or speak again, but to stay like that for ever. An infinite well-being had come upon her, the like of which she had never felt before.

Light breaths of the mild night air, soft as velvet, kept floating in and, faintly, exquisitely, touching her face. It was a caress, like a kiss of the wind, like the slow, refreshing whiffs from a fan made of all the leaves of the woods, and all the shadows of the night, of the river haze, and of every flower; for the roses thrown from below into her room and on to her bed, and the roses climbing up the balcony, all mingled their languorous perfume with the sane savour of the night breeze.

She drank in that sweet air, her eyes closed, her heart at rest in the still unspent dreaminess of the opium; she had no longer the faintest desire to die, but instead, a great, imperious longing to live, to be happy, no matter how – to be loved, ah ! – loved!

'Mam'zelle Yvette,' repeated Servigny, 'listen to me!'

She made up her mind to open her eyes. Seeing her thus reviving, he went on: 'Come, come! What does all this mean?'

'I was so miserable, my poor Muscade,' she murmured.

He gave her hand a fatherly squeeze. 'Well, that was a fine way out of it, wasn't it?' he said. 'Come, you're going to promise me never to do it again?'

She gave no answer but a little sign with her head, and a smile that he felt rather than saw.

Taking from his pocket the letter he had found on the table, he asked: 'Are we to show this to your mother?'

She frowned a 'No'.

And now he was at a loss what to say, for there seemed no way out of the situation. 'My dear little soul,' he murmured, 'one has to put up with many very sad things. I understand your grief, and I promise you—'

'Ah! you are good –' she stammered.

They were silent. He looked at her. There was a kind of swooning tenderness in her eyes; all at once she held out her arms, as if to draw him to her. He bent over, feeling that her heart had spoken; and their lips met.

So for a long time they stayed, their eyes closed. Then, feeling that he was losing his head, he raised himself. She smiled at him now, a real smile of tenderness; and held him, with both hands on his shoulders.

'I must fetch your mother,' he said.

'Wait one second, I'm so happy!' Then, after a pause, she said quite low, so low that he could hardly hear: 'You *will* love me, won't you?'

He knelt by the bed, and kissed the wrist she let him hold. 'I worship you,' he said.

There were footsteps near the door, and he sprang up, calling out in his usual voice, with its habitual touch of irony: 'You can come in. It's all over now!'

The Marquise flew to her daughter with open arms, and embraced her frantically, covering her face with tears; while Servigny, radiant and quivering, went out on the balcony, to take deep breaths of the pure night air, humming:

'Souvent femme varie
Bien fol est qui s'y fie!'